BLOOD MAGIC

——— DIVIDED REALMS ———
BOOK 3

KIM RICHARDSON

AWARD-WINNING AUTHOR OF *MARKED*

ISBN-13: 978-1537185125

ISBN-10: 1537185128

First edition: August 2016

MORE BOOKS BY KIM RICHARDSON

SOUL GUARDIANS SERIES
Marked Book # 1

Elemental Book # 2

Horizon Book # 3

Netherworld Book # 4

Seirs Book # 5

Mortal Book # 6

Reapers # 7

Seals Book # 8

MYSTICS SERIES
The Seventh Sense Book # 1

The Alpha Nation Book # 2

The Nexus Book # 3

DIVIDED REALMS
Steel Maiden Book # 1

Witch Queen Book # 2

Blood Magic Book # 3

THE HORIZON CHRONICLES
The Soul Thief

To my family and friends.

BLOOD MAGIC

DIVIDED REALMS BOOK 3

KIM RICHARDSON

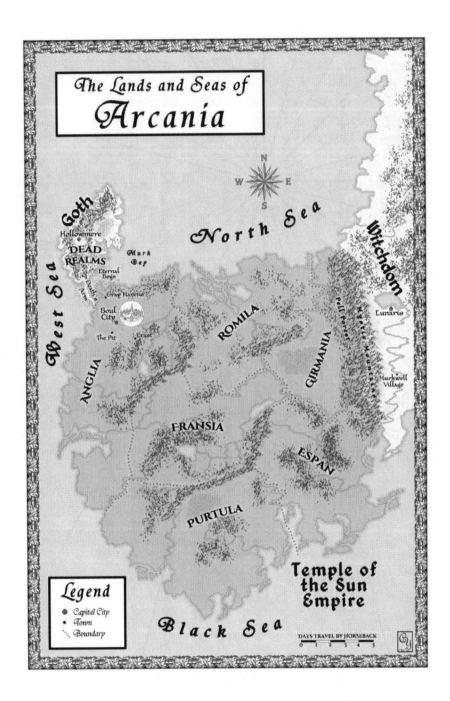

The Lands and Seas of
Arcania

Goth

West Sea

North Sea

Witchdom

Hollowmere

DEAD
REALMS

Murk
Bay

Eternal
Bogs

River

Death's

Gray Havens

Soul
City

ROMILA

Pell Forest

Mystic Mountains

Lunaris

The Pit

Exast

GURMANIA

ANGLIA

FRANSIA

ESPAN

Murkwell
Village

PURTULA

Temple of
the Sun
Empire

Legend

⊙ Capital City
• Town
⋰ Boundary

Black Sea

DAYS TRAVEL BY HORSEBACK

0 1 2 3 4 5

CHAPTER 1

WINTER HAD ARRIVED BY the time Fawkes led us back to Severed Hill Pass, the boundary that separated humans from witches, and Arcania from Witchdom. But when we entered the mountain pass, hundreds of pale and faceless familiars confronted us. We knew these specters would kill anyone foolish enough to try to enter or leave the nightmare land of Witchdom. My skin crawled, and I braced myself for another horrifying battle with these magical fiends.

But the Coven Council witches who accompanied us began chanting in Witchtongue. A fierce wind suddenly bit at the mountain peaks and loosened the rocks and boulders on the summits. A dark cloud coiled and swelled until the pass was hidden in impenetrable fog. Then the fog dispersed with a thunderous boom, and I saw that the familiars had faded away like a morning mist. It was as though they had never really existed at all.

The two Coven Council witches, Forthwind, who was a male witch from the Elemental clan, and his companion, Ysmay, who was from the Dark Witches clan, were perhaps as old as the mountains themselves. To my surprise, these two witches who were bent with age and whose skin was as wrinkled and rough as a century-old Anglian pine possessed more powerful and older magic than all the witches in our new army combined.

I shuddered as the last gust of their magic wind blew through my hair, but I couldn't help but be wary of my two new companions. They were more like coven gods than Coven Council witches. I was both fascinated and frightened by the effortless power of these apparently old and withered witches. I relaxed a little once I saw the smug smile on Fawkes' face and sensed his admiration for them. But I couldn't shake the knot I felt in my chest entirely because when I looked into the eyes of the Coven Council witches, I could see traces of something terrible.

My men and I were a bit overwhelmed that these two witches had had the power to annihilate the horde of familiars. After all, they had nearly murdered us all when we had come through the pass before. The rest of the witches in our crew, however, acted as if this was just another witch day — a walk in the park.

But there was something else.

The coven witches seemed to have another agenda. I could see a cold calculation reflecting back at me whenever I looked at them. There was none of the warmth that I had seen many times in Fawkes' or even some of the other witches' eyes. There was something else there, something cold and cunning, something they wouldn't share. Whatever I was to them, I would serve their purposes and not mine.

So while the old witches came along with us, I knew their real loyalty would always be to Witchdom and to the Goddess. They would never have come along if it hadn't benefitted them in some way. And I couldn't shake the feeling that I was just a pawn.

They had the power. While I was a half-witch and a steel maiden, my blood magic was no match for theirs.

Fawkes didn't show any lack of confidence in me. But I noticed a change in him. He had been haughty and confident before, but now he was like an obedient dog that knew who his real masters were. It was an unwelcome change.

As soon as we left Witchdom, it was clear who was in charge, and it wasn't me or Fawkes. After their little show of power with the familiars, which I suspected was also a warning, I understood that I was just another witch to them. If I was a seed, they were as old as the rocks in Anglia.

I was beginning my new life and continuing to discover my own magic powers. I would have to learn new rules about Witchdom and magic. The first rule appeared to be the same in all the realms—those with the most power *ruled*.

So I was troubled as I watched the Coven Council witches. Something didn't fit. The only thing I knew with certainty was that coming back home with an army of witches didn't serve me. It served *them*.

The journey home was cold. Damn cold. Everyone kept to themselves or spoke in hushed tones. The atmosphere was as cold as the winter's wind. Although we had fought on the same side, there was still little trust between the Coven Council witches and humans.

Fawkes and the other elemental witches did magic a little warmth for us, however. Even Celeste, who'd rushed away with me without a winter cloak or warm undergarments, needed a little magic to warm her up. My fingers were sore and chapped, and I was glad of my faithful companion, Torak. His long mane covered my fingers like gloves, and I savored the warmth of his body as we rode together. Torak and the other horses seemed to prefer the cold weather.

The witches had thick winter cloaks with fur-rimmed cowls, leather gloves, and wool riding clothes in their clan colors. While I had been struggling for my life in the witch king's trials, the witches had taken the time to pack properly. I spotted every clan color, and the witches' faces, ages, and skin color were as varied as Anglian oak leaves in autumn. They didn't speak to me. In fact, they pretty much avoided me like the plague. They avoided all humans. But every now and again, I spied the elemental witches watching me. *Studying* me. Sometimes they appeared to be indignant or confused, but mostly they looked hopeful. It was not an emotion I was accustomed to seeing in the faces of witches.

I'd heard my name whispered in blessings to the Goddess whenever I passed a group of witches, but my Witchtongue was still too limited to fully understand what they were saying. And yet I'd recognized the word, *guerierre*, which meant *warrior*. I also recognized the words *sien*, which meant *blood*, *sorceierre*, which meant *witch*, and *huhin*, which meant *human*.

I had done what High Witch Ada had asked. I had gone to Witchdom and brought back an army of witches to help us fight the necromancers. But I had not done so with the witch king's blessing. My witches had defied their king's wishes when they had followed me. Now I wasn't sure if they had actually followed me or had come along for some other reason. I held no titles or power beyond what my blood magic gave me. If they weren't following me, then who were they following and why?

I wasn't sure how the citizens of Arcania would feel about an army of witches marching through their country, but I didn't have time to worry about their feelings. Our goal was to end the necromancers' rule, to destroy the stone, and to bring back the balance. We needed to bring light back into our world before it was too late.

I might not have fully understood what Ada had meant when she had spoken of the *balance*, but I believed what I saw with my own eyes. For over four weeks, the sun had been masked by thick gray clouds, and we felt as though we lived in perpetual dusk. Before the black blight, the realm had been a land of warm, rocky mounds and thick pine forests that grew greener as the hills rolled inland and sharpened into towering peaks. Now the trees and meadows were dry and burnt, and the floor of the forest was a carpet of ash. Even the first signs of snow looked like gray ash. The earth had grown dark. The sickness was spreading.

I was relieved when we finally met up with Will, Nugar, and Lucas near the mountain pass outside the city. They were alive. But my relief was short-lived when I saw their gaunt, pale faces were covered with grime, and their bodies had become weakened and bent.

We stuck together like a family. Even Lucas seemed to warm up to me, although I still didn't fully trust the skinny bastard. There was still something twitchy in his eyes. Perhaps I stayed close to them because of the guilt I'd felt about losing the others. I wanted to keep my friends safe. They seemed to trust me now, too. But they didn't warm up to the witches. Who could blame them after what they'd suffered. They only spoke to Fawkes, and on occasion to Celeste. They figured out pretty quickly that she couldn't do magic, and they could relate to her better.

We'd lost Garrick, Max, and Leo on our quest. Leo's death hung like a heavy iron chain around my neck and pulled me into the depths of self-pity. I couldn't get the image of his wet, frightened eyes out of my head. I couldn't have helped him, but the memory of his death would haunt me forever. His life had not been irrelevant.

My revenge had been quick. And yet even after killing the witch queen, I felt nothing. No remorse, no satisfaction, no closure. It wouldn't bring him back.

My eyes burned with shame.

We woke to another dim morning on the twelfth day after our flight from Witchdom. We packed up and rode on. My thoughts turned to Jon, as they did every morning. He was in my nightmares and in my waking dreams. He had never left me. Ever.

The journey home seemed to be taking far longer than I'd remembered, and my sense of panic grew. Time was running out.

I felt eyes on me and realized the two silver and blue clad Augur clan witches had been watching me for the past twenty minutes. No doubt they had been trying to read my mind with their seer magic. I glared at them, and I had to restrain myself from baring my teeth. They eyed me briefly and then turned away with smug and knowing glances. I wanted to bash my witch blade into their skulls.

They still didn't trust me. After everything I'd done, I was still just a girl from the Pit to them—a human girl.

The wound at the back of my neck throbbed and itched. The pain had worsened over the last few weeks and was a constant reminder that there was still black magic inside me. It had never left. Sometimes I'd have blinding headaches as well, but they were probably due to a lack of sleep and food, and to the brutal beatings I'd received during the witch trials.

I had secured the witch queen's magecraft in a pouch tied to my belt. It was the size of a chestnut and was similar to those magecrafts that had enhanced the witches' power during my witch trials. Those magecrafts had kept me from healing, and the witches who used them had nearly killed me. Celeste had told me that the laws of magic forbade channeling power through a conduit, so I wasn't fool enough to bring it out in plain view. None of the witches appeared to have magecrafts, and I knew that Fawkes would surely take it from me if he saw it. Nonetheless it pulsed against my right side and kept me warm. I could feel its power sharpening my vision, refining my senses, and giving me strength.

My magecraft's strength was nothing compared to the Heart of Arcania stone. The Heart of Arcania appeared to amplify the bearer's own power, too. I knew the stone made me more powerful. I had sensed real magic soar in me when I held it.

Ada's voice echoed in my mind, *To use a magic stone you can gain great power, but there is a seductive, evil path to the stone's magic as well.*

But *I* was different. I was a steel maiden. Magic didn't affect me the same way it affected others. I had held the Heart of Arcania stone and lived. Others hadn't been so lucky. Perhaps I *could* wield the witch queen's magecraft, too. Only the Goddess herself knew. I needed more power to defeat the necromancers. Maybe my magecraft and the Heart of Arcania stone could give me the strength I needed.

Fawkes had managed to ride his giant bull elk right up beside me without my noticing.

"Is everything all right?" he said.

My heart stumbled a little, and I swallowed hard.

"If you mean apart from this blasted cold weather, and the fact that we don't know what's waiting for us once we cross into Anglia? No, I'm not. None of us are. But I have the feeling that's not what you meant."

My stomach turned over. His emerald eyes still unnerved me, but it was the suspicious look that threw me off guard. Could he sense the stone in my pocket?

"You seem to be struggling with something…internally."

His eyes narrowed slightly but shone with concern. "Is there something you wish to discuss?"

"No."

"Are you sure?"

"Yes, I'm sure. Stop staring at me like that. My feelings are my own, and they are *personal*. But if you must know, I'm just anxious, that's all."

Damn him for being so perceptive and reading my emotions a little too well. It was something Jon was good at, too.

A sudden burst of magic pulsed against my left side, as though the stone had sensed my discomfort and wanted me to know it was there. I kept my face straight and prayed to the Goddess that Fawkes hadn't seen the shock in my eyes or felt the spark of its magic.

As a steel maiden, I was perceived as a *lesser* witch—a witch without *real* magical abilities. I was a half-breed witch who played with blades and tangible weapons. I wasn't supposed to play with *real* magic. All the more reason to keep the magecraft secret, at least until I'd figured out how to use it.

Fawkes watched me with keen eyes. "You're hiding something."

I tried not to fall out of my saddle. "What?"

A faint blush of blood rushed to my neck and my face. I tightened my hands around the reins, but I couldn't think of anything to say.

Fawkes studied me carefully. His lips were drawn tightly in a thin line.

"I was trained to notice things long ago. I can tell when someone tries to hide something about their person. Something's different about you. I can't figure it out just yet. But it doesn't matter. I'll find out what it is soon enough."

Damn his sneaky ways. I bit down on my tongue until I could taste blood in my mouth. Luckily he turned his face from me and sighed.

We rode together in silence. I could easily see Fawkes as a family man, but I could also read the pain written in the lines on his face and around his eyes. They explained so much about him, his lost family, his life of solitude, and the hardness in his eyes. And yet, even after his family had been tortured by humans, he had still gone out of his way to save our lives. Fawkes was the one who had gotten the rebels out of the oubliette. He had saved them, not me.

Time and time again I tried to tell Fawkes how sorry I was about his family, but each time my lips were sewn together. I couldn't bring myself to say it. It felt too personal. Part of my reluctance was that I was afraid if I asked him about his family, I would release my own grief about my family as well. But mostly I was afraid to see his. Fawkes had become my pillar of strength, and I did not want to cause him any pain.

I had a fondness and respect for Fawkes that I had never felt for any other man, except maybe Jon…

Jon was always in my heart. The longer we were apart, the more I felt like my heart had been ripped to shreds. How long had it been since I'd seen him? Two months? Three? The thought that Jon might be dead was too crushing a defeat for me to bear, and I could barely contain my heartache and despair.

I tried to focus on what we had accomplished already, but I could not avoid a deep, festering dread that had been with me since our flight from Witchdom.

"It's not enough," I said.

Fawkes turned to look at me, his eyes narrowed. "What's not enough?"

"Us. This. We need more witches."

I watched his expression change. He knew I was right.

The six realms contained hundreds of thousands of people. How many had been infected by the black blight? How many had become priest soldiers? How many had been in league with the priests from even before the Great Race? Too many. What could a hundred witches really do against an army of thousands of infected humans, even if they didn't possess any magic?

Fawkes paused for a long while. I saw the gravity in his eyes. His lips parted and then closed, like he wanted to say something but couldn't.

"What are you not telling me?" I asked.

"More will come," promised Fawkes.

His expression became solemn, and his hands tightened around his reins. His words were weighted, as if he was thinking one thing but saying another.

"There are more witches on this side of the realm than you might think. They'll be the first to join us in Gray Havens. The rest will follow. Word of your victory has already spread throughout the lands. The witches will come. I promise. This is only the beginning."

I still felt he was holding something back, but I didn't press him. I just hoped he was right.

If no more witches came to our aid, we would all die.

CHAPTER 2

AFTER MORE THAN THREE weeks of strenuous travel, we made it to the northern borders of Anglia. My familiarity with the surroundings gave me some measure of comfort. But my sense of security was short-lived.

Two hours after sunrise the forest gave way to a clearing, and my breath caught.

When I had been forced to do battle in the witch trials, there was nothing I'd wanted more than to leave Witchdom. I had ached for home in a way I hadn't thought possible. I had ached for Anglia and for the Pit, even though I'd sworn I never wanted to return. I'd have given anything for the familiar smells, the hum of the overcrowded city, the beggars, the thugs, the whores, all of it. But the land I knew had changed.

The nearer we drew to home, the more the blight grew. It had spread like a black monster rising from the smoking ashes. It was everywhere. I felt it thrumming in the air like a dark song. Even the animals of the forest and the meadow had fled. No birds, no squirrels, no chirps or crows announced our arrival. Nothing. The air was hot and dry. My lungs burned with the heavy smell of sulfur and decay. The blight had begun in Anglia, and the beautiful landscape I'd left behind had been hit the hardest.

I'd been gone too long...

Torak tensed beneath me.

"It's all right." I leaned over and patted his neck. "There's nothing there. That's a good boy."

I knew his keen animal senses were probably telling him not to go any farther, to avoid this damned land, but he didn't falter when I urged him on. But I could barely function. I felt such fear and grief. I knew it would take another week to reach Gray Havens. I prayed that Jon was still alive.

I smelled them before I saw them. Torak shook his head. His nostrils flared. And then I knew what had upset him. Bile rose in my throat when we topped a crest on the road.

There were three of them. And from what was left of them, I could barely make out that they had been female. Even through the decay I could tell that these corpses had once been girls. Their naked bodies hung on wooden stakes. Flies buzzed on their swollen tongues, and maggots roiled in the deep gashes in their rotten flesh. Each of them had a sword through their skulls, and *STEEL MAIDEN* had been carved into their chests. And from the amount of dried blood in their wounds, I knew the words had been carved when they were very much alive.

I slowed Torak down, unable to look away from the horror of these innocent girls. I sensed myself slipping away into darkness. I would bleed the bastard priests, slowly, until I watched the light fade from their eyes. And I would rejoice in their deaths.

Fawkes was next to me. His eyes crackled with anger.

"Is this your priests' handiwork?"

"They're not *my* priests," I growled.

I steadied myself. I wouldn't look away.

"It's a message. The longer I'm out here, the more will die."

My heart ached for these poor women. "And they're going to keep killing innocent women until I give them what they want."

"But you said they already have the stone," said Fawkes, his voice empty of emotion. "What else do they want?"

"Me. Because I'm the only one who can take the stone from them."

I heard Celeste gasp when she saw the bodies, but I wouldn't look at her. If I looked at her, or at the men who had surrounded the dead women, and saw their pain, I would lose it.

"That's never going to happen," said Fawkes coldly.

"They want me to drown in guilt and to give myself up. But I won't. I'm not giving up."

The necromancer priests knew I'd return this way. What else had they planned for me? What other innocents had been tortured and died because of me?

"They're going to pay for this."

I slipped off Torak's back before I knew what I was doing. My legs wobbled, and I hoped no one saw how the scene had affected me. I straightened up.

"What are you doing?"

I turned and faced Fawkes. Will stared at me, his eyes wide and solemn. Nugar's mouth hung half open, and Lucas avoided my eyes. Celeste looked like she was about to be sick. I couldn't tell if the scene had affected the witches as much as it had the humans because they mostly hung back. The Coven Council witches just stared without emotion, as though the three dead women were a common sight, that they were nothing more than animals. But I also saw a flicker of anger in their eyes. They hadn't wanted us to stop. They would have ridden on without a second glance.

Their blatant disregard for human life infuriated me. I was starting to hate them.

I looked up at the big male Coven Council witch, already knowing his reaction to what I was about to say.

"I'm not leaving them like this. It's wrong. I'm cutting them down."

Fawkes leaned back into his saddle, but I caught the look that passed between him and the Coven Council witches.

"Elena. We don't have time for this. Leave them."

"I won't leave them for the animals."

He shook his head. "We cannot linger here. There's no time. We can't stop for every dead human we meet on the road. Besides, this might be a trap of some kind. We must go on."

I dug my fingernails into my palms angrily. I knew this wasn't a trap. Judging by the degree of decay, they'd been here for weeks.

"I'm not asking for your help or permission," I hissed. "I'm *telling* you. These innocent women died because of me. The least I can do for them is offer them a proper burial."

"Lots of innocents die in war. It's inevitable."

"Don't give me that horseshit." I turned on him. "These *innocents* weren't in *your* war. They had no idea what was happening. They couldn't have. They weren't prepared."

"Elena," said Fawkes, his voice gentle. "I know you feel responsible for this, but it's not your fault. You said it yourself. The priests did this only to get a rise from you."

"It worked."

Fawkes raised an eyebrow. "There are far worse things that death. We need to move on."

"Then go, leave!" I could see Fawkes' face flush with anger.

"Do whatever the hell you want. But this *is* important to me, and I'm not asking for you to stay or for your help. I won't leave them out here to rot, like their lives meant nothing. They meant something to someone. These were someone's daughters, sisters, lovers. They deserve better. And I'm not leaving until they get a proper burial."

I didn't wait to hear his response. They could all leave. I didn't care.

My stomach churned, and I did my best to ignore the flies and the putrid smell of rotten flesh. I hacked my witch blade against the rope that tied the first female's wrist to the wooden stake and sliced the rope. The body crumpled to the ground in a sloppy mess.

Stones crunched to my left, and I turned to see Will working to cut down the second victim while Nugar cut down the third. Lucas skirted one of the victim's heads as he tried to figure out how to pick it up.

With a powerful swing of his sword, Will freed the second victim's body. I nodded my thanks to the men. I didn't trust myself to speak just yet. We moved fast. We searched the woods for dried branches and kindling and used the wooden stakes and logs to build one large pyre for the three women. I wasn't sure if it was proper to perform the ceremony next to where they had died, but with their bodies so decomposed, we could barely move them at all. I didn't think the Goddess would object.

We placed their bodies carefully on the pyre.

I knew Fawkes wouldn't leave. The big brute loved me. But the others...

The Coven Council witches had not left. I was surprised they had stayed. Their resentment only appeared to have increased. Clearly I had disrupted their plans. But still they stayed. Why? Why wouldn't they leave me behind? It was obvious they wanted to go, but something held them back.

After I had placed the women's hands on their chests, I wiped my hands on the ground and stood back. None of the witches had dismounted to help me or to pay their respects to the dead, except for Celeste who stood next to me. They hadn't even bothered to get off their horses. I would not forget their indifference.

"I need fire."

It was a command. I was angry, and I didn't care if I was not showing the witches the respect they might have thought they deserved. I felt Fawkes' eyes on me, but I didn't look at him. I wasn't asking him.

But to my surprise three elemental witches slid off their horses. A plump, female witch, a male witch no older than me, and another taller witch with deep-set eyes that reminded me of Fawkes came forward. The Coven Council witches looked astonished but made no move to stop them. I almost smiled. Almost.

The elemental witches stood together in front of the unlit pyre and waited. My men shifted nervously, but I wasn't about to scold them for being self-conscious that the witches had come so close. They had helped me with the gruesome task of preparing the bodies, and they knew the importance of having fire.

I nodded my head, and the three elemental witches went to work. Their lips moved as they began their incantations, and then they raised their hands together. Yellow and orange flames sprouted from their fingers and raced along their palms. And then filaments of magic fire shot to the pyre like flaming spears.

Giant flames rose higher than the ancient trees around us, as though the Goddess herself was calling to it. Heat brushed my face, and I had to take a step back. The acrid smell of burned flesh mixed in with the sweet smell of wheat, pinecones, daffodils, and lilies.

Celeste raised her hands and, speaking in Witchtongue, offered a blessing to the Goddess. Her voice rose above the crackling of fire. Her beautiful and hypnotic tones sounded like the soft chords of a harp, and everyone fell silent, mesmerized.

Celeste was apparently gifted in both potions *and* prayers. Although I didn't understand the words, her blessing brought tears to my eyes. I was grateful. At least one of the witches understood that a soul, whether witch or human, was still a soul and needed respect.

I stared at the fire, trying to imagine what the girls had looked like and what they done before they were killed. Fire magic was mightier than regular fire and within a few minutes all that was left of the three women and the pyre were ashes that caught in the breeze.

I didn't speak to anyone as I returned to my horse and pulled myself up. Neither did I react when I felt Fawkes' eyes burning the back of my head. I kicked Torak forward.

We rode on, and my mood darkened with every passing moment. Our company of more than a hundred witches and men galloped through the barren land and made for the main northern road. The witches were silent; as was I. It was as though we were holding our collective breath, waiting to see what waited for us on the main road.

But after an hour of travelling westward, we discovered no red monks or temple guards, only flies, the smell of decay, and bodies.

So many animal and human bodies lined the road that they were impossible to count. I stared at the corpses, their limbs twisted in unnatural positions. Swords protruded from some of the carcasses, and some had severed heads, but mostly the dead were far too rotten for me to determine the real cause of death. The bodies of the children were the worst, and I quickly tore my eyes away. I swiped the flies from my head and wiped my brow. I spotted black veins on some of the victims' hands and faces, but most were so far gone it was impossible to tell if they'd been infected or not. Had the uninfected humans fought with those driven to madness by the blight? Had the priests been responsible? I didn't know. I could taste the copper tang of the blood that had soaked the ground.

We guided our horses carefully around the dead, afraid to get too close. After a few minutes, we came to a fork in the road. One road led southwest, directly to Soul City. The other headed towards Gray Havens.

My heart slammed in my chest, and I swallowed the bile that rose at the back of my throat. Had I been alone on my horse, I might have let myself be swallowed by fear, might have let my tears flow and wept until I was completely dry. But time was my enemy. I knew what I had to do.

I pulled Torak to a stop.

"Wait!"

I raised my hand, and the whole company pulled their steeds to a stop. They watched me and waited. I trembled and then straightened in my saddle. I needed to be confident, even though my reins kept slipping out of my sweaty hands.

I looked over what was left of our original group, and my eyes met Will's. I shook my head, and he nodded. He knew what I was about to do.

Fawkes rode up to my side.

"What is it? Did you see something?"

His gaze went over my head to the barren, sickly land before me. He looked as if he were preparing a spell to protect me. His concern was almost fatherly. And although I was moved by his worry, there was something I needed to do.

"No. That's not it."

Fawkes eyes narrowed, and he turned his attention back to me. Even his elk was staring at me now, with the same eerie emerald stare. Fawkes was not going to make this easy.

"Then why did you stop?" he said gruffly. It almost sounded like an accusation.

"We can't stop at every bloody sight on this road. The sooner we get to Gray Havens the sooner you can help them."

My throat tightened. The weight of everyone's stares was suffocating me. I knew this would go badly. But I wouldn't change my mind.

I waited until I had everyone's full attention, and I looked at Fawkes straight in the face.

"Because I'm going after Jon, and I'm going alone."

CHAPTER 3

FAWKES APPEARED TO PANIC momentarily before he turned to me with his usual frown.

"Are you mad?"

"Maybe."

"Do you have a death wish? Because it sure sounds like you have one."

I gritted my teeth. "I'm not planning on dying. And I'm not doing this just to piss you off either. I *have* to do this before it's too late."

I took a shuddering breath and added, "I have to go back for him. I owe him that."

I could see from the confused expressions on their faces that the other witches had no idea who I was talking about. But when I saw resentment in the eyes of the coven witch, Ysmay, my anger boiled.

I didn't have to explain to these witches the path I'd decided to take. It was my own path—my own destiny. And frankly, I didn't care if they approved or not. I wasn't doing this for them. I was not their pawn anymore.

I caught Celeste's face in the crowd of witches, and her reassuring smile kindled some hope in my chest, and a little courage.

Fawkes and the two Coven Council witches exchanged glances. While their expressions were stone cold, and their eyes showed anger and fear, it was not a fear for me, but rather for themselves. I didn't have time to ponder why. They probably thought me very foolish. But I didn't care. I'd done enough in the name of *witches*. It was time to do something for me. For those I cared for.

Fawkes leaned forward until I could smell the pine needles and moist earth of his cloak, until only I could hear him.

"Don't be foolish, Elena," he said. "There's a lot more at stake here than a young woman's heart. Don't you understand what it would mean if we lost you? You are the only steel maiden. You are the only witch who can handle the stone?"

His expression darkened.

"This is a war, Elena. A war between the realm of Light and the realm of Darkness. And you're a part of this whether you like it or not. You've been chosen by the Goddess. You're *her* soldier just like the rest of us. A soldier of light. Do you know what that means?"

"Of course I do."

I had no idea.

Fawkes' frown deepened. "It means you are *bound* to serve her. You are bound to this cause. You cannot escape your fate. None of us can."

The magecraft pulsed lightly against my hip, and I felt a warm sense of connection. It was as if I belonged to the Goddess. I really was her soldier against the darkness. I had been accepted. It was as though the stone itself approved of my endeavor.

Pride swelled in my chest. I'd never really thought of myself as a soldier, but to be part of something this big, even without magic, was incredible. The Goddess herself had chosen me, the girl from the Pit, to be her soldier. I was in a daze of momentary happiness.

I tried not to smile.

"If, as you say, the Goddess chose me, then she put me on this particular path as her soldier…she already knows what I must do."

"Think about what you're doing," said Fawkes with a troubled frown. "Think of the risks. He's not worth the risk."

I didn't try to hide my fury.

"He *is* worth it to me. I'm not changing my mind."

Fawkes' jaw tightened.

"We need to destroy the stone. And we can't do it without your help. If something were to happen to you…"

He paused and spoke to me more reasonably.

"The stone should be your first priority. Don't be foolish."

I mastered my uneven breathing.

"I'll be back for the stone. I promise. I just have to do this first. Besides, it's not like you'll go after the stone as soon as you reach Gray Havens. You'll need to make plans, very clever plans if you want to defeat the necromancers, and that'll take a while."

"You would risk all our lives for one human male?" he hissed. "I do hope he's worth it."

I bit back my anger. "Like I said, he is."

"I forbid it," said Fawkes firmly. "It's too dangerous."

I burst out into a nervous laugh. "Like hell you do."

I glared at him. "I'm no one's property. And don't even think of casting a spell on me to try to keep me from going. I would never forgive you if you did."

Fawkes' expression softened.

"What I meant was, it would be *unwise*. It's not safe."

I raised my brows. "You're probably right. This is stupid, and foolish, and goddamn dangerous. But I'm still going."

Fawkes watched me for a moment. Then he seemed resolved.

"Fine. Then we're coming with you."

I relaxed a little.

"There's a reason why I need to do this alone. I can't hide an army of witches. I need to blend in, and the witches…well…they'd stick out like a sore thumb. You would only draw unwanted attention. I have to stay under the radar if the rescue is to have a chance of succeeding. I'll only need a few of my men."

I could see the willing faces of my rebel men as they listened to the unfolding conversation.

"…and maybe even a witch who's skilled at brewing potions and tonics."

I could see Celeste tense slightly as she sat calm and collected astride her black and white spotted mare. Although I had only just come up with this plan, I knew in my soul that I *needed* Celeste to help me. And when Celeste urged her horse towards me, with her head held high and a spark of mischief in her eyes, I couldn't help but feel that I was doing the right thing to bring her with me.

Will, Nugar, and Lucas followed her example and steered their horses into a line next to Celeste. It felt right to be back together again. I knew they wanted to find Jon as desperately as I did. And I would not deny them the opportunity to do so. They deserved to find him just as much as I did. If this was our last chance, they should be part of it as well.

I gave a small nod of thanks to each of them. They straightened, pulling their shoulders back, and I could see their fierce determination. Their willingness to accept their fate with me was very reassuring. Maybe they weren't the Goddess' chosen soldiers, but they would fight for the light just as vigorously as any of the witches.

Fawkes raked a hand through his long, emerald stresses and glanced at the ground. I could see his jaw clench, but somehow, probably because we had an audience of witches, he managed to keep his anger under control.

"Elena, be reasonable."

"My reasoning is sound," I said. "And I'm not changing my mind. I'm just informing you of my plans. I don't care if you're not happy about this. You can't stop me from going."

Fawkes' forehead creased, and his eyes widened. "Then *I'm* coming with you."

"No. You need to see the witches safely to Gray Havens."

I knew this was the right thing to do.

"You've been gone from this land for over two months." Fawkes looked at me intently. "You have no idea how much the necromancers' magic has spread, how many are infected, or even if there's anything left of your beloved *human*."

"He's alive. I know he is," I said with enough conviction to hide my fear that I would be too late. I was not prepared to admit that I'd abandoned Jon to die alone, infected with a black magic that would turn him into a monster. He had saved me, and now I would save him.

"Do you even know where he is?"

I gripped the edge of my saddle until my knuckles turned white.

"I'll try Soul City first. It's where he was last. If he's not there, I'll make my way to the Pit."

I took a calming breath. But just thinking about that goddamn golden temple made my stomach churn. My vision reddened with fury as I remembered the high priest of Anglia, the necromancer in disguise, and how I wanted to end his life.

I had felt nothing when I killed the witch queen, but I knew my revenge against the necromancers, against that high priest, would begin and end with a smile.

I would have my vengeance.

"...and then I'll make my way back to Gray Havens...with Jon."

These last words were an effort. My throat was tightening, but I forced them out because saying them out loud made them more real. Goddess, I hoped and prayed Jon was still alive.

"Fine," said Fawkes, surprising me. "I'll expect you back at Gray Havens in less than a week's time. If you're not back then, I'm coming to get you."

"Fine," I answered. "I'll be there."

Fawkes shook his head. "But you do know he's most likely to be dead."

My heart sank. "Go to Hell."

Before anyone had the chance of seeing the wetness in my eyes, I spurred Torak into a run, and we sprinted down the road.

CHAPTER 4

WE TORE DOWN THE southwestern road leaving clouds of sand and dust in our wake. The sound of pounding hooves behind me echoed the pounding of the blood in my ears. It wasn't the entire witch army, but it was enough.

Celeste, Will, Nugar, and Lucas caught up to me, and we rode along together. I cussed Fawkes. Damn that male witch. While I cared deeply for him, I also wanted to punch him in the face. He knew the right buttons to press to send me into a fury. I knew he was only trying to prepare me for the worst, for what I'd been trying to avoid, what I'd been denying all along—that Jon was already dead.

Bastard. The tears fell freely down my cheeks.

I urged Torak faster. The cool wind soothed my hot face and my temper. We moved so effortlessly and fast that for a moment I felt like we were flying. My mastery of Torak provided me with great comfort as we neared the city, but my increasing dread began to overwhelm me.

"If we keep riding this hard, I'll have no more ass to sit on." Celeste smiled as she spoke.

She rode next to me, and her big mare easily matched Torak's speed. For a witch maid, she rode like a seasoned rider, and I wondered what kind of life she had before she worked for the witch king. Celeste was full of surprises.

She had started to wear her hair down, and it was tied neatly in a thick braid that reached the middle of her back. Wisps of hair framed her face, and even in the dim light she looked happier.

I slowed Torak to a trot, and the others followed my example. They looked relieved; no doubt their asses were sore, too.

"Thank you. That's much better," she said, and she rubbed her lower back. She turned to look at me and cocked an eyebrow. "So…are *you* feeling better?"

I smiled back at her. "Sorry I lost my temper back there. Fawkes has this damn magical way of making me *so* angry. It's like he tries to piss me off on purpose, like he enjoys infuriating me. He always seems to go out of his way to say the exact things that make me want to strangle him."

"You do know he says those things *because* he cares. If he didn't care, he wouldn't bother."

I sighed. "I know. He's like an overprotective father. And it's not that I don't need a little fatherly love, either. I do. It's just that I'm used to doing whatever I want, whenever I want, without anyone's permission. Except for Rose, who I always kept in the dark when I knew she'd give me a hard time, nobody has ever tried to tell me what to do. It's like he doesn't trust me. Like he doesn't believe I can do this."

"I don't think that's it at all," said Celeste. "I think Fawkes has a pretty good idea what you can do to save Jon. And I think that's what scares him. He knows just how far you'll go to get him back, and it scares the hell out of him. He wants you to stay alive."

I clicked my tongue. "I'm not planning on dying."

"No, but you are risking a lot. We don't know in what state Jon will be when we find him."

A quick panic rose up in me again, an aching pain that had my throat closing. But the mere fact that she had said *when we find him* filled me with hope.

Celeste brushed the strands of hair from her eyes and turned to look at the road ahead. "To Fawkes and most of the other witches, it's an unnecessary risk, to risk your life for the life of a human."

"Is that what you think?"

My words came out a little more harshly than I'd intended.

Celeste's soft eyes were filled with compassion.

"It is foolish," she said gently, "...but I would have done the exact same thing if I'd known my Jarin were still alive somewhere. I'd have gone to the ends of the world to save him."

Her eyes brimmed with tears as she turned her face away.

"I'm sorry, Celeste," I began. She had never mentioned her lover before.

"What happened to him?"

She shook her head and wiped the tears from her face.

"Now's not the right time. I'll tell you someday, just not today. We're *going* to find Jon."

She forced a smile, but I could still see the pain in her eyes. "The Goddess will show us the way. I know she will."

Celeste dropped her reins in her lap and pressed her palms together in front of her chest. It was a gesture of blessing and of protection from evil spirits and dangers that we might face.

My men were watching her. Will had a strange look in his eyes that I didn't understand. When he caught me staring, I'd swear I saw a blush on his cheeks before he turned away. Nugar and Lucas both squirmed awkwardly in their saddles, but their eyes filled with fear and doubt. Idiots. When were they going to accept the fact that witches weren't devils in disguise? Hadn't they been watching Celeste enough to know they could trust her?

There was nothing demonic or evil about Celeste's beliefs. They were all very natural and beautiful. Her faith was more like theirs than they realized.

"Great Goddess, creator of all that is," said Celeste as she began to recite the blessing. "We give thanks for the blessings and protection you've provided us this day and from this day forward. We honor the wisdom and love you've added to our lives. We give great thanks for your assistance, and we honor all the unseen forces that have provided us with support and blessing this day, and for this special request."

Celeste beamed at me as she wrapped her fingers around her reins. I knew she'd spoken in the common tongue for me because my Witchtongue wasn't up to par, not yet. She was convinced that the Goddess would help us and guide us on our journey. I admired her faith, but I wasn't so sure. I had the feeling the Goddess had abandoned us little people to our own devices.

Since our escape from Witchdom, Celeste had been instructing me in the ways of the Goddess, and I found myself ravenous for more. Fawkes had also begun my instruction in Witchtongue, having given me an ancient-looking book that contained the Witchtongue alphabet. And when he couldn't attend to my millions of frustrated questions, Celeste had volunteered to tutor me. She was less irritating than Fawkes, and our lessons were far more productive.

Writing and remembering all the letters didn't come easily to me, especially when my thoughts of Jon were a constant distraction. It didn't help that witches would come by and spy on my progress. While some nodded encouragingly at me, and others just stared, they embarrassed and infuriated me. And the coven witches were always watching. Even when they thought I didn't know, they watched.

"Pay attention!" Fawkes would bark at me.

"Your lines are too thick," he pointed. "Here and here and here. No, this is wrong. And what in the Goddess' name is this supposed to be?"

He pressed his large finger on my carefully drawn sentence. "It looks like the scribbles of a madman, not a written language. No, no, it's all wrong. Start again."

He wiped my parchment clean and erased hours of my work.

I wanted to murder him. I stared at him and felt the blood rush up to my face. I held my piece of charcoal like a knife—it would be easy to poke him in the eye. I didn't want all the witches to think I was an illiterate moron.

"You write like a five-year-old," he had said as he handed me back my piece of parchment. "You have to do much better if you ever want to learn."

And that's when my charcoal hit him square on the forehead. He winced as the piece bounced off his face.

I stood up, my hands tightened into fists. "Maybe I'd do better with a better teacher."

"Let's stick to your pronunciation for a while," he said as I stormed away, fuming. "Until your penmanship improves, we can stick to conversations."

"You know where to stick your conversations," I yelled over my head.

In my arrogance, I had thought that Witchtongue would come naturally to me, like my innate talent for blades. It did not. I was terrible, worse than terrible. And while my pronunciation was better than my reading and writing skills, I wanted to learn to write and read Witchtongue. To speak in well, I needed to read and write it well, too.

Celeste tipped her head back suddenly and laughed.

"I don't think I've ever seen the Coven Council witches look so put out. It's like someone told them they couldn't do magic anymore."

I loved that rebel side of her.

"I thought it was great."

I burst out laughing. "They probably hate me. What must they think of their champion now? The Goddess' soldier of light? I can only imagine what they'll tell the high witch when they reach Gray Havens. Ada's going to have my head. I don't think they expected someone like me. They expected a proper little witch who did what she was told. Boy were they in for a surprise."

"Well, they don't hate you," said Celeste with a smile. "I think you surprise them, that's all. I don't think they're used to someone so…bold."

I pursed my lips. "That's putting it lightly."

"I'm sure Rose will be happy to see you, regardless of what the witches tell her."

The thought of Rose warmed my heart.

"You don't know Rose," I laughed softly. "She likes to scold me as much as Fawkes does."

After a short rest, we rode hard and followed the well-used path that hugged the edge of the charred Anglian pine forest higher into the hill country where the air did not improve. No one spoke. We were each lost in our own thoughts, but we shared the same goal—to save Jon.

We rode on and on. My fingers were numb from gripping the reins, and my ass, thighs, and calves hurt like hell. Luckily my healing powers relieved the pain of my aching muscles. And even though the others couldn't heal their sore asses the way I could, they never complained. They were the real champions. They didn't stop, so neither did I.

Although we were alert for attack, after six days of riding and camping only during the nights, we met no enemies nor faced any ambushes. Except for the bodies, the road was deserted. It got to the point where the smell was so intense that we all made masks from our cloaks to help disguise the putrid smell.

The roads should have had a few travelers, or at least spies. The necromancer priests had hundreds of spies and assassins. Why would they leave the roads to Soul City unprotected? The road could have been crawling with the necromancer priests' infected minions. But there were none. There was only death.

It didn't feel right. It felt *wrong*. I sensed we were being watched when we made camp on the sixth night. But whatever it was, it stayed hidden in the shadows. A chill had spread through me, and it intensified as we neared that bastard city. If Celeste and the men felt it too, they didn't mention it. Still, they jumped to their feet with their hands tightly on the hilts of their weapons when they heard the faintest sound.

I watched Will give Celeste a small dagger and a weapon belt to strap around her waist. The flush on his face was obvious to me, to someone who knew him, and I had to bite the inside of my cheek so not to laugh. But if Celeste noticed Will's embarrassment, she didn't show it.

That evening, Will gave her a private lesson using tree trunks as targets. He showed her a few defensive moves and where to stick her dagger to make a kill. The intimacy between them had grown, and many furtive glances and shy smiles passed between them. They seemed very tuned in to each other. I didn't want to interrupt that.

Eventually Nugar and Lucas volunteered to help with her lessons, too. I think the men warmed to her far more quickly than to me because Celeste had no magic. She was more like them.

I wasn't upset. Rather, I was glad for it because now I knew they'd protect her with their own lives. And Celeste was a rarity that needed all of our protection. Her tonics could well cure the black magic that had infected all the humans. Hopefully. If they worked, they would make a great difference in our fight against the black blight and the priests. We needed her stay alive. *I* needed her to stay alive.

As I watched the newly formed friendships, I hoped that humans and witches could learn to trust one another again. Perhaps they never would. We didn't need to be friends to share the same enemy, but we needed to fight together. To win the war against the darkness, witch and human needed to stand together.

My headaches had worsened to the point that I could barely think. And nearly every night I lay awake staring up at a starless, clouded sky. Sometimes the headaches were so bad it hurt to open my eyes. As I lay on my bedroll listening to the low, steady breathing of my companions, my eyelids felt like they were made of lead. And when I finally gave in to exhaustion, all I remembered was the throbbing pain at the back on my neck.

CHAPTER 5

I'M MOVING FAST. I'm surrounded by fire and ash and shadow. There is no sun, only darkness. I'm lost. Moans and cries fill the air around me. I taste blood in my mouth. I'm searching for something, but I can't find it. The darkness shifts. Mist swirls around me and then parts long enough to reveal mountains of the rotting bodies of humans, witches, and animals. I'm standing in a red river. Bodies float past me, children. I try to move, but something grabs hold of me from below the surface. And then a figure emerges through the river.

At first I think it's a man. Then I see that his flesh is made of moving shadow and green fire. He is no man. I cannot run.

He has found me.

I woke up in a cold sweat. I opened my eyes to a pulsing headache the likes of which I'd never felt before. I felt a flash of blinding pain. The ground wavered for a moment, and before I registered what was happening, I rolled over and vomited.

"Elena?"

Celeste had been sleeping next to me and had an unfortunate close-range view of my stomach contents.

I wiped my mouth with the back of my hand.

"Sorry," I whispered.

I hadn't woken the others with my retching, and I wanted to keep it that way. Will looked my way, but to my relief he remained seated against the trunk of a colossal birch.

"I just felt a little sick. It's nothing. Go back to sleep."

What the hell had just happened?

I covered my mess with some earth and dried leaves and moved my bedroll to Celeste's other side.

Remnants of the dream were still fresh in my mind as though I had truly lived it, as though I had truly been there.

I winced because my wound throbbed, and I cussed it away. I was cold, hot, and then cold again. I knew I was running a fever. But I'd never been sick a day in my life. *What was happening to me?*

Glimpses of my dream flashed in my mind's eye: the red river, the dead, the thing that came out of the water. A wave of nausea hit me again and I struggled not to be ill again. I rubbed my eyes. *Was I going mad?* Normal people didn't puke their guts out after waking from a dream. Only it didn't feel like a dream. It felt *real*.

Had I seen a vision of the future? I couldn't have had a vision. Only the witches from the Augur clans were gifted with the Sight. As I struggled to come to grips with what was happening to me, I could feel Celeste watching me.

Her big, round eyes gleamed in the light of the small fire.

"I can make some ginger tea," she whispered. "It'll help settle your stomach."

"Don't worry about it," I breathed and forced a smile. "I feel much better now. I guess my stomach's tired of eating strips of dried turkey."

I hated lying to her. Celeste had always been open and honest with me. I was glad it was hidden in the darkness. On a whim, I had taken Celeste away from everything she'd known and brought her to a foreign land where everyone hated witches. Not only was the land slowly being infected by the black blight, it was mortally dangerous to be close to me because I was being hunted. The high priests wouldn't give up. Celeste could die, and I wondered if I'd made the right choice by compelling her to come with me.

"Get some rest," I said.

I lay back down and pretended everything was fine—that *I* was fine—when I looked and felt like I'd feasted on rotten meat.

I knew Celeste wasn't fooled. She lay back down, but I could see her eyes were open, and the tiny twitch of her jaw showed that her mind was racing.

I didn't sleep a wink for the rest of the night, but I took comfort in Celeste's soft and steady breathing. At least one of us would be rested.

The following morning was worse. I didn't puke my guts out, but the constant pounding behind my eyes made it hard to concentrate. White spots kept exploding behind my eyes, and no matter how often I rubbed them, they didn't go away, nor did the pain lessen.

Nonetheless, I wore my pain on the inside. I didn't want the others to see. I feared they'd make me turn around and go straight to Gray Havens so the witches could examine my head.

I *couldn't* be sick. *I* was a steel maiden. *So what the hell was wrong with me?*

That afternoon, on the seventh day, after a few hours of riding without a break, I lost track of time. The rhythm of the hooves had distracted my restless mind. But despite the stuffy hot air, the longer we rode, the more I felt a growing coldness.

The last time I had seen Jon, his face had been covered in thick, black veins, and his skin had been crusted and scabbed like he was suffering from leprosy. But his eyes had disturbed me the most. They were cold and black and foreign. It was like looking into the eyes of someone else, someone I'd never met before. There had been no love there. They were not Jon's eyes.

I tried hard to focus on his face before he'd been infected, his warm lips, his strong, hard body pressed up against mine. I tried to recall the musky smell that drove me mad and made me want to rip off his clothes.

We'd been apart for nearly three months. Anything could have happened during that time. I straightened up and pulled my shoulders back. My anger made me feel a little better; it stole my grief and absorbed my guilt. But I knew anger would cloud my judgment and lead to mistakes. I couldn't afford any.

I stuffed the memories into the empty place inside my heart. I would have to live with my grief. This was my last shot. I had to stay focused.

There was a sudden shift in the air, as though we'd crossed some invisible barrier from summer into fall. The air lifted and cooled, but not with the familiar coldness of winter. The chill was something else. It felt unnatural. Shadows loomed over us, and the sun hid behind a swarm of dark and angry clouds. There should have been about six hours of daylight left, and yet it was neither day nor night.

And then a smell like the decomposition of something that had been wholly unsavory even in life caught my attention.

Something was very *wrong*.

I whirled around in my saddle, but there was nothing on the road in front or behind us—nothing I could *see*. And yet the familiar feeling that I was being watched hit me like a splash of cold water.

"What is it?" Will called from behind me.

I turned and saw that his hand had moved to the hilt of his sword. The men followed his lead and did the same.

"I'm not sure," I said.

My eyes darted to Celeste's face pale.

"But something feels off. Whatever it is, it's not friendly."

I knew something was coming, I just didn't know *what*. I looked at the wall of trees that surrounded us on either side. At first glance they looked impenetrable, but I knew that anyone or anything could easily ambush us from their depths.

I knew the necromancer priests wouldn't leave this road unprotected. They would have expected me to come this way. I knew that sooner or later their evil would present itself.

"Be alert," I called. I scanned the forest again but saw nothing.

"It won't be just regular temple guards after us. Watch for sudden movements from the forest and the road. And trust your instincts. Whatever comes at us, if it feels foul, kill it. Don't think. Thinking will get you killed."

We had to be prepared for anything. For all I knew the priests could have sent an army of infected kids to rattle us and make us easier to kill. The bastards were that evil.

"Nugar, watch the back," ordered Will.

He kept riding on ahead and then circling back. Nugar tugged his horse around and positioned himself at the back. His battle-axe winked in the dim light, unsheathed and ready to throw.

Lucas eyed the forest. Everything was unnaturally still. Will's eyes darted nervously to me. The men were restless. My soldiers of light waited, anxious to kill whatever was out there before it had a chance to kill us.

"Is it the necromancers?" Celeste pulled her mare next to Torak and gripped the dagger that Will had given her. "Have they discovered us?"

Just as I was about to answer, a chill licked up my spine, and the wound at the back of my neck itched and stabbed. I knew the feeling all too well. When we'd first set out to Witchdom and neared Erast, the late Prince Landon Battenberg's home, I hadn't seen the evil that lurked there, but I had *known* it was there because I had *felt* it. It had also warned me of the high priests' black magic inside the golden temple. When the wound on the back of my neck throbbed, I knew evil was near.

There was black magic here...or something else...something *worse.*

The darkness increased until we could barely see each other. Darkness was coming from the west.

It rolled towards us like a great black wave. The trees moaned and cracked. At first I thought it was the black blight, but the trees didn't just sicken. They withered, dried up, and broke apart as though they'd been burned from the inside by invisible fire.

The darkening clouds hid the horizon. My heart slammed in my chest.

The clouds spread over the road. There was no going around them.

The darkness was coming straight for us.

CHAPTER 6

WHAT WAS THIS NEW THREAT?

And then, almost in unison, our horses snorted and slowed of their own accord. It was as if they too could feel something evil lurking inside the rolling black clouds, and they weren't going anywhere near it.

I scanned the unnatural darkness, seeking something out of place, something hidden. I saw nothing, and yet I could swear on the Goddess I felt eyes watching. I let Torak move at his own speed. We moved together through the dark, wondering how far it extended. Would we come out at the other end? We could hear strange calls and scraping noises from the forest. Torak whinnied at things unseen, and I couldn't calm him. It was hopeless. How could I kill what I couldn't see? There was no sky, no moon or stars to guide us—

Something crashed through the brush in the distance, breaking branches at it came nearer. Then it stopped. I strained to hear more, but the still of the darkness revealed nothing. Whatever it was, it stayed hidden within the woods.

I knew my companions were watching me. I had to find a way through this darkness. Jon was on the other side somewhere. And I *was* going to find him.

The magecraft throbbed against my side. *Was it urging me to use it somehow, or was this a warning?* I didn't even know how to use the damn thing. I didn't know any spells or incantations. I had memorized some words in Witchtongue like *good morning* and *thank you.* But that was about it. I prayed that my skill with the blade would be enough. It needed to be.

The darkness coiled onto itself and reached out with its rolling, swelling arms, as if it wanted to trap us in. The smell of rot was everywhere, but there was also a faint, acrid smell of something else, something viler and more evil, of something not meant for this world.

"Goddess above, what *is* that?" asked Celeste. "And what's that awful smell?"

Tears rimmed her eyes, and she began to cough.

"That's the devil's work, that is," said Nugar from behind us. "There's something foul and unnatural about it. This is dark magic."

"This *isn't* dark magic," I snapped. "This is something different. Foul and unnatural, yes, but it's not dark magic."

Celeste's eyes snapped back to me. "What do you think it is?"

I stared into the unholy black clouds. "Maybe something we haven't seen yet? I don't know. I don't like it."

Nugar stroked his long beard. "Well, whatever it is, in all my life I've never seen black clouds move like they know where they're going. Don't seem right."

"It's coming for us," echoed Lucas looking madly in every direction and unable to control his fear. I began regretting my decision to bring him along on this trip.

Will and I shared a look. My heart mirrored the panic in his eyes. We might not know what it was, but we knew it wasn't friendly. The others had seen our silent exchange, and they could easily read the terror on our faces.

Will drew his sword. Its blade glimmered slightly in the dim light. The sound of metal interrupted the silent, stuffy gloom.

"There are things in the dark that can get you," Will said solemnly. "Everyone, be on guard."

Lucas' eyes were wild with panic, and he rambled on about fire magic, and witches, and sorcery.

Everyone was looking around frantically for a glimpse of the devils inside the growing darkness.

Celeste's bravado had vanished, too. She wasn't a steel maiden or a soldier, and she didn't have combat experience. Her strengths were of the intellectual kind, brewing tonics and potions. I'd been selfish. She would have been safer with Fawkes and the other witches. If something were to happen to her now, I'd never forgive myself.

I tore my eyes from Celeste's pale face. I would keep her safe. I *had* to.

"Don't you think it's strange that it just appeared?"

Celeste's skin was pale, but her eyes were clear as she turned to look at me.

"It's almost as if it *knew* we were coming. Like it's been waiting for us, and now it's trying to keep us from getting through."

She had stolen my own words.

"A darkness that grows is an ill omen," she continued, "especially one that smells and reeks of death. I've seen my share of magic and the supernatural, but I've never seen this. Nothing good can come of it."

I knew she was right, but we couldn't run away. Jon was on the other side of this blasted darkness.

"You're right," I said, trying to still my nerves. "It is an ill omen. If the necromancer priests did this, then their black magic has grown more than I would have thought possible in such a short time."

"You think them capable of this? Of having such power?" Celeste's face was ashen. "I don't even think the witch king or even all the Coven Council witches combined would be capable of such magical strength."

I shrugged. "I'm not sure. Maybe I'm wrong, but the way the necromancers' magic was explained to me, they need to *borrow* it. They don't have blood magic. They're men, humans. Ada and the others never thought they could be a real threat because their power was minimal. They seemed to think that the necromancers' power wasn't strong enough *yet*. But now, with the stone."

I took in a breath. "I don't know. Maybe. But it scares me to think of how much power they've gained. Could they cast the world into darkness?"

"Goddess protect us if you're right." Celeste closed her eyes and mumbled a blessing.

I didn't want to think of the possibilities. It was madness. *How could we ever defeat such a strength?*

"This is my fault," I blurted and wiped at my eyes. I'd been carrying this burden for so long, I could feel it tearing at my soul bit by bit, and I was frightened that it would consume me completely. I should have listened to Rose.

Celeste shook her head. "Elena, don't be ridiculous. From what you've told me and from what I've gathered from Fawkes, the necromancers had been plaguing this realm long before your mother was born. How can any of this be your fault?"

"Because *I'm* the one who stole the damn stone in the first place!"

The words flew out of my mouth, hard and loud before I could stop them. I felt everyone's attention on me.

"Without the stone, these pricks couldn't have done this. Or any of it. Can't you see what I've done? How stupid and selfish I was! How I've condemned us all!"

My temper flared, but my anger wasn't directed at Celeste or the men, it was directed at me.

I did this. And somehow I had to stop it.

"They'll stop at nothing for the chance to kill me. They could have killed me before, but I escaped. They know I'm the *only* one who can touch the Heart of Arcania stone. I can take it away from them. They don't want me anywhere near it. If they're still in Soul City, we should let them think I'm coming for the stone. It's better that way. It'll give me the freedom I need to look for Jon."

I clenched my teeth as I formulated a plan.

"After we take Jon back to Gray Havens we can go back for the stone."

The words felt wrong somehow because part of me didn't believe that Jon was still alive. And I hated myself for that lack of faith.

"Elena, don't do this to yourself," said Celeste. "These mad necromancers would have figured something out eventually, with or without the stone. It was only a matter of time."

"She's right," said Will as he and Celeste shared a long look.

"Yes, maybe you sort of speeded the process a little," Celeste continued. "But you can't blame yourself for these devils. The Goddess knows your heart is pure, and it shines through your efforts. She will not abandon you."

It warmed my heart that Celeste thought so well of me. She was a true friend. But I knew what an ass I'd been, and of the selfish act that had gotten me into trouble in the first place.

My eyes burned, but I forced a smile.

"Well then, if the Goddess wills it, she'll guide us through this darkness. Let's keep moving," I said, more to myself than to the others. I had at least to voice the courage I so desperately needed.

I tapped my heels into Torak's flanks, and we trotted forward. The others followed closely behind me. I felt my warhorse stiffen beneath me as we entered the first thin veil of black shadow. I held my breath as I felt its tendrils brush against my face.

Then the darkness shifted, and through it came a familiar gray-white mist.

CHAPTER 7

WE HAD NO CHANCE. None. I knew all too well what devils lingered inside that mist. Demons.

But worse, I knew it was also a portal to the demon realm. The veil that protected our world from darkness had cracked, and a new portal had emerged here in Anglia. Somehow the priests had managed to splinter the veil.

For a moment no one moved. Struggling to control my rising panic, I did what came naturally. I got mad. There was strength in replacing my fear with my faithful companion, fury.

I stared at the unholy fog. There was no mistaking it. It was that same damned mist I'd encountered in Death's Arm. It was heavy and thick. Unlike the ordinary soft texture of mist, this was a choking smoke.

The mist kept coming. It spread out and rolled along the road towards us.

"Elena?"

Will's eyes were filled with alarm. "Is this…"

"Yes," I said, knowing exactly what he meant. Will had been there in the bogs when we'd first encountered the evil fog. "It's the same mist."

I gagged and breathed through my nose. Goose bumps rose on my skin. We halted and waited. But after the first few seconds, nothing happened.

"We should get off the road," said Will. "Try our luck in the forests."

"I agree," said Nugar.

He shifted in his saddle. "The devil's in that mist. I can feel it."

I couldn't see ten feet in front of me. The forest that had surrounded us had all but disappeared in the fog. But I could still see the dirt and pebbles of the road. There was still hope.

I turned in my saddle. "We'd get lost if we tried the forests, but I can still see the road."

I knew it was suicide to ride through the mist. But there was no other way to get to Jon.

"If you want to turn back, now's your chance. I won't force you to cross the mist. But I'm going."

I wouldn't let the priests win. To hell with their tricks, I was going to Soul City.

My companions looked as if they were as determined as I was.

"We agreed to come with you, and we meant it," said Will, as though answering for all of them. "We're not backing down. We're in this together."

I nodded of my head. "Stay close and alert."

We rode slowly and silently for about five minutes. I stared at the mists, and my fear increased with every step. Giant fingers of fog searched the road and forest as though they had minds of their own.

I steered Torak next to Celeste's mare, Bruma. I had to keep her safe. I had to accept what I'd done. I had to own it. And although it scared me, I was going to make things right. Even if it killed me, I would stop the priests. I would kill them all.

After a half hour of riding, I began to relax. Maybe I'd been wrong. Maybe this fog wasn't a portal and was something else we hadn't seen before. I was confident we could continue through the mist like this, all the way to Soul City. Maybe the mist worked both ways. While it hid our enemies from us, it also concealed us *from* them.

Steel maiden...

I jerked in my seat. My heart was in my throat. My companions didn't appear to have heard anything.

Had I heard correctly? Was I hearing things?

The mist was toying with me. It wanted to unbalance me, to lure me into its depths so that it might kill me.

My breathing came in rapid bursts. The smell of sulfur choked me. My eyes burned, and I had to blink the tears to see clearly. The smell of decaying flesh left a sour taste in my mouth, and bile rose in my throat.

I can see you...

The voice was clearer now. It was guttural and ancient. It had gotten into my head. I knew a dark entity was waiting for me somewhere down the road.

Sweat trickled down my back and my temples. My chest grew tight, and my breaths came shallow and fast. Something evil lurked beyond that mist. I couldn't see it, but I felt something inhuman in my bones.

I strained to hear the voice again, but instead I heard the sounds of battle. The cries of the dying sliced through the stale air around us. I smelled the acrid scents of fear and hate, the coppery tang of blood.

Somewhere deep within the fog, a great battle was being fought. I didn't know if it was coming from the demon realm or from somewhere in our world. The guttural snarls and growls of demons came from inside the mist.

"Do you hear that?" Lucas whirled around in his saddle. "What is that?"

Suddenly high piercing screams that could only have come from another world penetrated the fog.

Torak tensed beneath me. The whites of his eyes showed, and his ears flicked back and forth in a state of heightened anxiety. I remembered all too well how the horses had bolted at the first sign of danger from the mists at Death's Arm. If he bolted now, he'd throw me off for sure. I'd lose him for good.

With trembling fingers, I gripped the horn of my saddle and slipped off Torak's back. I pulled my witch blade from my waist.

"Get off your horses," I said.

I tried to keep my voice steady and calm to steady Torak. I wrapped my free hand around his reins.

"We walk from here on. But keep the horses close and tethered to you. Whatever's in there is frightening them and they might bolt. We can't risk losing them now. Do what you can to calm them."

Everyone dismounted, and I rubbed Torak's neck and side, whispering to him. But his eyes stared wildly. The horses were in a panic. They pulled, kicked, even bit, and soon I was drenched with sweat just trying to hang on to my own horse. Torak was strong, and if he bolted now, my skinny arms would be ripped out of their sockets.

We'd never make it through like this.

"We can't keep going," urged Will.

He struggled with the reins of his horse as it neighed and stomped its powerful legs, nearly crushing him each time.

"Our horses will be the death of us. There's no way they'll follow us through the mist. It's scaring the hell out of them."

I knew Will was right, but I couldn't face the alternative.

"I'm not abandoning Jon," I snapped.

Will swore as his horse kicked him on the leg. "I'm just saying…stop, you damn beast! I'm just saying, maybe there's another way…another route we can take."

I winced as the reins sliced a deep gash in my hands. I made a fist, but I was relieved to see the golden light seep through my wound. My skin tugged and pulled as it started to repair itself.

"Set them loose, and we'll make the rest of the journey on foot," said Nugar. He looked like he was about to butcher his horse with his battle-axe.

My heart thundered in my chest.

"No! It'll take us five times longer on foot. We need the horses."

"Then let's figure out another way to Soul City," growled Will. He was flushed and dripping with sweat as he tried to control his horse.

I kept moving. Going back was admitting defeat. I would rather die a million deaths than to admit defeat. But I knew this was madness. If our own horses didn't stomp us to death, whatever lurked in that mist would.

"Fine." I hoped my companions didn't hear the tremor in my voice. When I turned around, I saw that I had gone on far ahead of the others. I had moved forward when they had gone backwards.

"Let's get back to the fork in the road, and then we'll figure out another route. Maybe if we double back and use a less-traveled road—"

The mist grew denser. It rose like a massive white wall and circled me until all I could see was white.

"Elena!" Celeste screamed behind me. "Get out of there!"

But my legs were cemented to the ground. I couldn't move. My fingers slackened, and I felt the reins slip from my hands.

I was trapped in a world of fog and shadow and darkness. The road around me blurred and then disappeared. Everything became nothing, and nothing became everything. The spinning got faster and faster. It seemed to go on forever, and then it stopped.

My ears popped. I couldn't hear Celeste's screams any longer. All I could hear was the dull thudding of my hammering heart.

I had made a horrible mistake. The fog *was* a portal. And I had stepped into it.

CHAPTER 8

I HAD CROSSED INTO another realm. My world had disappeared, and my companions with it. I was surrounded by shadow and falling ash. It stank, a toxic combination of sharp and acrid.

And then, nearly invisible against the darkness, a creature stepped from the shadows barely ten feet from where I stood. It was vaguely human, with flesh of swiftly moving shadow, bones, and green fire.

It was the demon from my nightmare, and in spite of myself, I began to scream.

The demon stood over seven feet tall. The green fire that surrounded it subsided and vanished, and I could see gray skin under its thick chest armor, forearm guards, and a chain mail skirt. The demon was as well muscled and lean as a seasoned warrior. The only weapon I could see was a long sword that hung from its waist. And what I'd first mistaken as the points of a crown were actually six-inch bones protruding from its skull in a perfect ringlet on the top of its hairless head. It had high, protruding cheekbones and yellow eyes like burning coals.

It watched me without expression. But I would have been a fool not to have been frightened. Hell, I was frightened. I had accidentally crossed *into* Hell.

I didn't know much about demons, but I knew this one was male, unless they were sexless and they all looked like this. I was really frightened. This was not some mortal human or a witch, and I was certain I could not kill it. If I'd possessed magic like Ada or Fawkes, maybe I could have had a chance to fight my way out. But I knew I couldn't fight this demon. I needed to get away before I gave it the chance to kill me.

There was no sign of a doorway or evidence of any entry where I could have fallen through. I was in a tangle of rocks and darkness that was surrounded by mist.

I started to panic as my every breath burned my throat and lungs, like I'd swallowed shards of glass. I strained for breath and felt my blood gush to my head. I started to faint, and I knew I couldn't last long here. I couldn't even fathom how I had gotten here in the first place. I had simply *walked* into this realm.

I blinked to see. *Could I simply walk out the same way I'd walked in?* I needed to find the doorway back to *my* realm. *But what if I couldn't get back?*

"I've been waiting for you, steel maiden."

The demon's voice was guttural and ancient. The demon clearly knew who I was, what language I spoke, and apparently it had been waiting for me.

"I thought I'd use the language of the priests, so you would understand me," said the demon as though it read my mind.

"Although I hate to use such vulgar and revolting mortal speech, I will you use it with you…just this *one* time."

I tried to laugh, but my throat was full of blood, and I hacked. My body was not fit to live in here. And apparently my blood magic didn't work either. I didn't feel its pulse fighting off whatever this place was doing to me. I felt only an empty void inside me. I might be a fearless steel maiden in Arcania…but here…

White lights exploded behind my eyes. I pushed down on the panic that welled up inside me and strained to focus. The pain lessened a little, enough for me to stand up. I could feel wetness drip down the back of my neck, and I was sure my wound had ripped open.

"Why bother even speaking to me at all?" I hissed.

My throat tightened, and I spat the blood from my mouth. But as soon as my blood touched the ground it disappeared in a puff of coiling smoke.

I shook my head and focused on my surroundings. The mist and ash parted long enough to reveal rocky and ashen ground. I then I saw structures in the distance that looked like cities. I could hear grunts and moans somewhere in the distance. And then I noticed crowds of shadowy demons and creatures drifting in the air.

It was bad enough to fight in the real world, and although my limbs were stiff with fright, I kicked myself into action. I would not die here. I wouldn't.

I knew no one could help me. It was me against this world, this demon.

I staggered and nearly fell, but I managed to use my limbs and grasp my trusted witch blade.

"What is this place?"

The demon smiled and for the first time I saw the rows of black, needle-like teeth in his mouth.

"This is the Underworld, the realm of shadow and eternal darkness. It is the home of all creatures born in shadow and death, and it exists beyond your mundane terrestrial world. It is the realm of our Lord, the Creator of all darkness and shadow."

I had no idea what it was talking about and watched the demon through squinted eyes.

"Why did you bring me here?"

I knew the answer to that question, but I needed to keep him occupied while I figured out my next move. I had to get out of here.

The demon stepped towards me with the unearthly grace of a primal predator. Its face wrinkled in what I suspected was a sneer.

"It is of particular interest to me that a human half-breed, a *female* human half-breed, could be the cause of such trouble—remarkable for a mortal."

"What trouble? I've never even met you before now."

His eyes shifted to the magecraft in my pouch, and for a second I feared he was going to try and take it. I stepped back.

"The priests had promised to kill you…but time and time again they failed. You always seemed to slip away when you were in their grasp. But we're tired of waiting for foolish priests. So I've been searching for you."

He raised his arms.

"My power is lessened in the world of light and the living. I cannot reach as far as I would like…not yet…"

He stopped and frowned, as if he had said too much. "…which is why it took so long to finally find you."

Blood dripped onto my tunic from my nose.

"Because you want to kill me?" I growled.

The demon's eyes flashed. "Yes. How perceptive of you. Yes, yes. You must die. You alone possess the necessary skill to control the power in the stone. And these fool priests need to complete the ritual. We cannot have you interrupt that. You must die."

I didn't know what ritual the necromancer priests were intending, but if it involved an alliance with the demon realm, it was worse than I'd feared. Whatever they were doing, it was weakening the veil, the barrier that protected our world from the demon realm.

He took a step toward me and sniffed.

"The blood magic in you is very strong. Your death will bring great power."

He must have seen a spark of hope on my face when he added, "Witch magic does not live here. It lives in the world of the living where it can replenish itself. Your magic is useless here. You are powerless."

The demon cocked its head. "You are already dying. You know I'm right. I can see the fear in your mortal eyes."

"Are you a demon king?" I choked on my own voice.

A cold sweat dripped down my back, and I felt my witch blade slipping dangerously in my hands. I needed to distract it while I searched for a decent plan. If there was an *in,* there must be an *out.*

But why was the demon still in this realm? Why hadn't it crossed over to the land of the living?

"King?" said the demon, as though tasting the word on his tongue for the first time. "Not a king, but in your language I am a shadow knight, or perhaps a prince of darkness."

Shadows moved behind the shadow knight. I squinted through the wind and saw a horde of otherworldly creatures. I stifled a scream as their fleshy, crooked bodies shuffled towards me. The vile creatures looked like men who had half melted into reptiles. Their yellow eyes flashed hungrily, and they began to howl.

I took a deep gasping breath but coughed up blood instead of air. I struggled to control my rising panic. I had to be clever. I closed my eyes to shut out my fears and sought the calm within my core. I focused in the quiet of my mind. I was ready.

For better or worse, I gripped my witch blade and lowered my body into a defense stance.

The shadow knight eyed my weapon.

"How admirable," the demon purred. "A fight to the death? You will lose. Life cannot win in the realm of death."

My vision had begun to blur, and I blinked so that I could see more clearly.

"I won't die a coward," I spat and wiped the tears from my eyes. "I will fight."

My magecraft pulsed, and I was surprised to feel a spurt of heat on my side. The shadow knight's eyes darted to the pouch at my waist. He could sense it. *If magic wasn't supposed to live in this realm, what was he sensing?*

"You can't come through into my world, can you?"

I tried hard not to show my relief. There was still hope.

"It's why it took you so long to find me. Because you can't cross over."

The shadow knight's expression soured, but then he bared his teeth.

"Not yet. But soon. Soon your world will be ours. When the veil is broken, darkness will cross into the world of the living and crush it. The Unmaker's hatred of life is infinite. He will swallow you all. Your world will die."

The demons wanted our world, and the priests were helping them get it. Pricks. I should have killed the high priest of Anglia when I had the chance.

The shadow knight pulled out his sword. The black metal gleamed in the dim light.

"I shall enjoy feasting on your soft, mortal flesh. But first, the hunted must take part in the hunt."

The shadow knight raised his sword and bellowed in a strange language.

I knew what was coming. I leveled my weapon and waited. I held my breath, trying to keep steady and focused, even though my heart slammed painfully at my chest.

The ground beneath me trembled and the two nearest demons leapt at me with their terrifying jaws snapping.

Goddess, if you can hear me, help me.

I gripped my weapon and met the first creature.

Everything moved with the slow elegance of a dance. The demon was the size of my warhorse and came whirling at me with a cold and hungry rage. It pulsed and oozed like a trembling shadow as it advanced. It opened its enormous maw and howled in rage.

Moving on instinct, I pivoted, brought my blade up in an arc, and then spun again and swung it back down. My face and chest were splattered with something wet, but I could see that I had sliced a large gash across the creature's chest and cut off one of its arms. Its black blood sprayed the ground, but I never stopped moving.

I whirled and plunged the tip of my blade into one of the creature's eyes and pushed it into its brain. I pulled out my weapon, and it slumped to the ground.

I fought the urge to vomit as the demon's blood smelled like a mixture of feces and rotten meat. It burned my eyes.

I sensed the air move behind me, and I turned in time to block another demon who was reaching for my neck.

I could feel its hot breath on my face as I kicked out with all my strength. The demon went sailing backwards, and I fell hard on my ass.

I managed to push myself back to my feet in time to slash another creature's head right off.

I spun and skewered another through the mouth and out the back of its head. I yanked out my blade, but I cried out as it sank its teeth into my arm.

I staggered. My head pounded, and I struggled to breathe. But my legs grew stiff with exhaustion, and my lungs burned. I needed more air.

The ground wavered, and I could see white spots. I could hear laughing somewhere in the drifting clouds of ash, and I knew the shadow knight was near.

"Give up," I heard his voice.

"Your mortal life is over. Stop fighting the inevitable and give yourself up to the darkness. Your blood magic cannot save you, little mortal."

Bastard. I was furious. I wanted to slice the demon's throat.

I thought of Jon, and I hoped my companions would keep searching for him after I was dead.

Although the odds were against me, although I knew I could never win against these demons, at least not in their world, I wouldn't give in. I was a fighter. I always found a way…

Another demon came at me in an onslaught of flashing talons. I met it blow for blow, but I could barely see. I did my best to ignore the hot, putrid reek of decaying flesh. But even as I fought with everything I had in me and managed to fend off the demons, my body began to weaken of its own accord.

With every strike, kick, and punch, I grew more tired.

The mist moved and another creature sniffed at me with a long, elephantine nose. My energy was almost spent. I saw several small black eyes flash at me before it leaped.

I ducked and jumped back, but not fast enough.

Searing pain burned my stomach. And I gasped when I saw my wound. My blood magic wasn't working this time. There was no familiar healing sensation as my skin repaired itself. There was only pain.

I staggered back and held my chest with my hand. Blood seeped through my fingers. I raised my witch blade with my other hand, but I was weak, and my arm muscles burned with the effort.

I was going to die.

I tasted the coppery tang of my own blood and tried to slow my own panting. I winced at the raw pain in my throat. My lips cracked and bled.

The demon rocked back onto its hind legs, readying another attack.

I turned and ran in desperation.

I was surprised at my burst of speed, but it only lasted a few seconds before my body burned from the inside out, and I fell flat on my face on the cold, sharp rock.

I sensed a presence behind me. I flipped onto my back and jabbed out with my witch blade, but something grabbed my throat, and my arm went limp.

"Foolish little mortal," spat the shadow knight.

He lifted me up as though I weighed no more than a bag of flour. My feet dangled in the air, and he brought me so close to him that I could smell the putrid stench from his body.

"There's nowhere to run. Take comfort in knowing that your death will mean a great deal to the Unmaker. Your death will bring us power. Everything is connected. Your blood sacrifice is essential, just like the stone is essential. Our power comes from death and shadow. Your world will die."

I gasped for air. I tried to kick out with my legs. I knew I would bleed to death if I didn't die of asphyxiation.

But as I felt the darkness come for me, I also felt a warm pulsing in my core.

"I will taste your mortal flesh while your blood is still warm."

He laughed a sick wet laugh and pulled me closer to his mouth of razor-sharp teeth.

I did not close my eyes. I would look death straight in the eye.

The air around me shifted, and the pressure around my neck lessened a fraction.

The shadow knight pulled away from me with an alarmed expression.

My head lolled weakly to the side.

I heard shrieks and a loud clap of thunder. And then the demons scattered and ran.

The wind picked up, and I could feel ash and sand on my face.

And then I saw it, the tear in the veil. It was like a ripple in the air, or a drop of water breaking the calm surface of a lake. It rippled and grew, and the light intensified. As soon as the light touched the demons' flesh, they burst into flames and exploded into clouds of ash. The light burned everything in its path.

I smiled.

The shadow knight bellowed "No!"

He turned on me, and with a swing of his sword that would have brought down an army of men, he slashed in my direction.

But it never reached me.

The shadow knight jerked backwards, as though an invisible force had pulled him, and with a clap of thunder, the portal and the demons disappeared.

I collapsed to the ground.

I heard the snap of a bone breaking somewhere, and I pushed myself up on my elbows in excruciating pain. Pain was good. Pain meant I was alive.

I opened my eyes and winced at the light. After a few moments, my vision cleared, and I recoiled to see that the tip of a sword was pointed at my face.

"Now, what do we have here?" said one of the high priest's concubines.

CHAPTER 9

I WAS TOO SHOCKED to answer right away. But when I tried to speak I only coughed out some blood. I took a moment to compose myself.

I had met this woman before. She was the redheaded concubine who had helped bathe and dress me for the Great Race. It was her. I was sure of it, but I almost didn't recognize her at first. She'd lost her voluptuous curves, and her once porcelain skin was now sickly gray. Black circles marked the skin just below her eyes, and her red hair had lost its vibrant crimson color and had turned a dull mousey brown. She looked as though she had aged twenty years. If it hadn't been for her playful voice, I might not have recognized her at all.

"Helen?" I croaked with a throat that was still dry with blood.

The concubine sheathed her sword.

"Why is it that whenever we meet...you always look like hell," she asked.

I raised my brows. "Maybe that's because I was just *in* hell."

Part of me wanted to tell her that she, too, looked a little disheveled, but I thought it best not to.

I gulped down some fresh air and stumbled to my feet. My right ankle had been injured, and I had to steady myself. My head spun, and I swallowed hard to keep my stomach contents from spilling out.

"Elena!"

I turned, and Celeste pulled me into a tight hug.

"Thank the Goddess! We thought you were lost forever. What happened? Where did you go?"

She released me and stepped back to look me over. She could see that my ankle was bent at an awkward angle.

"Oh my. You're hurt."

I brushed her off. "I'll be fine. It's nothing."

I could already feel my blood magic pulsing warmth through me, healing me. *Thank you, Goddess*, I prayed. *Thank you for saving me.*

I thought I should thank her although I wasn't sure if it had been the Goddess or just damn luck that had closed the portal.

I looked over Celeste's shoulder and was relieved and delighted to see Will leading Torak and his own horse towards me. When Nugar and Lucas led their own horses in to view, I couldn't help but notice the apprehension on their faces.

What had happened while I had been in the demon realm?

We weren't alone. My men appeared to have been joined by a whole crowd of women, not just plain females, but gorgeous women with golden tanned skin. I recognized some of them. Kayla, with long golden hair, had been the head concubine, and Triss, who had been the youngest. I didn't recognize the others, but it was obvious from their perfect bone structure and bodies that they had all been concubines.

They looked like the true soldiers of the Goddess.

They led tan colored carthorses that also looked vaguely familiar. The women had shed their see-through robes and were dressed in practical pants and shirts. More astonishingly, they were bristling with weapons. Their eyes were hard and fierce, very different from the compliant expressions they had worn when they had been concubines to the priests. They looked as though they hadn't had a decent meal in a few months, but Helen looked the worst.

"We heard you screaming," said Celeste. "But we couldn't find you. It was like you just disappeared in that fog. Like it had swallowed you. We searched the mist, but it was like looking for you with our eyes closed. We couldn't see anything. And then a few minutes later the strange mist disappeared, and you were simply back again."

I squeezed Celeste's trembling hand.

"I'm here now, and I'm alive."

I squeezed it harder. "It seems the Goddess still has plans for me."

"We'd seen those dark clouds and that ghostly mist before," said Kayla.

She carried herself like a warrior who had been trained in combat and not in the art of pleasuring men. She looked down the road.

"We've seen folks walk into the mist, and children get swallowed by the darkness, but we've never seen anyone come out. You're the first."

For the first time since we had fled Witchdom, I felt real fear for someone other than Jon and me. Bile rose in the back of my throat at the thought of innocent children walking into the demon realm, and of the atrocities they must have suffered.

What if we couldn't stop this? What if it was already too late?

"How many more of these clouds have you seen?"

Kayla's perfect features contracted into a nervous glare.

"Not many a month ago, but for the last two weeks…a few every day. And they never settle at the same spot for too long. The clouds shift and reappear in different locations. Some are bigger than others."

"I even saw a group of twenty folks disappear all at once," said Triss. She rubbed her arm fiercely like somehow it would erase the memory.

Whatever these women had seen, it had left them shaken. Even though they did a good job of masking it, I could see their fear in the shadows below their eyes and in the twitching of their limbs. They were terrified.

And after what I'd experienced in the demon realm, I knew they had good reason.

Somewhere beyond the veils of our world, Hell was waiting to get in. And I couldn't let it. The fact that the portals couldn't stay open indefinitely gave me a little hope. If the portals couldn't stay open, the demons couldn't cross over to our world just yet. There was still a chance we could shut them out forever.

I had to *destroy* the stone.

"But what *happened* to you?" Will interrupted my thoughts. His eyes were wild and a sheen of sweat covered his face. "If you weren't here...then *where* were you?"

I took another gulp of good air and said, "I was in Hell."

For my blasphemy, Nugar and Lucas both made the sign of protection and forgiveness from the Creator. I glared at them. I expected them to be more open-minded.

Will's eyes narrowed. "You mean that you crossed into—"

"I went through a portal into the demon realm."

I waited for the fear and disbelief to fade from everyone's faces before I continued.

"Just like that mist we faced at Death's Arm. Only this time it wasn't the demons that crossed over, it was *me*. I saw what the other world looks like. Call it luck, or a miracle, but I barely made it back. I got a glimpse of what would come if we don't stop the necromancer priests."

"Hell in Arcania," said Will, stealing the words from my mouth.

I forced myself to stare at him. Looking away would mean I was frightened, and I wouldn't spread the panic and dread I felt. Not just Jon, but everyone living in Arcania and Witchdom was in imminent danger.

"What did it look like?" asked Helen, who seemed genuinely interested.

I didn't want to remember, but I'd never forget.

"Death—darkness and shadow and death. There's nothing living in that realm. There is only death. Whatever happens. Whatever we do. We can't let the demons cross over. Because if they do, our world will die, and we will die along with it."

An uneasy quiet settled on the group.

"Then we are all doomed," Triss whispered.

"No." I straightened up. "No, there's still a chance we can stop this."

"But how?" said Kayla.

"How can we defeat such darkness? Demons? We're just mortals. You said it yourself; nothing can exist in that realm. So what happens to us when they cross over and bring their darkness with them? It's only a matter of time."

Her tone was flat, and her expression hardened.

"We know about you. We know you're *different.* The priests never shut up about you. But what about the rest of us? How do we defeat this?"

"By not giving up." Celeste surprised everyone, including me. "By helping us with what you know of these so-called priests, these necromancers. Knowledge is stronger than you think. The Goddess is with us. Elena is proof. She will guide and protect us."

The concubines looked unconvinced. Even the men seemed shaken. Kayla stared at me indignantly.

The blood rose in my face. I was annoyed. I didn't have time for this. I had already wasted too much time trying not to die in the demon realm. We needed to keep moving.

"Yes, Celeste is right. That world is toxic," I said quietly. "I couldn't even breathe. It's a bloody miracle I even made it back alive and in one piece—but I *did*. I'm here for a reason. And I know exactly what I'm going to do."

"Which is?" I could see that Will knew what I was about to say.

"First we get Jon." I paused and smiled before I continued, "Then we kill the priests and destroy the stone."

As everyone stared at me, I turned to Kayla and asked her to clear up something that had been bothering me.

"But…how did you manage to escape the priests?"

"Easy enough," said the tall blonde. "We'd been training and planning to escape for most of our lives. All we needed was a diversion. This was our chance. You might not have seen us, but we were watching when the high priest killed Prince Landon. When the high priest claimed the Heart of Arcania stone for himself, we knew it was time."

"And you managed to escape the black blight?"

I caught Will's eye, and I knew he was thinking the same, *how could a group of untrained females escape without a scratch.*

"Is that what you call the sickness?"

Kayla's expression hardened as she inspected the men. Her eyes rested on Celeste for a beat longer.

"You seem to have escaped it as well."

She turned back to me. "We knew the priests were different from the rest of the noblemen in Anglia, different from men in general. Their desires and passions were *unnatural*. They spoke of demons, of black magic, of a time when they would destroy the light in our world and replace it with darkness. The high priest of Anglia spoke of a *coming of darkness*...when Hell would rise and dominate all life. We took your arrival with the stone as a sign for us to leave."

I tried not to react to the inference that I was somehow allied with the priests, and I continued to question Kayla.

"And the priests would speak to you openly about their plans?"

I didn't try to hide the skepticism in my voice.

"Of course not." Kayla's face hardened. "The bastards talk in their sleep."

Kayla dared me to contradict her. But I knew she was speaking the truth. Goddess knows, I didn't want to think about what those bastards did to these women. She probably had a lot more to say about the priests, all the women would. And I knew that knowledge would be priceless to the witches.

"If you're planning on killing the priests," said Kayla darkly, "then we can help you. We can be useful. We know things about the priests."

She smiled.

"I have no doubt about that." I returned her smile, and I agreed with her. I was certain that the concubines had many secrets to share.

"Whatever it takes," Kayla pressed. "All six of them need to die. And when the life snuffs out of the high priest's eyes, I will cut them out."

I raised my brows. I was beginning to really like her.

"I'd want nothing less."

I started to see Kayla in a different light now. Maybe her strength and pain had been there the first time I saw her. But she had been beautiful, and I had smelled like I hadn't bathed in years, so I didn't see. But there was no mistaking her loathing of the priests now. *How old had she been when the priests took her?* They had stolen her life, all the lives of these girls. I didn't want to think about her as a little girl with a dry old priest's clammy hands on her.

I suppressed a shiver and looked at the other concubines. The same determined hatred for the priests glimmered in their eyes. It was a familiar feeling. I wanted to avenge myself to those who'd wronged me, too. Who was I to stop them?

"Fine," I said, feeling more optimistic about this new alliance with the deadly concubines.

"We need all the help we can get. But first I need to do something on my own."

I wasn't about to risk their lives retrieving Jon. They would be useful, but not just yet. Besides I needed to be careful. The necromancer priests would be expecting me to come for them in a rage. But I wasn't that stupid. I would wait until the time was right. We'd only get one chance at this, and I couldn't afford to screw it up.

"In the meantime," I rubbed my temples as my head began to throb again. "You'll find food and shelter in Gray Havens. The witches' realm in Anglia is probably the safest place for you. And it's where we're headed next. We have friends there—"

I knew the concubines had more crucial information about the priests, and that kind of knowledge would be extremely valuable. I knew Ada and the other witches would find it out.

"But they're *witches*," said Triss, and she shared a look with Kayla. "How do we know they're not in league with the priests? We all know they worship the devil!"

Celeste choked "Excuse me?"

Triss straightened. "Why would you send us there? What game are you playing at?"

I felt all the eyes of the concubines on me, so I knew I'd have to make this good.

"I'm not playing games," I said. "And I'm not playing with your lives. Trust me."

I was speaking directly to Kayla now because I knew she was leading them.

"If you want to die, stay here and see how long you'll last on your own."

I met Kayla's glare.

"But, if you want to live, and if you want a chance at revenge, go to Gray Havens and trust the witches."

Triss scoffed. "Easy for you to say. You're not even coming."

"I'm half witch," I said.

Triss' eyes narrowed in suspicion.

"I am."

I waited while the concubines did a collective intake of breath.

"And Celeste here is a real witch. I don't have time to go into the details, but it's like you said. We're mortals, all of us, witches and humans. And we share the same enemy. Right now it's the necromancers playing at being priests, but I have a feeling you already knew that?"

I took Kayla's silence as a *yes*.

"We're on the same side, the side of the living, of the light. We need to stick together and share our strengths to fight them. The witches want the same thing as you—to kill those bastard priests."

Kayla was quiet for a moment before she spoke.

"I believe you survived for a reason, and I'll put my faith in that...in you. The Creator, or the Goddess as you put it, let you live. So, we will go to Gray Havens and wait for you there. We know the way."

"Good," I nodded. "Because I don't have much time left to convince you."

I made my way towards Torak, grabbed hold of his saddle, slipped my boot in the stirrup, and pulled myself up. I leaned over and rubbed his neck.

"Glad you're sticking with me," I whispered in his ear.

Celeste and the men mounted their horses.

My heart pounded as I anticipated another encounter with the mists and the demon portals. I might have survived by the will of the Goddess, but I suspected that my blood magic had helped, too. If we encountered another portal, Celeste and the men wouldn't be so lucky. Unfortunately, there was only a road, and it was surrounded by dead and decaying trees.

I turned to Kayla.

"Tell High Witch Ada that I sent you. She'll take care of you, especially when she finds out *who* you are. I'm sure they'll want to hear more about the priests and about what you know. They'll be grateful. Trust me."

Kayla considered it for a moment. "And where are you going?"

I turned my gaze back on the road. "Soul City. We're looking for someone."

My voice was pained, and I couldn't control it. "Someone we...someone *I* left behind."

Helen looked as if she already knew who I was talking about.

"Is that the handsome dark man you were with the night the prince died?" she asked.

My heart thrashed in my chest. "Yes. Jon. We're going to try Soul City first—"

"He's not there," said Helen, shaking her head.

"What? You've seen him?"

I kept my composure, but it was hard not to shake. My limbs felt weak. If I were standing, I would have fallen over.

Jon was *alive*.

"Yes," the concubine answered casually. "But he's not in Soul City. He's in the Pit."

"We just came from there," interjected Kayla. "It's where we've been staying for the past two months. But it got so bad we had to leave. The sick fight those of us who aren't infected, and the rest of us kill each other for scraps of food."

My jaw clenched tight. I was determined not to break down in front of these women.

"Are you sure we're talking about the same man? I mean, how would you recognize him?"

"It's him," said Kayla. "I remember him from that day."

She must have seen the relief on my face because she added quickly, "Just…be prepared. He's changed."

I knew what she meant. The Jon I had known was probably completely gone by now, and in place would be some sort of wraith, but I didn't let it dampen my spirit. He was alive. And that was the best news I'd heard in months.

And I would get him back.

"We better hurry," growled Nugar. He motioned to the darkening sky.

"There's not much daylight, but it'll only get darker the longer we prattle. We can make it to the Pit in a few hours if we get a move on."

I knew he was right. I turned to Kayla and said, "Thank you. See you in Gray Havens."

I kicked Torak, and we flew forward without another word. It was as though he sensed my urgency as he dug in his hooves and galloped as if the shadow knight himself were chasing us.

I held on to the hope that I could save Jon with Celeste and her tonic. We bolted down the dirt road, and I never looked back.

CHAPTER 10

WE HEADED SOUTH, aware that we only had a few more hours of daylight, if you could call it that. The shadow that had been cast over the sun, cast a heavy gloom over our task as well.

Even though it was the beginning of winter, there was no snow anywhere and the air was stale and warm—too warm. It was unnatural. It should have been damn cold, but the closer we got to the Pit, the warmer the air got. Trees loomed around us like leafless skeletons, and instead of snow, ash and rot covered the ground in blankets of gray. It was a blackened winter.

We rode hard, pushing our steeds. We followed the path that once hugged the edge of the dense Anglian pine forests. It was a road that had once smelled of pinecones and daffodils and wild roses. Now the air was heavy with the stench of rot, piss, and moldy leaves. The pines had lost their needles, and their bark was covered with the black spots of the sickness.

The gusting wind blew ash into my eyes, but I didn't dare slow Torak down. I had a primal need to believe in our quest. If I let my fear overtake me, it would all have been for nothing.

Familiar farms passed in blurs of grays and browns. I didn't even glance at the bodies in the fields. We didn't have time. Most of the nearby villages had been burned, and only stone chimneys and steel beams had been left standing. The looked like the carcasses of animals. Everything that hadn't been burned had been left to die from the black blight.

Sweat dripped down my back and between my breasts as I struggled to keep upright on Torak. My head pounded, and the wound at the back of my neck throbbed as we pushed harder and faster. I felt the warmth of my blood magic pulse through me, but my strength still hadn't returned completely. I hadn't eaten anything this morning, but I wasn't going to stop. Not for hunger. Not for anything.

By the time we neared the village, I was almost choking on my own dread. As it always was with the Pit, I smelled it before I saw it.

Only this time it wasn't the pungent smell of unwashed bodies, vomit, and piss. It was the choking smell of rotten meat, smoke, and death.

Through the blurry haze of tears and smoke, I could see the blackened frames of buildings that were once people's homes. Wooden posts were charred and broken. Rock walls were layered with soot, and the remains of tables and chairs had caved in on themselves and were glowing red. Where once merchants' shops and apartments had stood, only a pile of smoking ashes and scrap metal remained.

Anything that could burn had been burned. The tragedy was that it had been the men and women and children who had been infected with madness who had destroyed their own homes.

The ramshackle scenery of home should have given me some sort of comfort, but all I felt was cold and empty. There was barely anything left to remember it by.

I had hated this place. Loathed it. I had wanted nothing more in life than to get the hell away from here. But now, looking at what was left, I remembered all the years of hard work it had taken to make it somewhat livable. The home where Rose and I had lived was gone, and so was something in my heart.

I was crying for the Pit. It was ridiculous, ludicrous, and yet the tears wouldn't stop. I had never truly realized how much the little city had meant to me until I had seen it completely destroyed.

But what stood out even more than the demolished buildings was the lack of noise. It was too quiet. Goosebumps riddled my skin. Where once the tumbledown village had been overcrowded with Anglia's worst, where thousands of folks had been forced to live in too small a place, now the Pit was completely deserted.

I retched over the smell of burned meat and rotten flesh, over the blackish ooze that leaked through cracks in charred skin, and over the flies that buzzed around the bodies.

I could see that Will's eyes were red and full of anger.

Nugar sat on his horse; one hand gripped his reins as though they were the only things keeping him from falling, while his other hand grasped his battle-axe. And for the first time I could see real pain in his rugged face.

Lucas' shoulders bounced as he sobbed silently.

This wasn't just my home. It was theirs too.

"Look for survivors!" yelled Will, his eyes wild. "We'll take them with us to Gray Havens."

Before I could stop him, he urged his horse into the remains of the city. Nugar and Lucas were right behind him.

"Will! Wait!" I hollered, but they had already disappeared into a wall of smoke.

I cursed under my breath. I needed Will and the men with me. We could be ambushed. There could be hordes of the infected waiting around the corner.

I realized that they had been as anxious as I to return home. It hadn't just been about Jon either. I couldn't stop them from looking for survivors. They probably had family and friends still here, but I didn't join them. It was pointless. Anyone could see that there was nothing left but bones. The Pit and everyone in it was gone.

Eventually I headed into the smoldering streets and curving alleys, hoping to find some survivors, to find Jon.

I led Torak deeper into the bowels of the city, into what had once been Bleak Town. Celeste had ridden up beside me, and I knew she could sense my panic.

"I'm sorry, Elena. We're too late."

"What?" I said before I could make sense of her words. But I knew exactly what she meant.

"I'm sorry about your home. The concubines should have told us it had been destroyed. And it doesn't look like there are any survivors. We came for nothing. We should follow the others to—"

"No."

I knew Celeste was just trying to comfort me, but I was beyond comforting. I focused on the neck of the high priest. I imagined my hands wrapped around his windpipe, and I imagined my thumbs crushing the life out of him.

I will kill you for this, bastard.

"Elena?"

I couldn't let my emotions get the best of me. I had come here for one reason only. I pulled out my witch blade and grasped it in my sweaty palm.

"This isn't how it ends," I said. "He's still here. I know it. Come and stay close to me."

If Jon was still here, I knew exactly where he'd be.

Celeste and I led our horses slowly down the road, picking carefully through sharp metal and wood splinters that could cut through the horses' legs.

The Dirty Habit was the only building still standing. It had been the only inn in the Pit, and it had always stood out among the other buildings. It looked exactly the same as the last time I had set eyes on the damned thing. The panel siding had been scorched in an earlier fire, and the second floor was open and looked skeletal. It looked as if it had been entirely unaffected by the destruction surrounding it.

A trap?

My mind screamed that it was a trap, but my heart wouldn't have it. I began to fear that I would actually find him. *What had become of Jon?*

I slid off Torak's back. I heard the sound of hooves and turned as the men arrived. The gloom on their faces told me enough. I couldn't find it in myself to ask.

I looked up into Will's worried eyes. All my companions were taking my measure. Even the quiet Lucas studied me carefully.

"Wait," said Will as he dismounted.

The men followed his example and slid off their horses.

"You know this looks like a trap. There has got to be a reason why it's the only building left standing."

I didn't have to look into the faces of the others to know they were thinking the exact same thing.

After I had tied Torak's reins to a nearby post, I took a steading breath, despite the smoke and stench and said, "I know. Either there's a horde of red monks or of the dead, or Jon is there waiting for me, to kill me most likely. But I'm still going in."

I stared at the men. "It's why we came."

I waited for Will to reply, but he only clenched his jaw and looked back at the inn.

I waited for Celeste to climb off her horse. I reached inside Torak's saddlebag and retrieved the tonic she had prepared for me, for Jon. I placed the vial in her hand.

"If you're willing, I'll really need your help in there. You'll know better than me how to administer it."

Celeste gripped the vial purposefully.

"I told you I would help."

She gave me an encouraging smile, which I returned gratefully. She was risking her life, too. I just hoped I knew what I was doing.

"We need to move quickly," I said. "I don't want to stay longer than necessary. If he's not there…we leave."

The words felt final on my lips, and my eyes began to burn.

"And if things turn out badly in there, and if you can manage to escape, take the main road and go north until you reach Gray Havens. You can't miss it. Promise me."

"Okay, I promise." Celeste gave me a tight little nod. "But, we're *all* leaving together."

Will looked like he was about to protest. I could see that he was close to panic, but then he became resolved and made his way next to me with his sword in hand.

"Keep Celeste safe," I said. I knew he would.

Nugar and Lucas looked ready. I could see the fury that lay just under the surface of their resolve. I was glad for it. I needed it.

I looked back to the inn. Somewhere in that building was the man I loved, or what was left of him. I couldn't keep lying to myself. There was a chance Jon was dead.

Here I was, back again where it had all begun. My folly began here with the bet I made with Mad Jack, and my foolish stealing of the Anglian crown. At first, I *had* wanted to steal it, to prove a point. I wanted to show Mad Jack that even a scrawny female could do the impossible.

Celeste raised her hands to the sky and offered a blessing to the Goddess.

It was time. I smiled in spite of the dread in my gut. I *was* going to get Jon back. I took a deep breath and broke into a run. With my heart pounding madly in my chest, I raced up the steps and disappeared into the Dirty Habit.

CHAPTER 11

I RAN BLINDLY INTO the grim light.

As soon as I crossed the threshold, my wound throbbed, and I cursed under my breath. I ignored the pain as best as I could and raced through the hallway. My mind was a map, and I remembered where to turn and where to watch out for walls. I'd been in this place enough times to know it by heart. The others moved behind me.

The inside was dark, and I could barely see five feet in front of me. But I couldn't stop. I relied on instinct, kept my wits about me and kept my ears alert for any signs of an ambush.

I leaped over a fallen chair and headed straight for Jon's office.

A shape moved in front of me.

I barely had time to register what was happening before the shape came at me.

"Elena!" I heard Celeste scream from behind.

In the dim light I could just make out the shape of a large, burly man. Then I could see the sickness in his eyes and on his skin. I smelled his rot and then saw a flash of silver as he swung his sword for my head.

But I was ready for it.

Without pause, I pushed Celeste back and sprang forward. I met his sword with the side of my witch blade. I kicked him in the knee and deflected his attack momentarily. He came at me again, and I deftly avoided his flashing sword again. But this time he struck out with his other arm and punched me in the face with his fist.

I heard something snap on the left side of my face. I tasted blood in my mouth, and the pain from my fractured cheek brought tears to my eyes. But I never stopped moving. If I stopped, I would die.

I spun and attacked in a wild rage. I thrust upward, and my blade arced through the air and hit the left side of the man's head. I gagged at the rotten meat smell as I yanked out my blade, and blood splattered my face before he crumpled to the ground.

"Behind you!" howled Nugar.

Moving on instinct, I ducked, whirled, and came up behind another man. He turned around, but it was already too late for him. I shoved my witch blade into his right eye, and he went limp. I flung his infected carcass aside. I stepped over him, and then the shadows moved.

Ten more infected men emerged from the walls and came at us swinging their swords at a frightening speed.

"Keep Celeste safe," I growled at Will and watched as he placed his body protectively in front of hers.

I heard Nugar's battle cry. Lucas shouted a curse, and then metal clanked against metal as a new attacker came at me. The black magic had spread like a spider web across his face and made him even more terrifying.

When I heard Celeste scream from somewhere to my right, I lost it. I couldn't let anything happen to her.

My rage slithered up my spine, down my legs and arms, and into my fingertips. The aches in my head and limbs disappeared. My heart pounded, and the heat that pulsed through me sent new strength to my limbs, sharpened my eyesight, and enabled me to move with ease and agility. The magecraft in my pouch glowed.

Whatever magic this was, it filled me with power. I ignored Ada's warning not to give myself to witchcraft, and I embraced it as I embraced my fury. And the two blended together perfectly. I had become an unstoppable force, a perfect assassin.

Magic rippled through me. My body trembled, and I smiled. And then I was moving again.

I moved like I'd never moved before. I watched my own movements quicken into a blur of limbs that weren't my own. I didn't have to think of moving my legs or arms, they just moved of their own volition. It was as though my body anticipated what my mind wanted to do. I became one with the magic of the stone. Everything moved with the slow grace of a dance. I saw everything. I smelled everything. I felt everything.

I could have closed my eyes, but where was the fun in that?

The infected black eyes of my attacker gleamed with hunger and hatred. He came at me with primal fury. I whirled with cold grace and spun like a top with my blade out in front of my chest. I heard the slash of steel as it tore through flesh and muscle and bone. And all that was left of the thing that had attacked me was a crumpled mess.

I felt like my body had become independent from me in its efficiency. And I smiled at my new strength, my new magic. I embraced the smell of rot and decay because it was the smell of death.

I felt the next three of my infected assailants before I saw them. Without even turning around, I sensed their movements. I knew what they were going to do before even *they* knew themselves.

I pivoted in a blur of blades and arms and legs. Feinting left, I reeled and struck out at the first attacker. My blade crashed against his sword, and my arms shook as I countered the enormous force of the man's inhuman strength. But now *I* had magic too.

Without pause, I spun and evaded the killing thrust of his sword. He howled and whirled. But as he closed the distance between us to deliver another strike, I lunged forward and slashed my blade across his neck. The man toppled to the ground, writhing, and his black blood spilled onto the floor.

The air moved behind me, and I leaped to the side as another infected monster crashed to the ground where I'd stood a half a second ago. I never stopped moving and never paused to think. I just let the magic react and move me.

I blocked his sword with my blade, and our weapons locked. He towered over me and used his weight to crush me down. His bare arms were scaled and rotten, and foul-smelling gore oozed from his cracked flesh. He bared his yellow, rotten teeth, and his putrid breath brushed my face. He pushed down on me again, his face twisted in rage.

My focus was as sharp as a knife. I ripped open his belly just as another came at me. And another. I moved with precision. I spun, ducked, and sliced. The magic in me pulsed, and I reacted without question or pause. I was deaf to their death howls and indifferent to the foul-smelling blood and guts. I pulsed with magic and death, and I liked it.

I felt the eyes of my companions on me. I must have looked like a crazed woman, but I didn't have time to reflect on what had just happened.

I quickly took a head count and found Celeste first. The whites of her eyes glowed in the darkness. She was trembling, but she was unharmed. Will was at her side. His face was smeared in black blood, and the bodies of the dead were piled at his feet. Nugar's left arm hung strangely limp, and blood dripped from his fingertips. His large chest heaved as he breathed loudly through his nose. Lucas was panting for breath beside him, and the blades in his hands were covered in dark liquid.

"Is everyone okay?" My voice echoed strangely. I looked at my companions, but no one answered.

They looked frightened and confused.

Celeste's stare stopped my breath. She'd seen me fight in the witch trials and knew what I was capable of as a steel maiden, but she had not seen me fight like this. If anyone could figure out my new power, it would be her.

I was about to explain what had happened to me, but I hesitated. I *needed* the magecraft. I was stronger with it. I could wield its power. I could defeat whatever the necromancer priests threw at me with this new strength.

I said nothing. The magecraft was mine, and I was keeping it.

I surveyed the shadows and listened, but we were alone.

I heard a gurgling cough and leaped over the crumpled bodies looking for the last of our assailants who was still alive. I stood on his chest when I found him, and black liquid pumped out of his mouth.

"Where's Jon?" I hissed. "Where's Mad Jack?"

He smiled and black blood seeped between his teeth. His hairless head was covered in scabs and open sores. His diseased face hung so limply with gaping holes that it was impossible to tell how old he had been before he became infected. It was as though I was staring at a corpse.

The others moved around me as I leaned forward and pressed the tip of my boot against his throat.

"Tell me now, and I'll give you an honorable, quick death. If you don't, I'll leave you alive to suffer, and trust me, it'll be a long while before you die. You'll asphyxiate on your own blood. It's one of the worst ways to die."

He coughed a wet, sickening hack. "I don't know anyone...by that name."

"Liar!" I hit him and heard a satisfying crack. The man's black eyes rolled into the back of his head, and I grabbed the top of his head and turned it to face me. He seemed to focus again. His dry, cracked lips broke into a smile. I leaned forward until I could fell his warm, sour breath on my face.

"Just kill him and be done with it," said Nugar.

A sheen of sweat covered Nugar's forehead and temples, and now that he was closer to me, I saw the rip in his tunic above his left shoulder. He was losing a lot of blood.

Celeste must have seen me staring at his arm because she moved towards him and quickly tied a thin leather strap around his upper arm just above the wound. I was surprised that he didn't object.

I turned my attention back to the wounded assailant. While I was tempted to end this prick's life, I didn't want to kill him just yet. He could still be useful.

"What happened here?" I asked him.

Will and the others leaned closer.

"Where are the others? Surely you can't be the only one left. Where are the other men from the Pit? Where are the women and children?"

The infected man twitched beneath my weight, and I pressed my boot against his neck.

"Tell me, you rotten bastard."

"Dead," hissed the man. His voice was barely audible through the blood in his mouth.

"All dead." He laughed. Black liquid dribbled down his chin and neck.

I grimaced at the stink and breathed through my mouth.

"Then where are the bodies? We only saw a few back there. There should be more, a hell of a lot more. What happened? I'm not going to ask you again."

"Death," said the man. "And darkness. The Unmaker is coming. You cannot stop a God."

I swallowed hard.

"Where's your God now? Why isn't he here to save you?"

The infected man's eyes widened and he appeared to look at something above him.

"You're going to die, bitch," he gurgled. "You're all going to die. You're all going to—"

I speared my blade into his chin and pushed it up into his brain. His legs and arms twitched, and I waited until he finished jerking before I pulled it out.

"That was useless," grumbled Lucas as he wiped his nose with his sleeve. "We still don't know what happened here."

"Elena?" asked Will. "What was he rambling about? Did any of it make sense to you? What's this about the *Unmaker*?"

He was worried.

I wiped my blade clean on the dead man's trousers.

"I'll tell you what I know later. We need to look for Jon now."

I made to move, but Will's look pinned me to the spot.

"What?"

He looked away when he spoke. "Maybe...I think we...we've been gone a long time, Elena. I know this is hard...it's hard for all of us...but..."

I knew exactly what he was trying to say, and I couldn't prevent the tears that welled in my eyes. Maybe Will was right. They needed more explanation. They needed to rest. My relentless drive to find Jon was exhausting them.

I heard a quiet scraping sound. It cut through the tomblike silence of this giant room and drew my gaze to Jon's office.

I moved before anyone could stop me, before I knew what I was doing. I crossed the room and crashed into his office. Something caught my foot at the threshold, and I nearly tripped. I stumbled ungracefully into the room. I looked down and saw that I'd tripped over another infected body, one that I didn't remember killing.

And then I saw him.

A man sat on a chair behind a long wooden desk. It had been empty moments ago. His face was hidden behind a dark cowl, and his robe covered his strong, square shoulders.

My chest constricted with longing. I recalled vividly how Jon's warm lips had felt, how his sweet musky scent had driven me mad, and how his strong hands became soft as he caressed my body. How I loved him. I struggled to keep it together.

"Jon?" I cried. I reached out to him.

But I halted in mid-step as I remembered how he'd wanted me dead when he had become infected. If Jon was still infected, he could still be dangerous. I kept my distance.

"Jon?" I asked again, cautiously.

At first he didn't move, and then he lifted the cowl to reveal his face.

My breath caught in my throat.

"I knew you would come for him," said a voice that I could never forget. But it wasn't Jon's.

"At last, we meet again, Elena," said the high priest of Anglia.

CHAPTER 12

I JUMPED BACK AND would have fallen if Will's strong hands hadn't held me from behind. The others crowded behind us, and no one dared another step forward.

The priest, the necromancer I hated more than anything in the world, more than my bastard father, sat but a few feet away from me. Even in the semi-darkness I recognized the bastard. His voice had haunted me ever since I'd heard it the first time in the golden temple. I could never forget it.

At first glance he looked the same. His cold, self-important grin made my stomach churn. I wanted to cut that smile from his face. Under his dark cloak, his white silk robe was embroidered with jewels and golden thread, and the large sun symbol glowed in the dark like a star.

But he was different. He looked ill. I remembered him as a thin man, but now he was emaciated. Dark purple shadows made his pale gray eyes stand out. His skin had an unnatural grayish tint to it. It looked pasty as though he was running a fever. His thinning hair was plastered to his skull with sweat. His face was sunken, and his eyes seemed too large, his face too thin.

If I'd had to guess his age when I'd first met him, I would have guessed he was in his sixties. But now he looked like a two-hundred-year-old man. He had become so bent and gnarled that he reminded me of the Coven Council witches. His deterioration was supernatural. Something was feeding off his life force, draining his essence. Whatever black magic he was dabbling in, it was taking a toll on him. He was withering away.

The smell of rot was overwhelming. My eyes watered, and my throat burned. The reek of rot and death came off the priest in waves and consumed the air. My head started to spin, and I could hear the others coughing behind me.

In spite of his wasted body, his pale gray eyes were alert. They flashed with power and excitement. I wouldn't let his emaciated state fool me into believing he was weak. I knew his power was formidable.

He gripped a staff with a golden cage set on top with his skeletal fingers. And in that cage was the Heart of Arcania stone. My heart cracked a bit at the sight of it. I had been such a fool to have stolen it in the first place.

I felt a warm pulse from my magecraft, and for a moment I'd swear I saw the priest's stone shimmer in response to it. It was as though the stones were acknowledging each other. I stiffened.

Could the priest sense my own stone? What would happen if he took it from me? Two stones, no matter how powerful each was, would be better than one.

The high priest saw that I was staring at the stone, and I could see his yellow stained teeth as he smiled.

110

"Yes, glorious isn't it?"

He moved the stone towards his face and eyed it lovingly. His unnatural desire made me cringe.

"Go to hell," I spat.

I had found my voice, and although I wished it didn't tremble so much, I was relieved. If the priest had sensed the magecraft hidden in my pouch, he would have reacted to it by now. But he hadn't. I smiled at my small victory.

"Such power." The necromancer turned his gaze away from the stone and looked at me again. My blood turned cold.

"Such unlimited power in such a small thing, and a stone at that. Incredible really. You cannot imagine the gift you've given me, Elena from the Pit."

"I never gave you anything, priest," I laughed confidently. "But I'll give you the gift of death in a few seconds when my blade pierces your heart."

The necromancer priest sneered. "Death is inevitable in the world of the living. Every breathing creature, every living thing, every animal, every plant, even every blade of grass, everything will burn to ashes. Our Lord commands it. Death and darkness and power."

Celeste gave my hand a tug, and I let her pull me back a little.

My smile widened, and I watched the priest's face. "You look like shit. It seems death and darkness have already claimed you."

A scowl crossed his face, but his voice was cheerful.

"There is always a price to pay for great power. The more power, the higher the price. And as it happens, the price for infinite power and darkness in this world is death."

"The Creator would never bring death to those who worship truly," said Nugar.

He surprised me. I could hear the lethal anger in his voice.

Lucas nodded and murmured something inaudible. Tears trickled down his face.

"The Creator made this world and everything in it," continued Nugar.

He pulled out a silver chain with a sun pendant from beneath his tunic. It was the symbol of worship from the priest's own Temple of the Sun religion. I knew Nugar believed the priests were frauds, but I could see that it hadn't affected his faith.

"Why would he then destroy it?" Nugar continued. "Lies. You're nothing but a liar and an imposter. You don't serve the Creator."

The priest threw back his head and laughed.

"Ah. You mortals are so gullible."

He pushed his chair back and made his way around the desk. With a self-important look, he raised his voice as though he were giving a sermon.

"Accept the Creator as your shepherd, guide, and master, and he will lead you to true peace and true prosperity."

His eyes locked onto mine. "You misunderstand me. *Your* creator is weak. My Lord is the one true God. He is the Lord of Darkness and the Lord of all unmaking."

The priest's stone flared.

I heard Nugar curse, and I shared a troubled look with Will. He'd been right. This *was* a trap, and I'd walked right into it. What made it worse was that Jon wasn't even here.

I had been a damn fool, and I had damned everyone with me. Fawkes' face flashed in my mind's eye. What would he think of me now?

I took another careful step back, pushing Celeste with me. I was acutely aware that my other companions were following my example. And I didn't blame them. We weren't ready for this. We couldn't fight this necromancer priest on our own. Not when he had the stone.

The priest's pale eyes flared. "I was wondering when we'd get the chance to finish what we'd started."

I clenched my jaw and tried to control my breathing. I lowered my body slightly and put my weight on the balls of my feet so I could spring at any moment. I had to get the others out of here. We would never win this. Our best chance was to run like hell and pray to the Goddess to bless us with speed.

"And now you've left me no choice but come up with something more..." the priest looked about the room, "...more *creative*."

I moved to stand protectively in front of Celeste.

With a flick of his wrist, the wall behind the priest shimmered, and two red monks stepped into the room.

We had experienced the danger of these monks before, and I had nearly paid with my life. Their blood-colored wool gowns stood out in the dim light, as did the shaven bald spot on the tops of their heads. I wondered if the bald spot was a direct link to whatever dark lord they worshiped. I recognized the poison tipped talons that glowed on the gloves on their right hands. The priest's notorious assassins paused as if they were waiting for orders.

Their leering faces and elongated canine jaws were barely human. Their eyes were like black coals, and their faces were covered in black veins. They looked like the faces of the demons I'd seen when I'd passed through the portal. They were barely human, and I wondered if they were transforming into something else.

They moved like liquid night or wraiths from another world.

I fought the tug of panic and sensed my companions stiffen next to me. We braced ourselves for whatever was to come next. Celeste whispered a blessing for protection from the Goddess. I wished I knew it because I wanted to say it, too.

I grasped my witch blade so hard I could barely feel my fingers. My heart rate accelerated, but I wouldn't look away. I wouldn't show him fear. That's what the bastard wanted before he killed me. He was twisted in that way. Instead, I stared straight into those pale eyes.

"Come on then, you spineless prick. I'll kill your dogs before they lay a hand on me."

The priest reacted as though I'd just given him a compliment. But then my gaze was distracted by another shadow.

The air moved next to the priest. It was the same shadow I'd seen near the high priests before, a horribly deformed creature with long gnarled fingers and toes. Its body had a see-through quality, as though it was a specter, as though it wasn't really there. The ragged old pair of trousers and shirt it wore barely covered its dark gray skin, and its large, protuberant eyes locked onto mine, pleading.

The look on its face was haunting, and I didn't understand the pleading in its eyes. But then it cowered behind the priest and nearly disappeared altogether as it tried to hide behind his robes.

No one else seemed troubled at the sight of it, except for me. Even Celeste, who was a witch, didn't notice the specter. I watched as she looked from the priest to the monks, and she didn't appear to see it at all.

The priest smiled at my confusion, mistaking it for fear. He moved his arms around in the air dramatically.

"You know, for a *woman* you've proven yourself to be quiet an admirable adversary—the infamous steel maiden who passed through necromancer fire to steal the Anglian crown. The one who won the Great Race and brought me the Heart of Arcania. Such commendable skills. It's a shame I must kill you. But my Lord commands it. You must die. *All* of you must die."

I seethed. How long I'd waited for this moment. I wanted to gouge out his eyes and cut out that damned tongue. But the moment was wrong. It was all wrong. I was at a disadvantage because I cared for my friends. My love for them would get me killed.

"Let them go," I said.

My voice was surprisingly steady despite the hammering of my heart.

"You have me now. Isn't that what you want? What you've wanted all along? I'm why you're here. Let them go, and I'll stay."

"Elena, no!" Celeste grabbed my arm. "Don't do this. He'll kill you. You can't trust him."

I shook my arm free from her grasp, but I whispered. "I can buy you some time. You need to go. Now."

She frowned and mouthed the word *no*.

"I have a plan," I lied.

Truthfully I didn't know what the hell I was doing. But I knew I needed them out and safe.

Celeste looked at Will, trying to decide what to do.

"The mortals will die eventually," said the priest with contempt.

"Now or later. It makes no difference. Death is coming for all of you. None will be spared."

The red monks started to move.

I saw that Will had had taken up a defensive position on my left. He was a strong and experienced warrior, but he would die in a few seconds. He was no match for a red monk.

So I did the only thing I could do.

I slammed into Will and pushed him back.

"Get back! All of you!" I hissed. "They will kill you. Don't you understand? You cannot defeat these devils. You'll be killed!"

The red monks smiled when I called them devils. They probably were.

Will pushed me aside. "No. We're not leaving you."

"Yes. You. Are," I growled. "It's me he wants. It's always been me."

"No." Will stood his ground, but I could see Lucas making his way slowly towards the exit.

"There's nothing you can do," I said.

I looked from Will to the two red monks who had begun to circle him.

"You cannot fight his magic. Do you want to become an infected? Do you want to lose yourself to the darkness? This is exactly what he wants."

The necromancer's laugh burned in my ears. My eyes filled with tears.

"I can't have your lives on my conscience, too. It's too much."

"You can't fight the necromancer on your own," pressed Celeste.

I shook my head. "No. No I can't."

I leaned forward and lowered my voice.

"But I'm the only one who's resisted his magic before. I can do it again."

In truth, I had no idea if I could handle the priest and two of his bastard monks.

"I'll give you a head start. I've come face to face with what I started. And I need to fix it," I said.

"Do it. Go find Ada and the others and tell them."

I moved away from Will and the others. I didn't dare to look into Celeste's eyes. I moved farther into the room.

"Elena," called Will. "No."

I ignored him. I didn't trust myself to answer or to look their way. I had to be strong. I willed my anger to surface again. I knew that anger was my friend.

"Well then," I purred. I could feel dark fury welling up inside me. "It's like you said, they're just mortals. Why do you even care? Let them go. It's me you want."

I could see the cruelty in the faces of the monks, and my temper flared.

"So here I am. Come get me, you red shits. I dare you." I was furious.

The priest laughed and smiled at me wildly. "I will do no such thing, little witch."

I took a step forward.

"Let them go, you pale bastard, or I swear on the Goddess I will gut you like the pig that you are!"

The priest's smile widened at the fury on my face. He leaned slightly forward.

"Such a dirty mouth on such beautiful lips. You shouldn't have brought them with you if you cared so much about them."

He turned to the monk on his left.

"Keep the steel maiden for me. Kill the other female."

CHAPTER 13

"NO!**"**

My magecraft pulsed, and I launched myself at the monk on the left. I let the magic stone take control. I could feel it feeding on the darkness of my fury even as my strength and skill increased. I could not waver.

I leapt over a chair, and the room suddenly resounded with shouts, heavy boot steps, and the clash of steel. I knew my companions had retreated behind me. But I also knew I'd created an opening for the other monk.

A darker presence, cold but fierce had come over me. I liked it. And I let it consume me.

I spun my blade around. The monk held his sword defensively as he charged towards us. I smelled the rot and sweat from his body, and I saw a flicker of surprise flash across his face. I smiled because I knew what he was about to do next.

Feinting to the right, he brought his claw-like glove towards my chest. But I had anticipated him.

My blood magic raced through me with blistering power. I swung my blade low instead. The monk cried out as my blade hit his femur and sliced up into his groin. It severed the muscle in his thigh, and he tumbled helplessly to the ground. Black blood, thick and shiny as oil, flowed from the wound. It smelled like curdled milk.

The other monk had cornered Will, Nugar, and Lucas near the wall opposite me. I could see that they were protecting Celeste behind them. Something dark took hold of me and commanded me to bring death.

Without a moment's breath, I sailed across the room. The monk turned around as I slashed my sword across his back and down the back of his thighs. The monk cursed at the top of his lungs when he felt that his femoral artery had been severed. He called me every vile name I'd ever heard and brandished his sword in a last attempt to save himself. I whirled easily away from his sword, and I could see the fear on his face before I drove my blade into his heart. His last words died in gurgles of blood and stale hot breath as he slumped to the ground.

I did a quick inspection to see if the monk's poisoned glove had inflicted any wounds on the others. They were fine although I could see that Will looked bewildered.

I turned my attention back to the priest. His ugly face was screwed up in anger.

"I should have killed you long ago, witch whore."

I sneered. "Maybe you should have."

The priest closed his eyes, lifted his staff, and spoke some incantations in that same language I'd heard the day he first used the stone. The Heart of Arcania began to glow, and the hairs on the back of my neck began to rise. My magecraft pulsed as if it was about to burst out of my pouch.

"Creator save us," said Will from behind me.

The priest's stone pulsed, and a black radiance spun like a tornado around the room. It wrapped around me, wrapped around everyone in the room, and tightened until I could barely breathe.

His chanting grew louder and louder. His robes flapped, and a wicked smile stretched the skin on his gaunt face and made him look more like a beast than a man.

I couldn't let my friends become his infected wraiths. It was my fault. Tears streamed down my cheeks. My mind was in a fog. I had failed so utterly.

Before I could urge them to leave, tendrils of black magic floated from the priest's fingertips and slithered over his skin like hundreds of tiny shadow snakes. And then a surge of black power blasted out from the stone.

I pushed off and intercepted the fork of black lightning. It struck me in the chest and sent me sailing backwards. But I was on my feet again quickly, and I ran towards the priest with my blade still clutched in my hand. My magecraft scorched through the pouch and burned my skin. My blood pulsed in my ears, and I heard Celeste cry out my name.

My skin burned like ice as the dark magic pulsed through me. Smoke and the reek of burnt flesh rose from my clothes. Although my own magic had bloomed inside me, the dark magic didn't go away. It lingered inside, and I didn't feel any more pain. I wasn't sure what had happened to me, but I didn't have time to dwell on it.

The necromancer priest sneered at me.

"Steel maidens are more resilient than I imagined. But you cannot resist my magic forever. I will win. You will die. And this time you will stay dead."

I bared my teeth, aimed my blade at his right eye, and hurled myself at the pale bastard.

A tendril of his black power caught me on my left side, directly on my magecraft. I stumbled backwards, but I felt no pain.

I saw that light was glowing from inside my pouch. I stood paralyzed and watched as thousands of tiny white and yellow lights whirled around me in a glittering maelstrom and protected me.

A tendril of silver and gold shot from my magecraft.

The priest stared at my magic stone in confusion. A golden filament hit him in the chest. In a swish of black and white robes, the priest flew into the air and went crashing into the wall behind the desk where he had sat. He slumped to the ground.

I thought I'd killed him, but a moan escaped his lips, and his head rolled to the side. I rushed towards my companions.

"Hurry!" I yelled as I pushed Celeste through the doorway.

"Is the bastard dead?" Will turned back towards the fallen priest. I grabbed his arm and pulled him hard towards me.

"Don't be stupid."

I pushed him after Celeste.

"He's not dead. And I don't even know if we *can* kill him. He's already coming around, and we don't want to be here when he wakes up."

Celeste frowned. "How did you…"

"I don't know," I said.

The magecraft had reacted defensively, protecting me. I didn't even use a spell or incantation. It just countered on its own and attacked the priest.

"I'll tell you later, but we need to leave now!"

Lucas and Nugar disappeared through the doorway and into the main building. Will and Celeste were right behind them.

I was about to follow, but I turned and saw that the priest was still watching me. For a moment I froze and imagined he was about to send another filament of black magic at me. But he only blinked and frowned.

I turned to leave, but I could see that the Heart of Arcania was still pulsing, and my magecraft seemed to be responding to it again.

It wanted me to take it.

The priest's eyes widened. I could see clearly that he knew what I was about to do. Half of his face dropped as though he had suffered a stroke. Good. I was going to take the stone from him, and there was nothing he could do about it.

"Elena! What are you doing?" Celeste called.

But I moved towards the stone. Ada would have wanted me to take it. This was our chance. My heart raced. *I* wanted the stone. Not for them, but for *me*. I wanted its power.

I ran towards the stone. My foot caught on something and I pitched forward. Stifling a groan, I rolled off and inspected what I'd tumbled over.

"Shit." It was the dead infected fighter I'd tripped over earlier.

I don't know why, but I didn't move away. Something compelled me to stay and examine the body. His face was pressed against the floor and half hidden by his long black locks. There was something familiar about his face, the way his nose curved slightly at the tip and the height of his cheekbones. His skin was plagued by black veins and scabbed practically beyond recognition. But I leaned forward, and with a trembling hand I pulled away his hair and examined his face.

It was Jon.

My body trembled, and a wave of pain shook my soul. Something snapped inside me, and I began to sob uncontrollably.

"No. No. No."

My Jon was dead. I was too late.

CHAPTER 14

ALTHOUGH I COULD BARELY see Celeste's face through my tears, I knew she was kneeling beside me.

In the depths of despair, I bent over Jon. I touched his face. His skin was ice cold, like a corpse. Even though his eyes were closed, I could see there was no more life in him.

I had failed him. I was too late. He was dead.

Celeste put her ear to his mouth.

She looked up suddenly. "He's alive."

My lips trembled. "What?"

"I felt his breath," she said. "Barely, but it's there."

A grunt came from across the room. The priest's arms and feet twitched.

I spotted the shadow creature peaking at me from behind the desk. Its eyes widened when it saw me staring at it. It looked as if it was pleading for something. I turned my gaze away.

Celeste popped open the vial.

"Hold his head up and tip it back a little."

I gently placed Jon's head in my lap.

"Whatever you're going to do, do it fast."

Celeste nodded. She parted Jon's dry cracked lips and poured the contents into his mouth. The red liquid trickled down the sides of his mouth, looking strangely like blood.

"Is it going to work?" I couldn't stop crying, and my mouth tasted of salt.

Celeste looked hopeful. "I don't know. It might."

I grabbed hold of Jon's right hand. His fingers were as stiff and cold as icicles.

"Can you save him?" My voice shook with desperation. I didn't care how vulnerable I looked. All I cared about was Jon.

Celeste pressed her lips together and wiped her brow.

"I'm not sure. I'll do whatever I can to save him. But I'll need help from the other witches."

"Let's get him out of here," said Will.

He and Lucas each hooked their arms under Jon's armpits and lifted him.

"I will kill you!" came the priest's voice from behind us.

My heart sank. The bastard was already on his knees. He was shaking, but he had managed to recover this much in just a few minutes. I realized I couldn't kill him.

"Come on!"

We hauled Jon out of the inn. I couldn't stop staring at his lifeless face. The last time I'd seen him in the golden temple, he had been infected, but at least he had been alive. Now he looked dead.

"Tie him up on Torak. He can ride with me—"

"No," said Will. "He's heavy. And we can't risk him falling off."

He looked at me carefully.

"Elena, you're skilled with a blade, but you're not strong enough to help carry the weight of a man and fight—"

"Yes. Yes. Yes."

I waved my hand hurriedly at him, a little irritated at the truth of his words. I could wield a magic stone, but I couldn't hold up a grown man.

"You're right. I won't be able to hold him up. Just…just do it fast."

My skin felt tight around my cheeks. My tears had begun to dry in the stale air.

"If I'm right, the priest will come barreling through that opening any second now."

No one wasted any time talking. We worked fast. Jon was secured to Will's horse, and we took to the northern road. We rode hard and didn't look back.

The remains of the Pit passed in a blur of gray and brown and red. I was barely aware of my surroundings, barely aware of my own body. My mind reeled with questions.

What had happened to Jon? Had the priest done this to him? Was this the inevitable end? Did the black magic eventually kill its host?

But he was still *alive*. I clung to that hope and let it push away at my fears. I felt a new urgency. Now that I had found him, I had to save him.

If anyone could save him, Celeste was that witch. And there was no better place to heal the wounded than at Gray Havens.

Hang on, Jon...please don't give up...

I remembered that my group had looked as if they had been frightened of me when I had fought the infected attackers and the red monks. I had saved them, yet they were still afraid of me.

I wasn't sure how Celeste felt. She appeared to be more suspicious than frightened. I knew I would have to confess that I'd stolen the magecraft. But I couldn't do so until I figured out what was happening to me.

Undeniably, something had happened. I had felt something snap into place like pieces of a puzzle. The priest's stone had clouded my mind with a dark desire to possess it.

If I hadn't stumbled over Jon, what would have I done?

The scariest part was that I didn't know.

My love for Jon had distracted me from taking a stone that might have turned me into a monster. My obsession with saving him might well have saved me, too.

I urged Torak on and kept my eyes on Jon.

I swallowed and immediately winced at the pain in my throat. I could feel that my eyelids were wet. I tried to lick my dry lips before they cracked and bled.

I would never have described myself as a killer. But that's exactly what I had become back there in the inn, a death bringer. Those infected men had once been normal fathers, husbands, and brothers, but I had taken their lives away without a second thought. I should have been repelled by all the blood, but I had felt nothing but anger and hate.

And now I would carry the responsibility of bringing death to them all for the rest of my life. Those men hadn't chosen to be evil. They were sick because they had been infected. I had not.

It wasn't long before we reached the exit from Soul City, but I barely glanced up. Even if the temple guards had spotted us, we were traveling so fast they would need steeds with wings to catch up.

I focused on the road.

After a while, fingers of white mist slipped through the waist-high grass that lined the edge of the road. Like a predator, it hid behind a line of trees, and then it slipped down and jumped across the ground. I scanned the forest around us and the road behind. The mist was relentless as it filled in the road and navigated the curves as though it had a mind of its own.

It was cold against my face, like a fog bank, and for a moment I feared that this mist was another demon portal. Torak tensed beneath me, and his ears flicked back. The air grew wetter and heavier as the sun dimmed. While the sky had turned gray, I could see nothing unusual. And yet I couldn't shake the tension I felt that we were being watched.

We arrived in Gray Havens at dawn. We had climbed into cooler air, and the occasional patches of heavy mist softened the carpet of leaves on the worn road. For the first time in weeks, I heard the familiar tweets and chirps of birds and the warning chatter of squirrels.

I kept glancing at Jon for any sign that would tell me he was still alive. I hoped that Celeste hadn't made a mistake. But he never opened his eyes and only moved because he was being bounced around by Will's horse. Every time I looked at his pale, sickly face, a pang shot through my heart. I thought I had been prepared for the worst. I had told myself repeatedly that Jon was most probably dead. I thought I had accepted it.

But it was a lie.

Goddess above, please help him.

We entered the impressive forests and grounds of Gray Havens. The air was cooler, and a thin blanket of snow covered the grounds. The sweet scent of wet leaves and damp earth was the true smell of an Anglian winter. The witches had done a great job of keeping the black blight from penetrating their sanctuary.

I could feel that the air was alive with the gentle hum of magic. If the men were aware of it, they didn't mention it. Will's weary expression changed to fierce determination as we entered the witch realm. When Jon had first brought me to Gray Havens to save my life, Will and Leo had stayed outside the borders because they hadn't dared to enter. But now that Will had met Celeste and had been introduced to magic and to other witches in the witch realm, he had become more confident.

And while Lucas looked nervous, he didn't say a word or stop either.

I was worried about Nugar though. His skin had a grayish tint to it, and he looked about to topple over. He'd lost a lot of blood, and his injured arm hung uselessly beside him. I'd forgotten about his wound completely. The black blight wasn't the only infection that could make a man lose his arm. I just hoped it wasn't too late for Nugar.

Torak neighed loudly in his enthusiasm to be back. Apparently even horses realized it was a spectacular place. Anyone would be foolish not to think so.

But the sight of the castle did little to lift my spirits. It was all too much. I was deathly afraid that Jon would die, and my chest ached at the thought of seeing Rose again. I hadn't realized how much I had missed her until now. I was ashamed at how little thought I'd given to her all this time. But I'd make it up to her.

Kindling Castle was exactly as I remembered. It was a massive and ancient log structure. Soft yellow light spilled through its large windows, and the dark gray clouds overhead did nothing to lessen its beauty. It was a secluded paradise.

The grounds of the castle were dotted with thousands of small tents, and smoke coiled up from campfires. There were people, *humans,* everywhere.

A few curious folks bustled out of their tents as we galloped by. Their faces were dirty, but their eyes were clear of any infection. They were dressed in regular riding clothes, and most appeared to be survivors from the Pit. Not all the folks from the Pit were dead. We were all filled with hope at the sight of them.

But how did these people get here?

The witch realm had always been considered taboo. People had thought that the witches were devil worshipers. It was really hard to imagine that all these people had packed up and come to Gray

Havens willingly. Perhaps in their desperation they had finally accepted help.

I spotted some men clad in Anglian red and gold, but I also saw dark-skinned men and women whose features told me they were from Purtula. I could see makeshift flags from most of the six realms of Arcania. The purple and green flags emblazoned with two snakes coiled around a sword were from Purtula, the red dragon on a blue shield was from Espania, and the blue and white flags were from Fransia.

The orange and yellow colors of Romila, and the green, black and yellow colors of the Girmanian people were missing. Surely if the other realms had escaped to Gray Havens, the Romilians and Girmanians would have made the journey, too.

So why weren't they here? I felt uneasy. *Had they known about the black blight beforehand? Had the Romilians and Girmanians been in league with the necromancer priests all this time?*

It seemed that while the humans had sought refuge here, they were still frightened of the witches because they had camped outside and hadn't moved into the castle. I was sure that most of them would have fit comfortably inside the castle walls.

The tall, elegant and fierce-looking concubines stood out from the rest. Although we rushed past them quickly, I saw a look of surprise and a flash of something else I didn't understand on Helen's face.

As we approached the castle, I spotted Ada leaning on a wooden staff and standing on the gravel path right below the front entrance.

I knew it was Ada. Even from a distance I could make out her porcelain skin and shapeless dress of simple green linen. As we got closer, I could see that the high witch had a knowing frown on her wrinkled face, as though she'd been expecting us.

I stopped Torak and slid off his back.

The high witch wore her chain with a star and circle pendant, and wisps of white hair escaped from her usual neat bun. She looked as though she'd rushed out of bed. Something was wrong.

The high witch scrutinized me in a way that sent a chill right through me. She had the same scolding expression on her face that Rose would have when I'd get home late from one of my excursions.

But I was beyond scolding. After everything I'd done for the witches, I'd expected a much warmer welcome, a smile at least. I gritted my teeth and strained to keep my composure.

I could never guess Ada's age, and I wouldn't have dared to ask her. I'd gathered from her stories that she must have been a few centuries old. But I'd never noticed her age before. She had never looked a day older than eighty, until now. She seemed older somehow and paler. There were dark circles under her eyes that hadn't been there before. Although she looked tired, her familiar dark eyes were alert.

The expression on her face changed slightly when she saw Jon, but then it was gone.

"Elena, you can't stay here. You must turn around now and go."

This was not the welcome I'd expected.

"Like hell I will." My voice shook with rage. "Do you know what we've been through to get here? What I've done for you and all the witches?"

Ada's frown deepened.

"I must insist," she said. Her tone was final. "I've already made the arrangements for you and your company."

I couldn't control myself.

I shouted, "And *I* must insist that we bring Jon inside, and that *you* help him! What is wrong with you? Can't you see that he's dying!"

My voice cracked, and my throat felt raw.

The high witch drew in a breath.

"Something's happened…it involves you. And unless you leave this place now—"

"He's dying! Whatever it is, it can wait. I'll deal with it later. He's more important. I've risked everything to get him here. You must help him."

I searched her face. "It's Jon, Ada. You have to help him. If he dies…"

She watched me for a moment.

"Bring him inside," she ordered finally.

She turned and disappeared through the great doors.

CHAPTER 15

WILL AND LUCAS HELD Jon by his armpits, and I held his legs. We rushed him through the grand foyer under the soft yellow light from a large chandelier and down a corridor. The pounding of our heavy boots disturbed the silence, and no one spoke. Will and Lucas' faces were flushed with strain. Jon weighed a lot more than we'd anticipated. I could never have managed to hold him on my horse.

We followed the old witch who moved with a sense of urgency and never faltered. The banging of her staff echoed loudly in the deserted hallways. We hurried down a set of wood stairs and through more hallways and corridors. I'd never been in this part of the castle before, and because Jon was on my mind, I knew wouldn't remember the way back.

Celeste bumped into me when we finally stopped in a large shadowed room. At first I could barely see anything. Ada raised her staff and uttered two words in Witchtongue, and with a small rush of air, eight wall torches flickered into life and cast long shadows on the floor. It seemed that Ada could also manipulate elemental magic. Interesting.

Celeste noticed Ada's power, too, and raised her eyebrows at me.

Together we settled Jon into one of the two vacant beds in the room. The room was large but it felt strangely intimate and personal with everyone inside.

Lucas pressed his back against the opposite wall, keeping an eye on everyone, while Nugar leaned on the other empty bed. Will stood right next to Jon as if he were afraid to leave him.

I looked about the room. The shelves that lined the walls held assorted containers, vials, and potted plants. It smelled of sage and other plants I didn't know.

I couldn't help but remember when *I* was unconscious, and Jon had rushed me inside the log castle. It seemed so long ago now.

I scanned Jon's face to see if Celeste's tonic had helped, but he still looked dead. Pus leaked from his cracked skin. He looked worse than before. I was so worried that words stuck in my throat.

Ada lit three clay pots, and the smell of sage rose all around us. She moved to the head of the bed and pressed her hand on Jon's forehead. She closed her eyes in concentration. For a moment no one moved, and I hoped Jon would open his eyes with just her touch. But he didn't.

From what I remembered, Ada was from the White Witches clan. While they were guardians, first and foremost they were healers.

Ada looked at me. "He's much worse than I thought."

I almost threw up.

"But you...you *can* help him, right? Please, Ada. Please help him. I've done everything you've asked. Please."

My voice sounded weak and far away.

"What did you give him?" Ada asked Celeste. "I detect some belladonna, sage, pennyroyal, and Angelica root. But there's something else that I haven't smelled in a very long time."

"I gave him a pinch of brimstone powder and dragons blood," said Celeste. "I knew it could cleanse the dark entities from a witch's blood magic. But as I told Elena, I didn't know what the effects would be on a human."

The high witch raised her brows. "Dragons blood?"

I looked from Celeste to Ada. "Why? What's dragons blood."

"A poison," answered Ada. "A very deadly one."

My stomach tightened and I turned on Celeste. "How could you give him poison?"

"Because it was the right thing to do," answered Ada.

I turned away from Celeste and regretted the harsh tone I used.

"Dragons blood is very deadly, but if you use it properly and a very small amount, it's a very effective way to rid the body of other poisons."

Ada nodded her head in approval and looked at Celeste.

"Fawkes told me about you. He said you were a lesser elemental witch who was skilled with potions."

Ada confided in Celeste. "You'll soon find out that there are *no* lesser witches in Gray Havens. Every witch is equal, no matter if they can or cannot do magic. There are ways one can do magic without magic. Your skill with potions *is* magic."

137

Celeste's cheeks flushed red.

"We can use a skill like yours, especially now," said the high witch. "Can you make more?"

"Yes."

"Good. You'll need to start right away."

"What about Jon?" I searched his face, but there were no signs that the tonic had had any effect. I let my tears fall.

"Will he live? Can he make it?"

Ada's face was expressionless.

"He's a decent lad, a very good fellow, better than most. But there is much darkness in him. And like a poison, it's eating away at his life spirit. He should be dead. Any other man would have given up." She paused. "But not him. It seems something or someone kept him alive."

I could barely breathe, "And?"

"And," continued the witch. "This tonic might have been exactly what will save his life."

Celeste gave me an encouraging smile. But I couldn't smile back.

"But we'll need to rid his body of the black magic," said Ada. "If we don't, he will die. I'll need help from my witches."

I didn't understand why Ada looked so troubled. Before I could ask, as if on cue, six other witches slipped into the room. Some wore the white and gold clan colors and pentacle emblem of the White Witches clan, and the others wore the same shapeless linen or wool gowns as Ada. I recognized the long brown curly hair of one of the female witches and the deep-set eyes of one of the males. They'd ridden out of Witchdom with us.

Ada caught the surprise on my face.

"Your arrival isn't secret. Every witch in this castle knows you've arrived."

She opened her mouth to say more, but then she pointed to Nugar.

"Fix him up before he bleeds all over floor. See to it, please," she said to no one in particular.

The witch with the long curly hair steered Nugar to a nearby bench, ripped off his shirt and began to dress his wound. The big brute clenched his jaw and eyed her warily, but he didn't utter a single word as the witch cleaned his wound. I was impressed.

The other five witches settled around Jon's bed, and I leaned over him to protect him.

The witches looked to the high witch for instruction.

"Elena." Ada pressed a firm hand on my shoulder. "I need you to take a step back."

And when I didn't, she continued, "If you want him to live, you will do as I say."

I glared at her for insinuating that I'd hinder any chance to save Jon's life, and I stepped back, but just a step.

Ada pressed her hands gently on Jon's head. The other five witches followed her lead and pressed their hands to Jon's body.

I watched in silence as Ada began to chant. The others chimed in, and a sudden breeze tugged at my clothes as the chanting grew louder and faster. The air smelled of honey, of lime and oranges, of sweet syrup and spring. It was the smell of the witches' magic combining. It was a smell that was so sweet that I welcomed it.

Light traveled from the witches' palms to Jon's body until he was illuminated in a soft white glow. Celeste's voice echoed in a blessing behind me, and I, too, prayed that this white magic would counter the black. Even Will's lips moved in a silent prayer.

Jon's legs twitched, and then his right arm flailed.

My heart leaped to my throat, I leaned over him. "Jon? Jon? Can you hear me?"

His body continued to move, more erratically now, as the chanting increased. He was convulsing like he was having some sort of seizure. It was as though his body was trying to fight the healing magic, as though the white magic was hurting him.

Then it was all over. The wind died, and just as fast as it had appeared, the magic glow over Jon disappeared. I felt as though I had imagined it.

Ada jerked back, breathing hard. A sheen of sweat covered her face. The other witches panted, and I could see that their damp robes had stuck to their fronts and backs.

"The black magic is strong in him," said Ada as she wiped her face with her sleeve. "It's been infecting him for far too long. Festering inside him. We couldn't reach it."

My blood drained from my face. I knew what she was getting at. I swallowed hard. My throat was painfully tight.

"But you said Celeste's tonic had helped to save him. Do it again. Please."

"We can't, not without risking our own lives or becoming infected."

The high witch regarded me for a moment, and then she grabbed two medium sized bowls and placed them on the floor on each side of the bed. And before I saw what she was doing, she slit Jon's wrist with a small dagger. Black blood poured from the slit and trickled into the bowl.

"What the hell are you doing? Are you crazy?"

I lunged for her knife, but Celeste pulled me back with strength that surprised me.

"Wait," she said as she whirled me around to face her. Her tone was firm. "It needs to be done."

Lucas pushed off from the wall, and Will stepped forward. They both looked for my lead in case they needed to intervene.

I shook my head.

"Do you even know what she's doing?" I yanked my arm from Celeste, unable to stop my angry words.

Celeste's eyes were bright.

"I know that we all want him to *live*. We want Jon to live, Elena."

"By bleeding him to death!"

Ada ignored me and made her way around Jon's other side where she slit his other wrist.

I winced at the sight of the thick droplets of black liquid that poured from Jon's exposed wrists. I felt the sting as though it had been my flesh that she'd cut, as if my own wrists had been sliced open.

But Jon didn't even move.

I glared at the high witch. "Are you mad? He's not strong enough for this. You're going to kill him!"

I knew that what Celeste had said was true, and yet I couldn't stop the words from spitting out of my mouth.

Blood pounded in my head, and I didn't think. I just let the anger move me. I grabbed my witch blade as my rage poured from me like blood from Jon's bleeding wrists. I was losing it. I was in a senseless fury and wanted to attack the high witch. I wanted to kill her. I was going mad.

Ada looked at me with surprise. Her concern grew darker as she scrutinized me. She could sense something inside me. I feared that she'd seen the magecraft, but her eyes never left my face. Then I saw sadness in her eyes, and I felt ashamed of what I'd almost done and had *wanted* to do.

I sheathed my blade. I felt everyone's eyes on me. What a fool I had been. I grew frightened. I didn't know what was happening to me, and I feared I wouldn't be able to control it.

I wanted to tell Ada about my stolen magecraft, but I had kept it a secret so long that I said nothing. I wasn't even sure if confessing that I possessed a magic stone would be a good thing.

The high witch sheathed her tiny surgical blade into a secret compartment inside her sleeve and turned her attention back to Jon.

All of a sudden the room became too small, too hot. I managed to will the darkness within me to subside and concentrated on Jon's face. All I wanted was to see him smile again.

I was nearly overwhelmed by the foul smell of Jon's rotten skin and the amount of thick, black blood that poured out of him. My fingers shook as I rubbed the tears from my eyes, and my legs trembled, barely able to support me.

Blood. So much blood.

"You're killing him," I said, my voice barely above a whisper.

"There's a risk he might die," said the old witch, gently. "He must have been one of the first ones to be infected. The black magic has latched onto him and eaten away at his soul. We've done all we can with our white magic. The only thing left to do is to try and purge the sickness."

I moved to stand next to Jon. My eyes filled with tears at the sight of him. His blood trickled steadily from his wrists, and the two bowls were nearly half full. I had to resist the urge to reach out and touch him. His face was so gaunt and mutilated by the infection, and his lips were so cracked and blistered. I felt useless standing there. I couldn't do anything. I couldn't save him.

"We must first rid the body of the infection before it can heal."

Ada took my hand and squeezed, and I squeezed back.

"It's in the hands of the Goddess now. There's nothing else we can do but wait. If he lives through the night, he will live."

The high witch turned to me as she wiped her hands on a towel.

"Now that you've finally decided to show up, Elena, you must know that a lot has happened since you were last here."

She grabbed my arm.

"Okay," I said, trying to wiggle out of her iron grip.

The high witch shook her head seriously. "I wish we had more time."

I frowned. "Jon didn't have time. There was no better place in the world to bring him than here."

The high witch shook her head at me. "You don't understand. I was waiting for you to tell you…"

"What?"

The other witches avoided my gaze. The silence was chilling.

Ada looked both sad and frightened.

"There's been a new development. Something I couldn't have foreseen. Something beyond my control."

"Ada," I said, my voice was little more than a growl. "You're scaring me. What new development? Did something happen to Rose?"

The high witch's eyes widened. "You need to leave."

"What?"

"Until it's safe again. Listen to me." She took a deep breath and spoke urgently.

"There's a small cottage north of here that borders Murk Bay. It's well hidden, and you'll be safe there, for now. Take your humans with you. They must not be discovered here."

She turned to Celeste. "Celeste, I would have you stay here. We could really use your help."

"Of course, I'll stay," said Celeste. "I'll help any way I can."

Will looked as if he was unwilling to part with her.

"Good," said the high witch.

She turned back to me, "I'll send Fawkes to retrieve you when it's time. But you need to go now—"

"But we just got here." I curled my hands into fists. "What the hell is going on, Ada?"

"Let me explain," came a deep voice from behind me.

I turned and felt as though my own wrists had been slit, and my blood had been drained from my body.

Sagard, the witch king of Witchdom stared at me from the doorway.

CHAPTER 16

My BOWELS TURNED WATERY, and I felt ill. I turned and shielded Jon with my body. I inched my hand towards my witch blade.

My men stiffened at the sight of the witch king. I saw the hatred in Will's expression as he moved to protect Celeste. Lucas blended into the wall and contemplated the situation, and Nugar growled. The men had not forgotten that the king had thrown them down into the hellhole of the oubliette to be forgotten and die of starvation. None of us could forget the human hides that he used as wall art, and the human skin that covered his throne.

This king was a real bastard, the worst.

Even the other witches shrank away from him. I wasn't sure if he *was* their king in Arcania, since Ada and all the other witches in this realm were considered to have been banished. Whatever he was on this side of the world, they still cowered in his presence. And I didn't blame them.

The witch king's shimmering black coat billowed behind him as he ducked his head and stepped into the chamber. He was bigger than I'd remembered, but it may just have been that I was more frightened now.

He was clad all in black, with a red hand emblazoned on his chest, the Dark Witches clan emblem. His iron crown looked like the jaws of a beast, and his white hair draped over his shoulders and hung down to his waist. And although his face and features were ageless, his face possessed a perpetual frown. The large gray jeweled pendant that hung from his neck on a thick iron chain was his magecraft.

My magecraft hummed as though it was greeting his magic stone, and I willed it to stop. Now was not the time to make friends. If my magecraft could sense other stones, it made sense that the king's magecraft could sense mine...or rather his late wife's magecraft.

A tall witch with spiked yellow hair and yellow eyes followed the king into the room. I recognized him as the king's coven general by the branded hand on his forehead and the jeweled pendant that hung from his thick neck. And behind him stood six male coven guards with identical hands branded on their foreheads and magecraft pendants around their necks.

Surely all these magecrafts would have sensed mine.

Silently, they all moved into the room. The king's eyes never left mine.

I looked at Ada. The old witch's expression matched the king in her fury. She gripped her staff with white knuckles and looked like she was about to clobber him with it. She looked at the magecraft around the king's neck, and she frowned in disgust.

Her reaction only confirmed my own suspicions that if I'd told her about mine, she would have taken it from me. My magecraft pulsed in time with my heart.

Celeste moved silently away from the doorway. No one noticed her as all eyes were on me, but I could see that she was just as afraid as I was.

I kept my breath slow and quiet, desperate to control the frantic beating of my heart. But no matter how I tried, I couldn't calm down, not with the witch king right there.

My knees buckled. I *knew* why he'd come.

The witch king moved as gracefully as a panther as he stalked toward me. The pendant on his neck glowed with yellow power.

"Thought you could slip away, did you? Thought you could take something dear and precious to me, and that I'd let you go?"

The witch king laughed without humor.

Was he was referring to me or to the magecraft?

"I don't know what you mean," I lied.

I remembered the dreadful wedding ceremony all too well. He'd looked at me with longing and lust, like I was some rare prize. There was none of that desire in his eyes now. Only hate. I looked behind the king, hoping to see the silver hair of an ally, but I could only see the sour faced coven guards.

Had the king killed his son and heir, the prince who had saved me? I feared the worst for him. *And where was Fawkes when I needed him?*

His coven general spoke next.

"Elena Milegard, from the Steel Maiden clan," said the coven general, his voice deep and guttural. "You are charged with the murder of queen Enelyn, beloved wife of our king."

I swallowed hard. This was not going well.

"What proof do you have?"

I knew I was reaching, but what else could I do. I looked at Ada. She'd tried to tell me to leave, but I'd insisted she try to save Jon. That's exactly what she'd done. This wasn't her fault. It was mine. And I had to take responsibility for my actions.

"Two witches saw you kill the queen," said the coven general. "They saw her pleading for her life, begging for you not to kill her. And then you murdered her like the savage human half-breed that you are."

This was getting better and better.

"I seriously doubt that," I said casually. "The queen would never beg. You should know that."

The coven general's face colored and he frowned. "Watch what you say, half-breed bitch."

"Go to hell, stiff."

The room was silent, save for the light trickle of Jon's blood splashing into the bowls.

If I ran now, I knew my magecraft would propel me with enough speed and strength to make it out of the castle alive. But I couldn't leave Jon. I knew the witch king would kill him the moment I left.

The witch king kept looking over my shoulder, trying to see what I was hiding. He wasn't an idiot. It was pretty obvious to anyone standing in this room that I cared for whoever was lying behind me. I had betrayed my emotions by shielding him. I shouldn't have been so stupid.

"Who are these witches that supposedly saw me kill the queen?"

I didn't remember having an audience, but it had been dark, and anyone could have been hiding in the shadows. The fortresses courtyard was enormous.

"Two witch maids saw you kill her," answered the coven general.

His face showed no trace of his emotions, but I could see by the way he studied me that he was trying to evaluate my strength and plot his next move.

I raised my brows.

"They said that? And you believe them?"

I knew that anyone who had seen me would have seen the prince there, too. And no one had cared to mention him.

The coven general's smile would have sent little children running away.

"One of our most celebrated Augur witches linked into their minds, and he too saw what they saw. He revealed every detail of your murderous actions. His word is the only proof we need. Images cannot lie."

"Then if that were true," I started carefully, my throat aching. "He would have seen someone *else*."

I looked to the king for his reaction. His shoulders tensed, but his face revealed nothing. Either he'd killed his own son, or the bastard was protecting him.

The coven general straightened.

"Humans are liars. There was never any honor in them. They're no better than animals."

I wanted to spit in his face.

Nugar growled, and for a horrible moment I thought he was about to throw himself and his bad arm at the general. But Will placed a firm hand on the big brute. It seemed to do the trick.

I relaxed a bit. My jaw ached from the tension.

The general leveled his gaze at me again.

"*You* were the only one there. The two witches and the Augur all confirmed it. You killed the queen because you were jealous of her power because she was a real and powerful witch. And then you stole her magecraft."

Shit. Shit. Shit.

Ada's dark eyes were on me before the general had even finished his sentence. I swallowed hard and avoided her gaze. If I looked at her, she'd see right through me. But the look on Celeste's face told me that she'd figured out why I had suddenly acquired such strength.

The king stepped forward and spoke to Ada.

"For someone so adamant that witches should abstain from conduits," he said, "it appears your apprentice seems to think otherwise."

"Elena would have no use for such a trinket," said the high witch. "She is skilled at a lot of things, but she is not a murderer."

My face darkened, and I prayed no one saw the guilt I felt.

The witch king sneered.

"Oh, but you are wrong, Ada. Seems like your new pet is a murderer. She is a murderous half-breed, which proves that witches and humans should never breed. She's going to pay for what she's done."

I leaned against the metal frame of Jon's bed and held my breath as Ada and the witch king had a staring contest. After a long silent moment, the king looked away from Ada, and his dark eyes settled on me.

The coven general spoke again.

"Elena Milegard of the Steel Maiden clan. You are found guilty of the crime of murder and are hereby sentenced to death. In two days, you will be beheaded."

"What?" I choked on my own tongue. The room began to spin.

Ada stomped her staff.

"I will not allow this."

"You have no authority here," growled the king. "Be thankful. I only came here to take one life. Keep pushing me, and I will take others. It's my right as king."

Ada pressed her lips together. Her eyes glistened. She would not help me out of this because she couldn't.

I stood my ground.

"It was self-defense," I pleaded. "She tried to kill me. I acted only to save my own life. And if your witnesses truly saw what happened, then you would know what I say is true. She attacked first, and I defended myself. It's not my fault she ended up dead."

The witch king's eyes flashed with hatred. "You will die."

"But it was self-defense," I howled.

The king's expression warned that I should back down, but I couldn't.

"I was on my way out of your damned fortress, and she jumped me from the bushes. She tried to kill me. She wanted to kill me because she knew you had feelings for my mother."

The king's eyes widened.

"She wanted me dead. Don't you see? You know it's true. I can see it in your face. You knew how much she hated me. You had your guards watch her before our wedding day because you knew she'd try to kill me."

But the king remained silent. He nodded to his general.

I turned to Ada.

"Ada!"

My voice caught in my throat. I could see that Ada's eyes were rimmed with tears. This was it. I'd lost.

"Take her to the holding cell."

The six coven guards came at me. Their magecrafts flashed with power. I flinched, but I didn't resist when they grabbed me. It would have been foolish to try anything. Their grips were like tight metal cuffs around my arms.

Will looked as if he might move forward, but I gave him a warning glare, and he stood down. My men had suffered enough. I didn't want them dragged into this. The only comfort I had was that the king didn't seem to care about my men or Celeste. I wanted to keep it that way.

As the guards dragged me past Ada, I whispered so only she could hear, "Protect Jon."

They hauled me out of the room before I could say anything else. They dragged me through the castle corridors like a common criminal. I had been convicted without a trial. My blood ran hot in my hatred for the witch king. He might think he had me now, but in his anger he had forgotten something.

I still had the magecraft.

CHAPTER 17

Turns OUT, the castle *did* have a dungeon, or something very close to it.

The coven guards hauled me down a long set of stairs and into the cellar of the log castle. The only light came from torches that were barely lit. Unlike the prison cells in the golden temple, which smelled of vomit and piss and desperation, this cellar smelled of mold and forgotten food and damp soil. The floor itself was old packed dirt, and the walls and wood posts were covered in thick cobwebs. The ceiling was low, and I had to duck to avoid knocking myself unconscious with a wooden beam.

I knew they were going to search me and confiscate my weapons. I couldn't let them get the magecraft. It had saved me from the necromancer priest, and I still needed it. *If the witch king and his cronies wore them, why couldn't I?*

I would have to make Ada understand that I was keeping it for the greater good.

So I looked for my chance as they pulled me into the dimly lit cellar, and I tripped over my own feet. I slipped out of their grasp, and as I pitched forward my clever, thieving fingers slipped the magecraft out of its pouch and into my boot.

"Stupid, half-breed bitch," said one of the guards as he yanked me to my feet. "Can't you even walk?"

I winced as the magecraft's metal clasp pinched the skin on the side of my calf.

"It's not my fault I can't see in the dark," I said, searching their faces for any indication that they had seen what I had done. Their faces revealed nothing.

"Move!"

The magecraft's sharp metal clasp sliced into my skin, and I could feel the warm wet blood drip down my leg. But then I could feel the familiar warmth of my healing magic as it worked to counter the cut. I was grateful for my blood magic, but I was also grateful for my tall leather boots.

My new home was stacked with bags of rice, grain, soft meat preserved in jars, used and broken furniture, dusty old books and rat droppings. It wasn't a *real* prison cell, but it was probably the only room in the entire castle with no windows and a very large iron door.

If I were them, I'd have put me in here, too.

It seemed that stinking prison cells were my lot in life. That's *if* I were to have a life. I wiped off a small wooden bench so I could sit on something other than damp soil and rat poop and took a look at my leg.

My sock and calf were wet with blood, but my wound was already healed. Only a small white line was left as evidence of a cut. I pulled my sock off and examined it up close, wrinkling my nose at the copper smell. It must have been a deep cut for so much blood. I tossed the wet sock into the corner and slipped my boot back on. I wasn't about to put on a blood-wet sock. Unfortunately, my change of clothes was still in Torak's saddlebag with the rest of my supplies. The leather of my boot stuck to my skin, and I could already anticipate the chaffing it would cause, but I had no other choice.

While the guards had taken away my pouch and all my weapons, they'd missed my magecraft.

I smiled as I held it and let it swing like a pendulum.

I could hear water trickling nearby and the sound of tiny feet scurrying in the walls as I sat in the corner of my new prison and watched door. The only light came through the cracks between the door and the wall.

I knew with all certainty that someone was going to come through that door, I just didn't know who or when.

They wanted to execute me in two days because I had fought back when the queen had tried to kill me. I wouldn't give up so easily. The Heart of Arcania was still in the necromancer's possession, and I was the only one who could get it away from him. I was also the only one who'd seen the other side and seen our real enemy. I had to warn them somehow.

I didn't have time to feel sorry for myself. People depended on me. Jon depended on me. Somehow I *would* make it right.

Ada had done all that she could for Jon, but she had also said that all we could do now was wait. Wait for Jon to wake up, or to…

I couldn't bring myself to say it. Even to myself. The high witch had said that Jon should have been dead, but that something or someone had kept him alive.

He was going to be okay. He had to be. I couldn't panic.

Why had the witch king come to Gray Havens? Surely he could have had me killed by his coven guards without having to make the journey himself. My mother had escaped, too, but the witch king had not left Witchdom to come after her. So why make the journey now? I had killed his wife, but I knew he had not been devoted to her. He had intended to take me as his second wife. It didn't make sense. I was missing something.

The hum of voices echoed from somewhere on the castle grounds. I jumped from the bench and pressed my ear to the door. It was chanting, and it wasn't in the common tongue, so I knew it was the witches. It was the same rhythmic chanting I'd heard from the witches who had followed us out of Witchdom. I still didn't understand *what* they were saying.

A stack of old books caught my eye, and I crossed the room without thinking and picked up a large leather bound book. It cracked as I opened it, and I flipped through the thick yellowed pages. As my eyes adjusted to the darkness, I could make out that it was written in Witchtongue. Even though I couldn't read it, I rummaged through the pages, not knowing what I was looking for.

Another flat-looking book caught my attention. It looked like one of the history books from Rose's book collection.

I rubbed the dust from the cover with my sleeve and opened it to the first page. It was hard to see, but it looked like a map. I ran to the crack in the wall next to the door and held the book in the light. It *was* a map, a very detailed map of Arcania. It looked like one of the maps from Rose's collection, but upon closer inspection, I realized that this book was older than any book I'd ever seen.

The ink was faded and had been completely absorbed into the paper in some parts. But what really drew my attention was that there appeared to be no reference to the six realms. Even though it had been written in Witchtongue, I could easily make out the shape of the country and the markings for villages and towns that I recognized. I recognized Lunaris, the capital of Witchdom, but no borders indicated what territory the witch realm occupied. Only the mountains were indicated.

I changed position to get a better view. I didn't know what I was looking for, but something compelled me to keep looking.

I flipped through the pages until I found a drawing that depicted a battle scene. The artist had depicted the fear and desperation on the faces of the fallen in a way that was hauntingly accurate and disturbing. There were two types of warriors, some with swords and some without them. I strained to decipher the words scribbled below each drawing, but the ink was smeared and worn, and it was impossible to make it out. Still, it was obvious that some great battle had been fought between the nations.

Flipping through more pages, I found more detailed battles and even some images of children. One drawing depicted three horrified women strapped to a stake and staring aghast at the flames that burned at their feet and up their bodies. The images were disturbing. They were all depictions of death, and most of the dying and the dead were witches.

Was this an accurate depiction of the past? What had really happened?

From what I'd learned from the witches, the steel maidens had been forced to help in the fight against the steel and metal weapons of the humans. I could find no drawings of witches with weapons in the book.

As disturbing as the drawings were, I found that I couldn't stop flipping through the pages. I felt I was about to discover something important. I skipped a few more pages until I landed on a drawing that made my blood run cold.

It was a map that occupied two pages, and it depicted ships from the north, south, and west, all converging towards Arcania. The boats all flew miniscule flags, but the images had deteriorated, and I couldn't identify the symbols. But I could make out the symbols on the ships. I could see heraldic badges with lions, trees, eagles and snakes, horses, swords and a dragon. They were the emblems of the six different realms I knew today.

The next page showed the ships on the shore and it was clear that human soldiers with long swords were engaged in the mass murder of witch children and their families.

I knew in my heart that I was staring at the truth. Fawkes had been telling the truth all along. I'd been lied to all my life. We had all been kept in the dark. The original humans of the six realms had come to Arcania from another land. And it looked as if they had murdered the witches who lived here when they had invaded.

CHAPTER 18

I SPENT WHAT FELT like an eternity in my small prison. My only visitors were the occasional field mice, and they barely paid any attention to me. They were more interested in filling their bellies with rice, grain, and giant furry black spiders. I was beginning to think everyone had forgotten about me.

After the first hour or so, I had the feeling that Rose would probably come to see me. I missed her. Even if the first words out of her mouth were scolding, her familiar face would calm my nerves. I smiled just thinking about it.

But she never came. No one did.

They'd thrown me in here without food or water. Worse, there was no bathroom, or even a chamber pot. I cramped with the urge to go, but I wasn't about to soil myself. I had no doubt that was what the king had intended. He wanted me to lie in my own filth.

Bastard.

Rose couldn't know that I was here. They were probably preventing her from visiting. The witch king had probably thrown her into a similar cage, just to piss me off. Even so, why hadn't Fawkes come? Surely the king would have let his old coven general, his friend, come to see me. And yet, no one came.

I was livid, lost in the thundering rage of a darkness that stormed through me. It was a tangible thing, and it wrapped around me like a blanket. It was almost like a release when I fed it. Anger had become my companion, and I liked it.

Why shouldn't I be pissed? I had done what the witches had asked of me. I had helped to defeat the darkness that the priests had unleashed. And yet I was still treated like an animal, like a criminal.

The king would pay for this.

But first I needed news about Jon. Only then could I make the necessary plans...

I kicked the ground angrily. I could still hear the chanting outside as I sat on my bench and clutched the large book. I couldn't stop thinking about the lies we'd been told since the beginning. Prince Aurion had been right. I was naïve. I knew nothing. But that was going to change.

Now that I had seen the book and knew what had happened, it made sense that the witches would hate the humans.

But no matter what had happened in the past, there was a new threat, a threat that endangered the lives of everyone. We would have to stand together if we wanted to live.

On my way to the castle, I had seen humans and witches who looked as if they were prepared to forget the past and have a future together. I just hoped it would be enough.

I heard the sound of heavy footsteps. I dropped the book, stuffed the magecraft inside my boot, crossed the room in two strides, and flattened my back in the shadows against the wall next to the door. I had only my fists and my wits to defend myself.

The heavy iron door scraped as it swung open. I held my breath.

Yellow light spilled into the room from the single torch my visitor carried. He spun around to face me. His silver hair sparkled like tiny stars in the light of the torch. His face came into view.

"If it isn't my favorite witch who's gotten herself caught."

Prince Aurion stood in the doorway. His beauty always surprised me. He was too perfect, too gorgeous. So very *unnatural*. Any breathing female would be a liar not to notice that he was a perfect specimen of the opposite sex. My anger melted away.

The prince turned to the two coven guards at the door.

"Leave us."

The two guards looked at each other before obeying their prince. They pulled the door shut behind them. I couldn't hear the sound of boots fading into the distance, so I knew they remained just outside my door.

Idiots. If I'd wanted to escape, I would have done it by now.

Prince Aurion sauntered into my prison. His gray tailored coat showed off his muscular body. His pale skin and sparkling silver braid shone in the darkness.

He turned to me with a sly smile on his elegant face.

"What are you doing standing against the wall?"

I scowled at him. "Waiting for you, of course. What else?"

I pushed off the wall, but I kept a safe distance between us.

The prince smiled. "It's nice to see you again, Elena. I've missed you."

The deep purr in his voice set my cheeks on fire, and I was glad of the dim light in the room.

"What are you doing here, Aurion? Did you come for front row seats to my execution?"

I noticed he held a platter of food in his hand. My mouth watered.

Aurion set his torch in the empty bracket on the wall. When he turned around, he had lost his smile.

"Seriously, Elena? After everything I've done for you, you still think I'm in league with my father."

I shrugged. "I don't know what to believe anymore. I've travelled across the country to seek help from the nation that could help in our fight against the darkness. And now this same nation has thrown me in a cell to await my death."

The images of humans killing witches in the book still haunted me. I had an uneasy feeling that there was more I didn't know.

His face was soft. "Here. I thought you might be hungry."

He settled the platter on top of a rice bag. I stood next to him and salivated at the cheeses, nut breads, sliced apples, grapes, dates and strawberries. I moaned and then I blushed when I realized he had heard me.

"Thank you," I said between mouthfuls. "This beats eating spiders."

The prince's teeth gleamed in the dim light when he smiled.

"Rose? Have you seen her?"

He looked perplexed.

"She's an older human with gray hair. Thin, but hopefully a little less thin than the last time I saw her. She's staying here in the castle. Ada promised to look after her while I was away. She's very dear to me."

My voice wavered. I was surprised that I'd let my guard down so quickly.

Aurion nodded. "I think I've seen her. She was with the human men you brought with you to Witchdom. And that witch maid is with them, too."

"Celeste." I let out a shuddering breath. "Thank you."

I devoured a slab of goat cheese spread on a slice of sweet bread. I sucked on my fingers. Rose would probably have had a fit if she had seen me doing anything so unladylike. I grinned and sucked on my fingers some more.

Thankfully the prince hadn't noticed my lack of decorum. He stared at his magecraft ring and rolled it around and around on his finger.

He stopped and scrubbed at his face. "Have they told you anything?"

"All I know is that your father is pissed at me for killing his wife and wants me dead. Sure I hated the bitch, but I was *leaving*. She attacked first."

Now I had sticky fingers and nothing to wash them with, so I settled for rubbing them on my pants.

The prince looked me in the eye. "I told him the queen attacked first. I told him *you* and *I* both acted in self-defense."

I exhaled loudly. "Yes, well your daddy seems to think otherwise. He told everyone that I acted alone, and that I set out to kill her on my own. That I murdered her."

"That's not what happened."

"Try and tell your father that," I growled.

Prince Aurion shook his head. "My father's always looked the other way when it came to queen Enelyn. Ever since my mother's mysterious death, he knows I suspected Enelyn of killing her. But I could never prove it. It's been one of the reasons we drew apart. That, and his obsession with killing humans. He and I will never agree on that."

The pain in his voice made me move towards him with the thought that I might be able to provide him with some solace. But I stopped and pretended to be interested in the pile of books instead.

"I'm tired of being used," I said as I turned to face him. "I'm tired of being lied to."

"I haven't lied to you."

I raised a skeptical brow as the prince smiled impishly and said, "Yet."

He moved closer to me and spoke more intimately.

"You know I had to tell those lies...for your sake. I didn't enjoy lying to you."

"Sure you did."

Aurion set his jaw. "There's still something I want to know."

I swallowed but remained face to face with him. "What?"

He was so close that I could feel the heat from his body and smell the sweetness of the soap on his skin.

His face was inches from mine now, and his breath was cool and minty.

"Did you take the queen's magecraft?"

I opened my mouth to prepare my lie, but somehow the words wouldn't come.

The prince flashed a smile. "You did, didn't you?"

His eyes rolled over my body, slowly, making their way up my thighs and lingering on my chest.

"Where is it?"

He leaned forward, and I braced myself as he ran a finger along my neck and slowly moved it down towards my collar bone, searching.

Blood rushed to my face. I slapped his hand away and stepped back.

"I don't have it."

The lie was weak and obvious, but I couldn't think of anything else to say in my stuttering defense. My eyes moved to the ring on his finger.

"And why should you care? You have one already."

The prince stared for a moment. "Because my father wants it back."

"Why?" I asked. The magecraft pinched my skin. "He has one and it's a hell of a lot bigger."

Aurion's smile widened. "Why have one, when you can have two. But mostly he wants it because tradition says it belongs to the Dark Witches clan and to the next in line to receive and wield a magic stone."

I didn't like where the conversation was going. Like hell I was going to give the magecraft back. I suspected that Aurion wanted the stone himself, not for selfish reasons like his father, but for something else.

"Don't you find it strange that the witch king came all this way?" I asked him. "Why would he come all the way to the realm he hates to be surrounded by thousands of the humans he hates, just to kill me?"

The prince peered at me. "What are you saying?"

"I'm saying that I don't think the king came here only for me, and certainly not for the magecraft I've supposedly stolen."

"Then what?"

I shook my head. "I'm not sure. But it can't have been just for me. He could have sent an army after me. Why come himself?"

The prince watched me, his eyes far away, but he said nothing. If he knew, he wasn't about to tell me.

"You still haven't told me why you're here," I said, desperate to change the subject. "Why did *you* come here to Gray Havens?"

He smiled and his gaze intensified. "Isn't it obvious?"

I looked away as heat rose from my neck to my face.

"Stop playing games, Aurion. I've less than two days to live. And if you say you care about me, if we're *friends*, you'll tell me."

I noticed that he frowned at the word *friends*, but his cool smile returned quickly.

"I came to keep you safe," he said.

I believed him. The emotions that showed in his face and eyes sent warmth through me.

He searched my face. He could tell by my reaction that I knew what he wanted, but that I couldn't give it to him. Whatever joy had been in his eyes vanished, and only a cold calm remained.

"Safe from your father?"

"That's part of it," said the prince. "After my father discovered his queen was dead and you were missing…" He walked the room. "Well, you can image his outrage. You had made him look like a fool. Weak. He killed every human he could find after that."

I remembered all the wretched humans working in the fields.

"What? Why? Why would he do such a thing?"

"Because he can," said the prince coolly. "But I suspect because they reminded him of something, maybe you, maybe something else. He's been looking for you ever since."

His gaze shifted. "There's something else you should know. The decision to have you killed wasn't my father's."

"Really! He has a strange way of showing it."

His face hardened. "It was the Coven Council's. They pushed for it. My father only wanted you punished."

"Lovely." I couldn't help but shiver.

"Still, they convinced him. They said a…"

He looked away from me.

I leaned forward. "Said what? You can't just start a sentence and leave me in suspense like that. What did they say? Don't worry about hurting my feelings. I can take it."

The prince rubbed his temples.

"They said a bastard half-breed should die for killing a high born. It would show weakness on the part of my father if he let you live."

Anger shot up my spine, and I felt that white-hot pain behind my eyes again. My head felt like it was on fire. My vision blurred, and I felt dizzy and cold and hot all at once, and then I stumbled.

"Elena, what is it?" Prince Aurion was at my side. "What's wrong?"

Steadying my breathing, I rubbed my temples.

"It's nothing. Just a headache. Probably because I've been cooped in here and breathing this foul air. It'll pass in a moment."

My headaches were getting worse.

Was I getting sick? What did it mean if my blood magic couldn't rid me of a simple headache?

"And what's the other part?" I asked, my headache subsiding a little. "The other part of why you came."

The prince cocked his head. The angular bone structure on his face was thrown into stark contrast in the dim torch light. "Because of the assembly that's been called."

He had my full attention now. "What assembly?"

"The meeting that was called by the Coven Council, my father, and the high witch of Gray Havens. We're to meet with the human representatives of the realms, whatever high-ranking nobles or officers are left, and the rebel leaders. They've suspected the necromancers, the priests, for a very long time."

I thought of Jon, and my heart ached. But he was too sick to speak for the rebels. They must have picked someone else by now...

"It's a meeting to decide our fate," continued the prince. "We are beginning preparations for the war against the necromancers. We need a good plan if we want to defeat these *priests*."

I whirled and grabbed his arm. "Aurion. I *need* to be at that meeting."

He raised an eyebrow. "That might prove to be a problem since you've been accused of murder."

I stepped back and let go on his arm.

"Damnit, Aurion, this is important. I have important information they'll need."

I suddenly realized how often and intimately I'd used his name. *What was I feeling?*

"Like what?" The prince looked calm, but his eyes twitched restlessly.

"Like I've been *inside* a demon portal and lived to tell."

His eyes widened, but he still kept his composure.

I started to yell. "I've seen what we're up against. I've felt it. Lived it. It's bad, Aurion. Really, really bad. I know what the necromancers are planning, and your leaders have no idea."

Aurion rubbed his face. "I'll see what I can do."

"Why are they doing this to me?" I asked.

I was uncomfortable at how intimate his voice had become.

"I won't let them hurt you, Elena."

I squared my shoulders. "I can take care of myself. Just get me a seat at this meeting."

The prince smiled.

"Consider it done."

He made to leave but then turned around and added, "Oh, and by the way, I thought you'd like to know something."

"What?"

"Jon's awake," said the prince.

He closed the door behind him.

CHAPTER 19

*J*ON'S *AWAKE.*

I could barely keep it together.

Aurion had said it, and I knew it to be true because the prince had looked a little sad and had avoided my eyes when he had spoken. In my heart, I cared about the prince, probably more than he knew, but it would never be in the way *he* wanted. It would never go beyond a friendship. I could never feel for him the way I felt for Jon. I didn't know how to express this to the prince without hurting him. I still needed him to get me into that meeting.

Jon was awake!

What did it mean? Was he awake and still close to death? Or was he awake and on the way to mending?

I had been completely preoccupied for hours thinking about Jon when the door to my cell squeaked open again.

Prince Aurion held out his hands to me. "Quickly, before they change their minds."

I practically ran into his arms. I knew a hug was a bad idea so I settled for a squeeze of his arm.

"I don't know how you've managed it, but I'm grateful."

"We can talk later about how much you owe me," said the prince with a mischievous gleam in his silver eyes.

I followed the prince and four coven guards through the castle's underground cellars. I was queasy and nervous when we reached the fresh air of the main floor.

Would they believe me?

The prince was gleaming in immaculate clothes and boots. He smelled of sweet fruit and something musky, while I stunk of rot, blood, mildew, and sweat. I was embarrassed. I looked positively dreadful—exactly like the savage they expected me to be.

The prince didn't seem to mind that I looked and smelled like a farmer's barn. The demons wouldn't care what I smelled like either. And I was sure some rose water and a silk dress wouldn't impress them. The guards allowed me a few minutes to use a lavatory on the main floor, and I nearly collapsed with relief.

Afterwards, I could see our reflections in the windows as we walked down another long corridor, so I knew it was late in the night. The castle bustled with the movement and voices of the many more witches who were being accommodated here now. I couldn't recognize their faces.

Were these some of the witches who had come with us from Witchdom? Or were they witches who had come afterwards or even before?

Fawkes had said many more would come, and by the looks of it, he had been right.

I asked Aurion if Jon would be present at the meeting, but he said Jon was still too weak to do anything. Still, I made a mental note to seek him out after the assembly. One thing was for sure. I wasn't going back to the bowels of the castle now that I knew Jon was alive.

We arrived at a large set of double doors, and I could hear the sounds of a heated discussion from within. The prince gave me an encouraging smile and pulled open the doors. I struggled to control my nerves.

The meeting chamber had high ceilings and no windows. The walls were lit with torches, and a large chandelier carved in the shape of antlers hung from the ceiling. The air smelled of candles, sweat, and incense.

I felt the pressure of eyes bearing down on me as soon as I walked in, and the air was suddenly thick with silence.

The assembly sat in tall, carved wooden chairs around a giant oak table in the center of the room.

I was surprised to see the witch king at the head of the table. He made no attempt to hide his scowl, and the hate in his eyes was in plain view. The coven general glowered at me, too. Fawkes sat two chairs from the king's left, and Ada sat on the king's right, next to the two Coven Council witches, Forthwind and Ysmay. The other four Coven Council witches looked equally stern.

Fawkes scowled at the king. Will lifted his chin in a cold greeting. He sat next to a large man with a red beard whom I didn't recognize but must have been one of the rebel leaders.

Three men and one woman also sat at the table. Humans. The woman was dark-skinned, with a stern face and eyes as black as night. She was wearing the purple and green colors of Purtula. The man next to her wore the red dragon emblem of Espania on his tunic. The other man had a pinched face and gray hair, and he wore the blue and white colors of Fransia. The last was a thickset man with tawny hair who was clad in the red and gold colors of Anglia.

There were no representatives from the Romilian and Girmanian people. Only four of the six realms were here.

While no one rose to welcome me, no one seemed put off that I looked like I'd just been retrieved from the dungeon. I felt like I'd just interrupted something important, a secret meeting where I didn't belong. I wasn't even introduced, and I felt like a fool, a little girl in a room of adults.

But I hadn't been a little girl in a very long time. My anger flared, and my jaw ached. It took enormous control to keep my mouth shut. I wanted to curse them all.

I had to remember that I was a soldier of light. I was doing this for the scrawny kids from the Pit, for the witchlings, for Jon, for Torak, and for the forests of Arcania and the bugs that live there. I was doing this for all of them. It was the witches and humans without titles that mattered. Not these pompous bastards.

The king looked satisfied to see my discomfort. If I had my witch blade, I would have carved out his eyes. But I didn't, so I showed my teeth and winked at him instead.

The king turned an ugly shade of purple, and I was surprised he didn't turn his dark magic on me right then and there.

The prince took the seat to the left of his father, and I pulled back a chair and sat next to Fawkes. His frown deepened.

"Thanks for coming to get me," I whispered and rubbed my sweaty palms on my pants. "A great friend, you are."

"Didn't Prince Aurion get you out? I thought—"

"I thought you were my friend." My heart pounded in my throat.

Ada bowed her head in greeting, waited a few more seconds, and then called the assembly to order.

"Welcome, and thank you for coming," said the high witch. "To those of you who don't know, Gray Havens was originally formed on the western side of Arcania by a small group of witches who served the Goddess and the elemental forces of nature. After the Great War, our coven expanded to become a haven, or more accurately, a neutral ground for all witches *and* humans."

Ada took a deep breath. She looked ancient and tired in the candlelight.

"The human nations and the witches have never before sat together with a common goal. We are gathered here today to pool our power and knowledge so that we can rid our world of the threatening darkness.

"With the use of the Heart of Arcania stone," continued the witch, "the necromancers can unlock access to the demon realms by creating openings in the veil that protects us. Our magic shields are weakening all over our world. Soon they will collapse, and the veil will not be able to repair itself. If this happens, there will be nothing to stand in the way of the necromancers' black magic. It won't matter if you're here in Arcania or in Witchdom—the darkness will spread to us all."

Blood rushed to my face as all eyes turned to me, as though all this evil had been my fault. Of course they were right, I *was* partly to blame—but I had no control over the necromancers. Somehow I *would* make it right.

"Why should we care what happens to the world of *humans*?" spat the witch king.

His general nodded in approval, and I could see agreement in some of the Coven Council witches.

The humans, however, looked horrified by the witch king's betrayal.

"I say," continued the king, "let these mere necromancers rid our world of the humans. It was never theirs to begin with. We witches should put our efforts into protecting our own borders and our own people. Let the humans die. It is all they deserve."

"I refuse to be spoken to in this way by a devil worshiper!" spat the representative from Fransia.

I shifted uneasily in my seat, and I could see that Will's face had darkened, too. I was not surprised at the malice of the witch king.

The Fransian representative turned to Ada and pointed an accusing finger at her.

"The Creator said that the devil's purpose in inventing magic was to lure humanity away from the truth. Is this what's happening here? You said to come here because we could help each other. You said we should ally ourselves with the witches—that it was our obligation to do so in order to survive. Was this a trick?"

He pushed his chair back and stood to leave. The rebels and all the other humans stood as well.

"Did you call this meeting to make us out as fools!"

Ada jumped to her feet and raised her hands.

"Please, sit down," she said to the humans. Her voice was surprisingly soft and full of compassion.

She glared at the witch king. "The king does not speak for all of us."

The witch king looked smug, as if he was pleased to have offended us all.

After an uncomfortable moment, the human representatives took their seats. Ada waited until they were all seated again before settling down herself.

"Let me remind you, witch king," said the high witch. "You may be the witch king of Witchdom, but you are *not* king of Anglia or any of the other human realms."

My breath caught with hope and surprise, but a shadow crossed the king's face. He said nothing.

Ada turned back to the table. Her face was flushed.

"We called this assembly because this plight affects us all. Witch *and* human. We need each other to win this war."

She hesitated for a moment, and when she spoke again her voice was grave.

"It worries me profoundly that the necromancers have acquired so much power in so little time, and it cannot be just the stone. There's something else."

"Like what?" asked one of the Coven Council witches. "We all sensed the Heart of Arcania stone's power. But it was only *one* of the great stones. Do you suggest they have found others?"

I shifted in my seat. My magecraft pulsed against my leg. I remembered that Ada had mentioned there had been more than one magic stone, but they had been destroyed. I was certain she hadn't meant the smaller ones that had been cut into magecrafts. But what if she was wrong? What if the necromancers had managed to find another stone?

"I'm not sure," said Ada. "Maybe it's something we haven't seen yet. Another stone might explain why the black blight has spread so fast, and why so many demon portals have been opened."

Forthwind and Ysmay bent their heads together, whispering, and more than once their eyes settled on me. A chill crawled up my spine.

"If not just the stone," asked Fawkes, "then where's the source of their power? We know they've been borrowing it for centuries. So where are they borrowing their magic from? We all know these necromancers don't have blood magic, so to manipulate any magic stone they need to borrow a source of magic from somewhere. And I have the feeling they're borrowing it from somewhere in *this* realm."

"Yes," said Ada. "I believe that to be true. Somewhere in this realm there must be a spring of magic. There must be a crack in the world where the fountain of power spills to the surface."

The king's expression changed from boredom to caution. He caught my eye and glared. But I didn't look away. I wouldn't let this bastard intimidate me.

"These necromancers?" asked the prince, and I turned my attention away from the king. "Have they been *outside* this realm?"

"Yes," said the high witch. "They've been in all of the six realms for many years."

The prince shook his head.

"I meant, since the darkness spread. Have they ever moved away from Soul City? If I were to make an informed guess, I would suggest that the source of their magic came from somewhere inside that city. The darkness did originate from that area, so it would be logical to think that the highest concentration of magic would be there, too. The darkness would have spread faster if the priests had traveled to the other realms to unleash their wickedness. They might even have traveled to Witchdom."

"They would never have reached Witchdom," growled the king.

The prince glanced casually around the table, as though giving time for this new information to settle.

"So we should ask ourselves why? Speaking strategically, if I were them, and I had endless power, I would have struck out everywhere at once. But they didn't."

The prince continued, "I can only guess that they *couldn't*. Somehow they are bound to that city."

"He's right." I spoke before I could stop myself. I knew the prince was right. "Their source of power must be there."

It made complete sense to me. The necromancers had stayed in Soul City and hadn't been out since this mess had started. Maybe they *couldn't* leave.

Ada confirmed my suspicions.

"According to our spies, the necromancer priests have stayed in and around Anglia. Perhaps they've stayed *in* Soul City. I'm sure we can find out."

The witch king studied his son.

"My son's assessment rings true," he said, ignoring me completely.

"Even if they wanted to try and take a piece of Witchdom, their magic wouldn't be strong enough. It's like I've been saying from the beginning."

The king smiled, but his eyes were cold.

"Witchdom is well protected. The magic in this world, and in Witchdom and the mountains that protect it, is far older than theirs. These necromancers have nothing on us. They will die before they enter *my* world."

"The magical borders that protect our land has shifted," said a female Coven Council witch.

"We felt the darkness reach inside our borders. You had already left for the human realm. It was a message that they were coming."

The witch king shook his head.

"It's an empty threat. Their power won't reach beyond the mountains. You're mistaken."

"But what if it could?" asked the prince. "What if you're wrong, father? Who knows how many witches will die before we stop them. What happens when they get stronger, bolder, and set their sights on Witchdom? What if they launch another black blight at us, even bigger than the last? We are not immortal. The witches would not survive such onslaught. Are you willing to risk the lives of hundreds of thousands of witches?"

The witch king frowned. "You don't actually believe this nonsense, do you?"

I shifted in my chair. The tension between the king and his son was unsettling.

After an awkward hesitation, Prince Aurion clenched his jaw and said, "I do. Our greatest weakness has been that we know so little about the necromancers. What other secrets do they have? What other evil lurks with them? I believe this is just the beginning of something far, far worse."

"It's true," I began, but my voice was drowned out by the shouts of alarm across the table.

I tried again. "What's coming is—"

"These necromancers," barked the coven general, his voice as oily and grave as his face, "are nothing more than humans. And humans are easily killed. I propose we go in and crush them when they least expect it. Eliminate their source of power, and they'll have nothing to fight with."

"But why are they doing this?" asked the Purtulese woman angrily

"They were practically kings in Purtula. They had everything they could ever want: power, women, gold. They were practically Gods themselves. Why this darkness and evil? What more could they want?"

"Isn't obvious?" asked a coven witch male with a tremor in his voice.

He pressed his gnarled fingers on the table. "Because it wasn't enough. They want *more* power. They want to kill those of us in power and rule in our stead. They want to dominate both realms, Arcania *and* Witchdom."

"You're wrong," I interjected. My voice rose with my temper. I was tired of being ignored. "*They* won't rule over us."

The witch king slammed his fist on the table and made everyone jump.

"Shut your filthy mouth. You're only still here...still breathing...because my son says you have important information to share. But all I see is a murderous human whore—"

"Let her speak," Fawkes' expression was murderous as he scowled at the king. "This is neutral ground. Every person in this room has the right to voice their opinion."

He gave me an encouraging nod. "And Elena has just as much right as anyone else to speak."

The witch king stared at me angrily. "Fine. Let the bastard speak."

My indignation mounted at the king's words and the self-satisfied look in his eyes.

Prick.

My eyes moved to the others gathered around the table.

"The priests won't be in power. The demons will."

"The demons?" asked a pasty-faced man from Anglia.

Fawkes turned in his seat to face me.

"How do you know this?"

"Because I've seen it with my own eyes. I've been to the other side."

I looked around the room, but I couldn't tell from their stricken expressions if they believed me or not.

"I've been through a demon portal and walked their world. And I've had a conversation with one of their leaders."

I gave the room a moment to absorb this information.

"The necromancer priests haven't been acting alone. They've been doing their Lord's bidding. He's called the Unmaker, and if I were to guess I'd say he was the lord of the underworld. This Unmaker is their master. He's been guiding them all along. The necromancers have been assisting him in his plan to rise into the world of the living. The stone was only an amplifier of magic. It sped up the process. It's why they needed the stone, and why they drew up that ridiculous race in the first place. The demon also said something about blood sacrifices. I can't figure that part out. Whatever they're doing, it's all about opening a hole in the veil that would be large enough for them to bring the Unmaker into our world—"

"*Exterminatore*," said Ada.

She looked at me. "It means destroyer of life, in Witchtongue. But in common language, it is the Unmaker. He is the lord of the underworld and master of darkness. He is not a creature, Elena, but a *God*."

The room erupted in shouts and shrieks. But what froze my blood was the knowing looks shared by the Coven Council. It was as if they already knew, or at least suspected as much.

"A God?" I stared at Ada and fear shivered up my spine. "But that can't be."

"Why not?" Ada looked calm. "Whether you believe in the Goddess, or in the Creator, you must believe in the Unmaker. Where there is light there is also darkness. One cannot exist without the other. The Unmaker is the polar opposite of the Goddess, and his hatred of life is endless."

"Nonsense," hollered the witch king. "How can you believe her? She's a murderer. She killed a witch *queen* and ran away like a coward. If she were innocent of the crime, why did she run? Because she was guilty."

He scowled, and his magecraft pulsed with magic.

"Why would you believe this half-breed?"

He leaned towards me on the table. "I should have killed you when I had the chance—"

"I believe her, witch king," answered Ada. "News has reached us that the temple guards have been rounding up the surviving humans and taking them to Soul City."

I knew the humans at the table must have been her source of information.

"We've heard reports of hundreds of human sacrifices."

"Why sacrifice humans? What does it have to do with the Unmaker?" I asked.

It would explain why the streets and villages had been deserted when we had rescued Jon. It would also explain why the surviving humans had fled to Gray Havens. But I couldn't put the pieces together. I thought the priests had wanted to create an army of the infected, not kill them.

"If you think of the stone as the key to unlock the doorway to the underworld, then blood is the path," said Ada. "Blood is life, and the Unmaker needs a substantial amount of it to cross into our world."

"But how do we stop him?" I was starting to understand better.

Shadows flickered across Ada's tired face.

"I'm not sure. The Unmaker is the ruler of darkness. His weakness is light. That is all I know."

As I opened my mouth to ask another question, the doors burst open and Celeste came barreling in. She was in a panic.

My stomach fell when she looked at me.

"It's Rose, Elena. Something's happened to Rose."

CHAPTER 20

I GALLOPED OUT THE door behind Celeste, and the witch king shouted, "Fools! She's trying to escape, and that one is helping her!"

I didn't know if Ada and the others believed him or not, but they sent a band of coven guards after me. Surprisingly, the guards ran alongside and didn't try to stop us.

My entourage struggled to keep pace as I flew down the corridors behind Celeste. She ran with the grace and skill of a thief, but I suspected she was running with the same fuel as me—fear.

Oh, Goddess, no! Rose!

I wondered if hearts really were capable of breaking. Mine was. My magecraft sliced into the skin on my leg as I ran, but the pain kept me from crumbling into sobs. Celeste's face was a mask of terror, and I knew it was bad.

I pushed harder and ran faster.

I hadn't asked for permission to go to Rose. I had just run. The hell with them. If they had tried to stop me, I would have punched and kicked them out of my way. I'd had enough of this horseshit. I wasn't the enemy. If they couldn't see that, I wouldn't waste any more of my time trying to help them.

My vision blurred as we ran, but I could see witchlings in their shapeless gowns jump out of the way as Celeste and I came barreling down the hallway. More witches rose from their seats in sitting rooms as we ran up a set of stairs.

I could hear the low rhythmic thrum of chanting. Although the sound was as low and hollow as distant thunder, it was just loud enough for me to hear.

They were chanting my name.

My skin crawled as I listened, but I didn't think about what it might mean. I just focused on finding Rose. Celeste hadn't even told me what had happened to her. I just ran.

The last time I had seen Rose, we had not parted on such good terms. She had still been angry with me about my stealing the first stone. I could still remember the I-told-you-so look she had given me. She'd been right all along about that stupid Anglian crown. I should have never taken it. But I would make it up to her. Somehow I would.

We charged around a corner and up another level. A group of witches was gathered outside a bedchamber. The door was open. We charged towards them, and the look of sorrow and pity that flashed on their faces nearly sent me sprawling on the ground.

I couldn't look at them. My breath was ragged. My throat was parched and I could not get my breath.

I reached for my witch blade, but the coven guards had taken all my weapons away. If Rose wasn't safe here, I would take her somewhere else. I would take her East, yes, towards the mountains.

My legs were suddenly full of lead, and I could feel myself falling. But Celeste hooked her arm in mine and pulled me with her. We stumbled across the threshold together.

The world slowed down around me.

There was blood on the bed, the walls, and the floor. In the center of the room the blood pooled around the rug under Rose's mangled body. Her mouth was gagged, and pasty patches of scalp showed through her blood-clumped hair. Her glassy eyes stared lifelessly at the ceiling. Her throat was cut from ear to ear.

I knew she was dead.

My eyes stung with tears as a shuddering cry escaped my throat. The ground wavered, and I vomited where I stood. I shook with a pain I'd never felt before.

I staggered next to her on the rug and fell to my knees. She was completely naked. Her chest had been carved, and her internal organs spilled onto the rug. There was so much blood. Her skin was bruised, and her arms were covered in defensive wounds. She had fought.

I gazed at the woman who had once been a mother to me. She had been kind, perfect in my eyes. I had been damn lucky to have known such a vibrant, fierce, and loving soul. The woman who had practically raised me was gone. And when it would have mattered most, I hadn't been there to save her.

The others fanned out around the room, careful not to come too close. I couldn't even look at Celeste.

Great gashes had been carved into Rose's chest so violently that they almost obscured the letters. But there was no mistaking what they spelled.

STEEL MAIDEN

CHAPTER 21

M Y WORLD WAS RED and black, blood and despair, and I blinked the spots from my eyes.

The letters had been carved into Rose just as they had been carved into the women we had encountered on the road. The necromancer priests had sent me a message. They could reach me anywhere. Somehow the necromancer priests had managed to infiltrate Gray Havens. Rose's death was proof that we had an assassin in our midst.

The throbbing in my ears crowded out all of my other senses. I couldn't feel anything. My teeth clacked together as a wave of hot and cold rushed through me. My muscles ached, and my bones and joints seemed felt as if they had been wrenched to their limit.

Rose...

I sobbed uncontrollably. I rocked back and forth as I stared at Rose lying there, her body ripped apart. I hoped this had been a bad dream and willed her to move. But Rose would never wake ever again.

I heard someone calling my name.

A girl? A woman?

It was faint and muddled as though it was coming from far away. I shook my head to make the sound go away.

I rocked and rocked and rocked.

Maybe it was someone she knew?

From the way the sheets were sprawled all over the bed, I knew she'd been sleeping, and that she had struggled. I trembled as I reached out and placed my hand on hers. It was still warm. Some of her fingers were blue and bent unnaturally. Bile rose in my throat again, and I forced it down.

The castle was bustling with strangers. Anyone could have done this. Any one of them could be the assassin.

"I'm so sorry, Elena." Celeste pressed her hand on my shoulder.

I looked away from Rose's face. My throat was raw, and my every breath felt like it was coming through shards of glass.

"It…should have been me. Not her."

Celeste squeezed my shoulder gently, but she didn't answer.

A dull pain throbbed where my heart used to be.

"Did…did you find her?" I could taste the bitter salt of my tears in my mouth.

"No, one of the witchlings did. She was bringing her a cup of tea."

The throbbing in my head intensified until the pain was nearly unbearable. I cried out as my head pulsed with fire. I hit my head over and over again, but the pain wouldn't stop.

"What's wrong with her?" someone asked.

"Stay out of this." Ada's staff hit the floor with a thump.

193

I turned and saw that Ada's eyes brimmed with tears, too.

She stared down at me with a strange expression on her face. And before I could stop her, she pressed her palm against my forehead and closed her eyes.

Her hand was cool against my skin. My throbbing headache vanished, and I felt a soothing cool like a bucket of cold water had been poured over my head in the hot sun. Just like Fawkes' magic, Ada's magic smelled of sweet honey and lemons and lilacs and early spring. It caressed my face like a cool breeze, and I let her soothing magic enter me.

When Ada removed her hand, I felt as though I had just woken from a long sleep. I felt energized. And my headache was gone.

I blinked up at the high witch. Her expression was grave.

"This is how she reacts to a little blood?"

The witch king strode into the room, followed closely by his coven general and Prince Aurion. The prince looked aghast as he took in the room, and even more so when he saw me.

I looked away from him and watched as Fawkes and the Coven Council witches crowded into the room.

Fawkes' face paled as he gazed at Rose's body. He frowned, and something dark flashed in his eyes. I knew he didn't care much for human life, but he had changed over the last few weeks. I couldn't help but wonder if he was remembering the way his own family had been murdered. When he turned to me, his eyes gleamed with moisture, and at the sight of his tears, I began to sob all over again.

The room was packed with witches whispering to one another. I spotted a golden-haired witchling who must have been the one who had discovered the body. She was pressed into a corner, sobbing, and a teacup and saucer clattered in her trembling hands.

While some of the witches looked appalled, others, like the king, looked unimpressed and bored. It was as though Rose's mutilation and death had been nothing but a spectacle. A show.

The witch king's laugh sent a chill through me.

"A steel maiden who becomes ill at the mere sight of blood, is no *real* steel maiden. She's nothing but a trickster and a fool."

Celeste gasped, and I could have sworn I heard a growl coming from somewhere deep inside Ada's chest.

"Why all the sad faces?" questioned the king. "And tears?"

His face darkened as he surveyed the faces of the witches.

"Did you shed tears for your queen? Did you? How dare you shed tears over *her* loss? *She* murdered my wife! Your queen!"

The witch king crossed the room and stood over Rose's body. All the hairs on the back of my neck stood up. I watched as he examined the words that had been carved into her skin. His face was expressionless. It was as though he were reading a report about his crops. When he whirled around, there was only hate in his eyes.

"Have you forgotten your history?" he hissed.

His magecraft glowed with yellow power. The witches cowered and wouldn't look at him.

"The humans killed our families and burned our children *alive*."

He hesitated for a moment, as though gathering himself.

"Crying over an old, human woman," spat the king dismissively.

And then he turned to me and said, "Every human and half-breed deserves to die."

"Father," growled Prince Aurion. "Show some respect for the dead."

The prince's silver eyes were full of compassion and understanding.

"Show some respect for the dead?" mocked the witch king. "Never. Never for any human."

Ada slammed her staff on the floor. The sound resonated into my bones.

"That's enough, Sagard."

Ada and the witch king glared at one another. She would not be cowed by him.

"I will remind you again, witch king, that you are far away from Witchdom. And here in Gray Havens, all humans are welcomed. We are all equal in the eyes of the Goddess, no matter how many magic stones we possess."

The king frowned.

Color rose in Ada's face. "Rose was a guest here, and I will not have you tarnish her legacy by your prejudice."

The king smiled. "You always did love the humans more than your own kind."

His eyes widened suddenly. "Yes, I remember that human you fell in love with, the one that saved you from his own kind? He turned you against your own blood."

I looked at Ada, searching to see if there had been any truth to the king's words. Her face was stone, but her knuckles were white.

"What happened to him?" The king turned his gaze to the room.

He scowled. "Oh, yes, didn't his human friends turn on him? Yes. That's what happened. They burned him alive, didn't they? I remember that he screamed for mercy as he begged for his life. He said he wished he had never met you and that you should burn in his stead? That must have been painful. And still you stayed."

I felt sick to my stomach at how the king enjoyed taunting Ada. He wanted to hurt her.

But she didn't move. She didn't even blink. My heart broke for Ada. And I knew why she'd been so kind to my mother and me.

The witch king shook his head. "Pathetic."

"Father!" The prince's skin glowed in silver light as his ring pulsed with power. He glared at his father.

"Think, father. Don't you realize what this means? It means there's a traitor among us."

The king shared a look with his general, but I couldn't interpret his expression.

The witch, Sylvia, draped a clean bedsheet over Rose. She'd stitched up the back of my neck when Jon brought me here the first time. I wanted to thank her, but the words wouldn't come. She gave me a tight smile.

When Ada turned to me, all traces of fury had disappeared from her face.

"Rose will receive a proper burial. I promise."

She gave me a weak smile. "But first, you must follow me to my chambers. I need to have a look at you. Something's…something's not *quite* right."

"That wasn't the deal, high witch," said the king.

His dark eyes were expressionless, like a wolf stalking prey, confident, deadly.

"You'll put the animal back in her cage where she belongs, or *I* will."

"She's ill," pressed Ada. "I will not have her put back in that moldy old cellar, not when she's sick. I need to treat her first."

"Why do you care so much for this half-breed? How can you believe a word from that vile, traitorous mouth?"

"The witches of your kingdom believe in her." Ada straightened. "That they followed her here is proof. Proof that the prophecy *is* real."

I shifted uncomfortably. "What prophecy?"

The witch king's frown deepened.

"Even so. We don't need her anymore. Others will come. We have more than three thousand witches. Her use has ended, as has her life. She's no more use to us."

"What's he talking about?" I could see that Ada was conflicted.

"What is he talking about?" I demanded again.

Ada looked at me. "Elena, I'm sorry. I wanted to tell you."

My fingers curled into my palms. "Tell me what?"

"You must try to understand the situation."

Ada spoke quickly, and I couldn't tell what she was feeling.

"We had to make a choice for the good of the realm, for the world. The Goddess commanded it."

"What choice?" A new dread crept inside my chest.

The king motioned to the coven guards.

"Put the bitch back in her cage. Get rid of the body."

"No!"

Something snapped in me. I jumped to my feet and whirled around, fists ready.

"Don't you touch her! You bastard!" I shouted and sobbed at the same time.

The coven guards laughed. The one closest to me mimicked me and made fists with his hands. This was a joke to him, to all of them. Rose's death was a joke.

I felt darkness awaken inside me. I couldn't control it. I welcomed it.

And then I attacked.

CHAPTER 22

BEFORE I COULD STRIKE, the king blasted a stream of power straight into my chest. I was thrown back into the wall behind where it exploded into a shower of splinters, dust, and plaster pieces. I blinked the dust out of my eyes and tasted blood in my mouth. Something, a rib or my spine, had snapped. I couldn't feel my legs as I slumped to the floor, and I suspected that my back had been broken.

I could hear screams and shouts as I blinked the world back into focus. The king was towering above me with a self-satisfied smile on his face.

Celeste and Fawkes came to my side. They talked fast, but I could not hear them for the pounding rage in my ears. My head burned and my limbs were heavy and cold.

But then a familiar warmth started to surge through me. As my healing powers worked to repair my broken body, my magecraft began to pulse and throb as well. It awakened a cold and wonderful energy that flowed into my veins, mixed with my blood magic, and accelerated the mending of my body.

I smiled. I couldn't help it. I felt amazing.

"Elena?" Celeste's hand covered mine. "She's smiling. Elena, can you hear me?"

"Get away from her," said the witch king. "I'm going to finish this half-breed once and for all. Kill her!"

Fawkes stood and shielded me with his body. The breeze of his elemental power caught his cloak like the wind, and fire curled around his palms.

"I can't let you do this."

"You dare defy me?" growled the king.

His magecraft glowed as he advanced. He flicked his fingers, and a magic filament struck Fawkes. He staggered, but he did nothing to deflect the blows.

Fawkes straightened.

"I'll do what it takes to protect an innocent life." The strain of the king's blow showed on his face.

The king threw up his hands.

"Innocent? She's *not* innocent. She murdered my wife, your queen. I can see now that she's poisoned your mind, too. I want her dead. The laws of magic are simple. You take a life...you pay with your life. I've lost my patience with this half-breed!"

The witch king raised his arms.

"No!"

A cluster of orange and yellow fire danced around Fawkes as he spoke.

"You cannot kill the last steel maiden. Think of the consequences, the repercussions should you do this. Think of our future. She needs to live."

My blood thumped with pride. At least Fawkes believed in me. I wished I could see his face more clearly. I felt a tug inside me as my bones snapped back into place.

"This bastard witch killed my wife!" the king bellowed.

The coven guards nodded their approvals, but the coven general had moved away from his king and stepped silently into the shadows. I could see his lips moving as he began to conjure a spell.

"She killed a queen. She deserves to die!"

"Queen Enelyn tried to kill *her*," said Fawkes. "We all know what the queen was capable of, and what she'd done to others. You know this."

I saw the prince's face flush as he clenched and unclenched his fists.

"Father," said the prince, in an effort to diffuse the situation. "Let's take a moment and discuss who our real enemies are."

The witch king moved away from his son. His black eyes flashed with madness.

"You've always been a fool, Fawkes, a weak fool. There's no place for fools in my new world."

With a flick of his hands, the king shot a blast of black tendrils at Fawkes.

"Father, stop!"

But Fawkes was ready this time, and a shield of fire rose up before him. The king's dark magic collided with the wall of fire and deflected back at him.

My face burned at the intense heat, and the smell of the magic overpowered the smell of Rose's blood. I brought my knees up to my chest, and then rolled onto the balls of my feet.

As I waited for my blood to circulate freely through my limbs again, the coven general moved.

Fawkes turned to his left, but it was too late.

With a solid strike of yellow magic, the coven general hit him straight in the chest, and Fawkes burst into flames. His defensive magic wall had been shattered, and he was thrown back. He recovered quickly, but not fast enough as the general lashed at him again, and again, and again.

Fawkes howled in pain as he convulsed and fell to the ground. The smell of burnt flesh rose in the room. The magic fire extinguished itself, and the general looked triumphant. He stood over Fawkes who twitched in pain as tears streaked down his cheeks. The general began to chant, and raised his hands to strike again.

"Stop!" Ada intervened and shuffled towards Fawkes. "Stop this madness!"

But the general aimed his flaming fingers towards Fawkes.

Ada was too far away to stop him, but I was close enough.

I heard Ada scream for me to stop, but I was already moving.

They would not hurt Fawkes. They would not touch Rose.

Before he saw me coming, I leapt across Fawkes' body and caught the general in the gut with my shoulder. We fell on the ground together, but I was in a rage and was back on my feet in an instant. He smashed me in the face with his fist, but I reeled back, barely feeling any pain, and as I kicked out I heard the satisfying crunch of breaking bone from his ribs.

Although the general cried out in pain, it was Fawkes' wailing that rang in my ears.

I was going to kill that bastard.

Ice-cold power soared through me, and I embraced it. It was just like when I had fought the red monks. My senses sharpened, my sight became more acute, and my body became stronger and more agile. I had been energized by dark power.

Four coven guards came at me all at once. I could see the power glowing from their magecrafts.

But I was ready for them.

I let the darkness guide me like before. My legs and body moved in harmony with everything in the room. I owned that room.

Filaments of magic materialized all around me as the king's henchmen focused their magic on me. Like wisps of mist in the damp air, their magic searched the room to kill me.

Prince Aurion came running towards me.

A blast of light came at my heart, but I stepped aside, and it collided with the wall. I moved behind a coven guard and watched the surprised look in his eye as I snapped his neck. He dropped at my feet.

I jumped, spun, and ducked like a skilled dancer. More magic tendrils shot towards me, but my body reacted more quickly than ever before, and they could not hit me. I never imaged that I could possess such skill.

I was the bringer of death. And I wanted more.

Another guard stepped towards me. His magecraft pulsed, but he was no match for me. The magic in my soul was stronger.

My rage had become a living thing, a driving force. I was going to kill these bastards.

The guard struck, but I struck faster and harder. He collapsed in a heap of ripped flesh and shattered bones. Blood flowed down my face and fingers, but it was not my own.

"Elena, stop!" warned a familiar voice.

But I couldn't stop. I didn't want to stop.

Before I could stop, the last of the coven guards had howled in agony, sobbed and cried out for their mothers, and then fallen dead at my feet.

I stood breathing rage. Sweat poured down my temples and my back. I beamed at my skill. Someone was laughing, and then I realized it was me.

I searched the room and found Celeste. I didn't understand why she looked so frightened.

Had I not just saved everyone? Fawkes?

Everyone just stared at me. The room was suddenly still.

What was the matter with them?

And then something hit me in the back of my head. I saw black spots, and then I tumbled into darkness.

CHAPTER 23

I COULDN'T TELL IF I was lying down or floating. Then I started to spin.

Is this a dream?

I thought you couldn't feel pain in dreams. I dreamed of light and darkness, and I felt heat and pain.

My heartbeat pounded in my head. I tried to open my eyes, but they were crusted shut.

Where am I? What's happening to me? How long have I been here?

Finally, I managed to open my eyes, and I had to squint to make out anything. My world spun and tilted. I felt nauseated. I closed my eyes again and waited until the nausea passed.

I reached out and gripped the sides of something soft. Yes. A bed. I was in a bed.

I pulled myself upright, and after a few moments my eyesight had adjusted to the light.

I was in a room with wood paneled walls that smelled of pine. I was still in the castle. Thank the Goddess.

But how did I get here?

My memories were jumbled together like dreams that fade away when you wake. I couldn't remember.

I remembered that the witch king's magecraft glowed, as he was about to strike me…

But then something occurred to me. I lifted the soft bed cover and looked down at myself. My clothes were gone, and I was wearing a simple white shift and clean undergarments.

My boots!

"Shit."

I swung my legs off the bed, and a spell of dizziness nearly sent me to the ground. I steadied myself with the bed. Bile rose in the back of my throat, and I waited for the nausea to pass.

I moved more slowly as I made my way over to the dresser. I yanked open the drawers and rummaged through them looking for my clothes, but all I could find were stacks of neatly piled linens.

I spotted a closet, and I lunged unsteadily towards it. I swung open the door. Spare robes and trousers hung on wooden hangers, but they were not my clothes. A basket on the floor was piled full with multicolored slippers. My heart sank. No boots. No magecraft.

"Looking for this?"

I spun around.

Ada stood in the doorway, and my magecraft was hanging from her index finger.

"That's *mine*," I said.

The anger in my voice surprised me, and I reached out to grab my magecraft. But with a swift flick of her hand, Ada secreted it in one of her many hidden pockets.

"I don't think it ever belonged to you," said Ada sternly. "No magic stones belong to anyone."

"Give it back," I said.

My head throbbed, but I ignored the pain. "It's mine. I won it."

"I think you've had it long enough." Ada's tone was final. Her skin sparked with white power, and although she was shorter than me, I felt as though she were the tallest woman in the world.

I didn't shrink back from her, despite her height. Instead I look a tentative step forward and reached for the stone again.

"You knew better," she said.

She shook her head, "I'd warned you before about any magic stones. You knew that while you could touch them, you could *never* wield them. And yet you doubted me. You had felt the wild and dangerous magic of the Heart of Arcania stone, and yet you took one for yourself?"

I was furious, and I lunged for the stone. "Thief! Give it back!"

Ada flicked her fingers, and an invisible force pushed me back. I felt like I was underwater, fighting a strong current, and I couldn't break to the surface. I tried to twist away from her, but it was hopeless. I could feel my own magic countering hers, but it was ineffective. Finally I stopped fighting. The fury in Ada's eyes matched my own.

"Don't make me hurt you," she bellowed. "Control yourself. Control *it*. Or I *will* put you in a cage."

Before I realized it, I was moving towards her again with my arms outstretched—

Ada slapped me hard across the face. "Snap out of it!"

It worked. I staggered back. The impact sobered me right up.

What was I doing?

The darkness lifted, and I could think again. The true meaning of her words really hit me. It was as though my head had been full of water, and now it was clear.

My anger had clouded my thoughts until I had become someone else. I had become someone angry, someone who wanted to kill for the pure pleasure of it. I knew then that I was different, that I had some black magic in me, but it had been made a hundred times worse by the stone. I was going through some kind of withdrawal. I yearned for the rush of my magecraft. And I didn't like the emptiness I felt without it.

I craved that magic power.

I felt sick to my stomach when I realized what I'd become. I was embarrassed that Ada had seen me behave so badly. I couldn't control my tears. But Ada continued to lecture me.

"Haven't you seen what the stone has done to the witch king?" she asked. "He believed he was strong enough to control it. But every time he uses it, he loses a piece of himself. He has become unrecognizable as our king. Look at how he nearly killed one of his oldest friends. That's what the stones do. They corrupt the mind, and then the stone controls you."

She sighed heavily.

"As a steel maiden, you are more prone to turn to that dark path because dark blood magic flows in your veins. You would be seduced by that darkness willingly and completely, and we would never be able to get you back. You would be lost to it, forever."

Ada's shoulders slumped a little, and for the first time she looked drained.

"You disappoint me, Elena."

Her words stabbed my heart. Shame colored to my cheeks, and I swallowed hard, trying to control my emotions.

"You don't understand," I said.

My voice was still strong in spite of the tightness in my chest.

"It can help me, help *us* win this war. I can do amazing things with it. It makes me stronger, better."

"No, Elena," said the high witch. "Not better. Never better."

"But you saw what I did—"

"What about Rose?" said Ada. "What do you think she'd feel about what you've become?"

My eyes filled with tears.

How could I have forgotten about Rose? I hadn't thought about her once since I had woken up. This wasn't me. I didn't want to be like this. Rose...

I blinked the moisture from my eyes. I felt ill.

"Is Rose...have they..." I couldn't say it.

"Rose's body was taken care of," said Ada gently. "We have prepared her funeral ceremony for tonight. I wanted to make sure you were *well* enough to attend."

The memory of Rose's mutilated body caused the room to spin again. My stomach tightened into a knot. I couldn't breathe. Rose was gone.

And then the memories came flooding back.

My blood went cold. I swayed and shifted on my feet, and I had to stick out my arms to balance myself, for fear I might tumble over. My stomach twisted as I clenched my fists. I had lost a mother and a protector. Rose had kept me fed and clothed and warm. She had kept me hidden and safe.

She had been brutally murdered because of *me*.

I remembered the words that had been carved into her flesh, the gag in her mouth, the blood. There had been so much blood. I fought against the nausea that stirred within me.

And then I remembered the coven guards. I had killed them all with my bare hands.

I was a monster.

Perhaps I *was* a monster, a killer. Maybe the Goddess had intended that her soldier should be a killer. Even so, I felt nothing. I didn't feel any remorse for the witches I'd killed.

The assassin who had killed Rose had denied me the chance even to say goodbye, to apologize for being a stubborn ass, but mostly I lost my chance to thank her properly. To tell her how much she had meant to me. How much I loved her.

Just thinking about it, even now, caused my furious blood to pound in my ears.

"We've kept you under a sleeping spell to help your body heal from some of the damage done by the stone. And by the bump Fawkes gave you."

"That was him?"

I remembered something hitting me in the back of the head. I would have to pay him back when I had the chance.

Ada appeared to perk up a bit.

"With a little push from our witches in the White Witches clan to speed up the healing process, your own blood magic did the rest."

Her face turned solemn. "The stone had made you sick, Elena."

I gaped at the old witch and shook my head.

"I'm not sick, honestly. I feel perfectly fine. Better even."

I wasn't about to tell her about the dizziness I had felt just moments ago. Besides I felt steadier on my feet now that I was fully awake.

Ada took me into her confidence a little more.

"I felt a change in you. The darkness has been growing in you ever since you were touched by the necromancer's black magic. It has been dormant perhaps, but it was still *in* you, in your blood magic. And now I'm afraid it has nearly taken control of you."

"It hasn't, I swear," I argued.

I knew quite well that something had been brewing inside me, but I had always thought it had been malnutrition, exhaustion, and the stress of searching for Jon.

Ada raised a quizzical brow. "Your headaches? They are the manifestations of the *awakening* of the black magic."

Instinctively I reached out and brushed my fingers against the scar tissue at the base of my neck. The wound the red monk had given me with his poisoned talons felt rough and angry. It still throbbed constantly and had never truly healed.

Ada saw that I was rubbing my scar.

"You said it would never heal," I said.

Despite their efforts, the witches had not been successful in removing all the black magic.

"Yes, I did. But if you had been left alone, you probably could have lived a life without it taking control. Your blood magic is strong, and it would have protected you. But things have changed."

"What do you mean?"

"The stone you carried with you didn't make you better, it made you worse. It magnified the power of the black magic that was awakening inside you. It sped up the process and changed you."

Ada cocked her head.

"And if you don't relinquish the stone, it will consume you. If the darkness takes you over, you will no longer be Elena. You will have become a creature of darkness."

Ada looked at me sympathetically.

"Your headaches and the darkness you felt are both black magic. Rotten and evil. It's seducing you. It's the worst kind of magic, and it doesn't belong in this world. That's why everything it touches withers and dies. The more black magic seeps through the portals, the more our world will die. And it will happen one piece at a time. One witch, one human, at a time."

I thought of the demons with a cold shiver. It scared me to death that I could lose control. I was a witch and a human. I didn't want to become something dead.

"What's going to happen to me?"

Ada regarded me purposefully.

"You won't turn into a creature, if that's what's worrying you."

"Well, at least that's a small comfort."

But was it? Was it really? I was lying to myself because what little comfort I'd been able to feel had been derived from that damn magecraft.

How was I supposed to defeat the necromancers now?

The magecraft had been the aide I had so desperately needed and wanted. With it, I was an unstoppable force, a dark force maybe, but at least a strong and powerful one. It had given me the power to beat the necromancers. Now, I was back to being just me, a half-witch with no real magic, not the kind that mattered.

I stared at my toes.

Ada would never give back the magecraft, and I doubted I'd get my hands on another. I had the chance to kill the high priest back at the inn. But I had saved Jon instead.

Had I made a mistake?

Before I had taken the stone I'd sworn to avenge the deaths of my friends. I was resourceful. I would just have to find a way to kill the necromancers without magic...

"I believe we removed the stone from you just in time," said Ada.

She crossed the room and stood next to me. I believed she had mistaken my silence for fear.

I heard the rattling of a metal chain somewhere beneath her robes. She caught me staring at a spot below her right elbow, and she moved her arm behind her back.

"If you had spent any more time under the influence of the stone's wild and untamable power, we would have been unable to rescue you. Breaking the link between you and that stone was the first step on your way to recovery. In a way, your headaches helped."

"Helped? Apart from making me feel like my head was splitting open, I don't see how they could have helped. They just hurt like hell, most of the time."

"I'm sure they did, but the headaches *were* a sign. They helped me *see* how much the black magic had awakened. You were suffering, my dear, because your blood magic was trying to protect you from the black magic. You are a steel maiden, and your blood magic was telling you that something was very wrong."

I rubbed the back of my neck. "But it's still there. Isn't it?"

"I think…" She eyed me carefully. "I think your blood magic is very strong, Elena. It's why the stone affected you so effectively. I imagine it was having a feast on your blood magic."

"Sounds disgusting."

Ada's eyes narrowed slightly. "Well, you'll have to control your urges. When you can control your mind, your own blood magic will do the rest. But you will need training."

I shook my head. "Maybe after this war. There's no time for any kind of training now."

"Training of the mind is essential to suppress the black magic. You're no good to us in this state."

I frowned at her, and she continued. "Your black magic is wild and unpredictable. Until you can control it, there's no telling what you can do or what you will do. So first, you must learn to control it. Then we'll see if you're fit to help."

I was about to object that this training would be a waste of precious time, but I knew the old witch wouldn't have it. So I just played along, for the time being.

And then something occurred to me.

"The prince wears a magecraft. The stone is set in his ring, but he's not like his father or that horrible witch queen," I began. "Don't look at me like that. I'm not making excuses. I'm just saying that the prince doesn't seem to be controlled by his ring. And I'm sure there are others like him."

"Yes, that is true," said Ada. "Not all magic stones are created equal. The king has had his for more than three centuries, and you can see how much damage it has done to him. The prince only started to wear one thirty years ago."

Ada smiled when she realized I was trying to figure out how old the prince actually was.

"The prince's blood is mixed. He has less dark magic in him than you might think because he takes after his mother. It will take longer for the magic in the stone to take hold of him. And the stone he wears is quite small. I have reason to believe he doesn't use it. Still, in the end, it will consume him, just as it has his father."

"I hope not." I didn't like to think that Aurion might become as vile as the king. While I didn't know him that well, his actions had led me to believe that he was the opposite of his father.

"It's something else entirely in your case," said Ada. "When the black magic in you mixes with a magic stone, the combination is dangerous and deadly. The events of that night cannot happen again. You must understand."

216

I didn't, but I decided to leave it for now.

I asked instead, "What are you going to do with it?"

I couldn't help myself. I still felt attached to that little stone. I tried to act calmly, and to be normal, but I couldn't deny the addictive power of the stone. It still pulsed in me. It made me want to reach out and rip off the old witch's robe just to look for it.

A tiny smile formed on Ada's lips. "That, my dear, you'll never know."

"Figures." I sighed.

I felt naked without the stone and the extra power it provided me.

What was worse, I still felt a yearning hole in my soul where Rose had once been. My heart ached for her, and I felt as if I might cry again. I couldn't break down now. I had to keep my tears in check and my wits together. I needed to find her killer. Nothing else mattered.

"How long have I been in here?" I asked coldly.

"Two days."

"Two days!" My stomach turned over. Two days was an enormous amount of time. The murderers would have had plenty of time to cover their tracks. They were probably long gone by now.

Maybe they'd left something behind.

"Have you found any leads on her murderer?" I knew Ada would have told me first thing if they'd caught Rose's murderer.

For the first time Ada looked away from me. "No. Fawkes and the prince gathered a search party. They searched everywhere and interrogated everyone who had access to the castle. They even questioned some of the humans. But they couldn't find any evidence of her killers anywhere inside the castle. The witchlings were the only ones who had been allowed in Rose's room. And they're just girls. It's not in their nature to do something so atrocious."

"So they stopped looking?" My anger rushed back.

Ada looked back at me.

"I'm sorry, Elena. I know this is difficult for you to understand. But there is no more we can do right now. I'm afraid the culprits have disappeared."

Ada rested her hand on my shoulder. "Don't feel that you are responsible. Her death wasn't your fault."

"Like hell it wasn't," I snapped. "The necromancer priests killed Rose to get at me. It was deliberate and cowardly, but her blood is on my hands nonetheless. I'm the only one responsible for her death. Me."

"Elena, listen to me—"

"I need to go." I rushed past her, but the old witch stopped me with a grip like iron.

"You need to rest," she ordered.

I yanked my arm away.

"I need to see the room again." My voice broke. "There's got to be something there. Some evidence of who did this. There has to be."

"I'm afraid you'll find nothing," she said. "The room's been thoroughly cleaned."

"It doesn't matter. I still need to see it."

I slipped out the door before she could stop me.

CHAPTER 24

I SPRINTED DOWN THE hallway as though a pack of shadow knights was at my heels.

It took a few seconds before I realized that I was barefoot and wearing only a thin shift. I tried to get my bearings. I knew Rose's room was in the upper left wing of the castle. I was just a floor below.

As I galloped up the stairs I heard a rip, and then I felt a cool breeze around my back and my ass. Witches and witchlings gasped and jumped out of the way as I ran past them. I wasn't about to stop. I would knock them over if I had to. I could already feel blisters burning the balls of my feet, but I didn't care. My breath was ragged in my throat, but I felt surprisingly energized, even without the magecraft. I tried hard not to think about my magic stone and pushed myself to run faster.

I skidded to a stop at a large wooden oak door. With a trembling hand I reached up, turned the doorknob, and pushed it open.

It looked like a totally different room, so empty and too quiet. I stood on the threshold, unable to move. I only realized I was crying when I felt the warm tears trickle down my cheeks.

Was I ready for this?

I took a deep breath and went in.

The air smelled of lavender soap, candles, and rosewater. The windows were open, and the breeze that ruffled the linen drapes had blown away the smell of blood. The polished wood of the large four-poster bed glimmered in the soft light of the setting sun. The bed was made. It was covered in a beautiful colored quilt emblazoned with autumn-colored leaves and topped with large pillows.

I'd last seen Rose on the ground next to the bed. The images of her death were still so fresh in my mind that I could almost make myself believe it had been a dream. My pain made it real.

The rug was gone, and so were any traces of blood, or any signs of a struggle. The broken chairs had been replaced, and the room was spotless. Everything had been wiped cleaned or fixed. It looked like a normal guest bedroom, inviting and ready for the next guest. The curtains were drawn, and I could see the human camps dotting the lush castle grounds outside.

Could the killer still be here?

The killer must have been bold and arrogant, and was probably a skilled assassin. It would have taken a lot of guts to kill someone in a castle that had been bustling with so many witches. They could have easily been caught.

The killer must have known the castle layout very well to have managed to kill Rose and then to slip away without being seen.

Still, the killer had made his move. My gut feeling was that he was still somewhere on the castle grounds. I suspected he would want to hang around so he could see me crumble and give myself up.

Never. I would *never* give up. If I still drew breath, I would find her killer.

My witch intuition, the voice inside me, knew that her killers were still here. I was sure of it.

Somehow the killers had managed to elude the magic searches of Fawkes and the prince. The necromancers must have helped them somehow.

I crossed the room, searching for clues. I tried to imagine how the killers had come in. There were only two ways into Rose's bedroom, through the window or the door. I gazed at the big oak door. I half expected to see Ada waltz in, but I realized she was giving me time alone, not just to try to discover the truth, but also to grieve.

Had the door been locked?

No, because Celeste had said that one of the witchlings had gone to fetch Rose some tea. She had discovered her when she had returned. So although the door had been closed, it had been unlocked.

Rose had probably been awake and reading by candlelight. She had been so vulnerable. I didn't want to think about it.

I wiped away the sweat on my forehead.

Focus, Elena. Focus.

If her killers had come through either the door or the window, she would have screamed. But no one had heard a thing. Which meant…which meant the killers had been hiding in her room.

The hairs on my body rose. Yes, that was it. I knew I was right. I had hidden for hours and hours just to steal something I could trade for food or for books. No one had ever found me. I could control my breathing, even in the tightest of spots. So it was very possible that the killer had hidden somewhere inside the room.

And now I knew another thing for certain. There could only have been *one* killer because two or more couldn't possibly have hidden in here. But one...one most definitely could.

The room didn't have a closet, and there was no way the killer could have hidden in the lavatory. I moved to the window and peeked over the windowsill at the gravel three stories below. Although the wood exterior looked slippery, an experienced climber could have used the logs as footholds.

One of the humans camping outside would have spotted someone climbing up or down. Perhaps the killer had been cloaked in darkness.

The killer could have escaped through the window. That was a possibility. But I still didn't think they had come in that way.

If the killer had used the door to get into the bedchamber, it would have to have been someone who could wander the castle hallways without calling attention to themselves. But it still didn't explain how he had attacked Rose without her making a sound.

I moved to the door and then turned on the spot, searching. The room wasn't grand, so where? Where did the killer hide?

And then it became so obvious I felt I must have been stupid not to have noticed before.

The bed.

The coverlet draped the bed and practically grazed the floor. Anyone could have hidden under the bed and no one, not even Rose, would have suspected anything. Why would she be suspicious? She was supposed to be safe here.

I had told her she would be safe…

I pushed my feelings aside. I wouldn't discover the killer if I became an emotional mess again.

I stared at the spot under the bed. Rose's killer had been only inches away from her, waiting.

It had been a well-planned attack. The killer had known exactly what he was doing. *So the question was who? Who would do this? Was the killer a witch or a human?*

My instincts leaned towards the humans. They were the only ones who'd allied themselves with the necromancers. I didn't believe it could be a witch. But apart from the small group of humans who had attended the assembly, I hadn't see any humans roaming in the castle. But that didn't mean there hadn't been any.

This was a personal attack. These killers hated me, and they wanted me to suffer.

Who was cruel enough to kill and mutilate the body of an old woman? So who? Who would do this? Who would take the time to carve the words, STEEL MAIDEN, into Rose's chest?

Celeste and my men were the only ones who had seen the dead women beside the road. Their chests had been carved in the exactly the same way Rose's had been. I had never trusted Lucas. More than once I'd seen hatred in his eyes.

Did his hate for me run so deeply that he'd take it out on Rose?

It didn't fit. His hatred was aimed at witches, not humans. No. It wasn't Lucas. I didn't trust him, but I didn't think he was capable of doing this.

Who would benefit from hurting me?

What if I'd been mistaken, and this hadn't been the necromancers' doing?

My blood turned ice cold.

The witch king.

Of course, it must have been him. Who else would have been sick enough to murder and mutilate Rose? The witch king. He had probably heard the rebel men talk about the murdered women we'd encountered on the road. The witch king would have wanted to know every detail of our trip.

I knew the king wanted me dead. I suspected he would want to get even first, to kill someone dear to me, just as I had killed his queen.

I heard footsteps from the hall. I turned and gave a little gasp.

Jon stood in the doorway.

CHAPTER 25

I STEPPED BACK.

The man who stood in the doorway watched me with sparkling, dark, clear eyes. Although his face was marred by a few scars that would fade with time, there were no traces of the sickness. No black, angry veins, no blistering welts. His face was paler and thinner than usual, but it was still beautiful. Patches of scalp showed through his short black hair. He wore a loose white shirt and pants, and a sword hung from his weapon belt.

And then he smiled—a beautiful, casual gesture.

Heat exploded in my chest, my limbs, everywhere. I lost a shuddering breath that was mixed with a sob. I sprung across the room and flung myself into his warm, strong body.

For half a second I thought I'd hurt him. He was probably still sick. But then his strong arms wrapped around me tightly, and he lifted me up. I laughed and cried and buried my head into his neck. I breathed in his musky male and lavender scent, and I tasted the salt of my tears in my mouth.

Jon squeezed me tighter.

Right there and then I thought I'd die of happiness, burst into a million pieces of myself.

Jon was alive.

"Elena," he breathed. His hot breath caressed the nape of my neck and sent waves of goose pimples rolling over my skin.

My entire world narrowed to the touch of his lips on my skin. I wrapped my arms around his neck and kissed him, softly at first, but then harder as if my desperate need for him could not be satisfied. He returned my kiss with equal fervor, but then he pulled away and trailed soft kisses up my throat before he nuzzled his face into the crook of my neck.

I moaned, and then his lips crashed against mine again. I couldn't kiss him fast enough or hard enough. I dug my fingers into his back, pulling him closer and pinning him to me as if I could prevent him from leaving me ever again. Hot tears poured down my face like a stream that would wash away the weeks and months of torment, of not knowing if I'd ever see him again, let alone kiss him and touch him.

Finally I wrenched my lips from his mouth. We were both breathing hard, and his lips were red where I'd abused them. He let out a shaky breath, his eyes wide and burning with hunger for me.

"I can't believe you're here," I said.

My voice was small and hoarse. "I feel like I'm dreaming, that this can't be real because I don't deserve it."

I swallowed hard. "I thought I'd lost you."

He watched me with an unflinching gaze. "You're not dreaming. I'm here now."

His gaze dropped, and then his eyes were on me again, searching.

My heart throbbed in my throat.

"You cut your hair? I like it. Brings out your eyes."

Jon smiled and raked his fingers through his hair with such a boyish gesture that it made him seem years younger. "Yeah. Most of it was gone anyway. Your friend Celeste did it for me."

My heart warmed at the mention of Celeste. She had been a true friend and had looked after Jon when I'd been indisposed. I searched his face. I could scarcely breathe. It was a miracle he was standing here before me looking so strong.

"How do you feel?"

"Better than I should," he said. "I can't say that I'm fully healed, at least not yet anyway, but I know I'm getting stronger every day. The priest's magic did a number on me. Ada said that my body and mind had been broken, and that I had been consumed by the infection. I shouldn't even be alive. But I am."

He paused for a moment, but he never looked away from me.

"They told me what you did," he said awkwardly.

I caught my breath. *Shit. Here it comes.*

At first I thought he was about to curse me for coming back for him, for risking the lives of his friends. Given the chance, I would have done it again in a heartbeat.

But then his face lit up with a smile that crushed my heart.

"You saved my life," he said gently and took my hand in his. "And I'm grateful, Elena. Truly. You have no idea. The idea of a life without you…is no life at all."

Waves of delightful heat pounded through me, and shivers raced along my spine.

I released a breath I hadn't realized I'd been holding.

"Now we're even."

He gave me a tight smile.

"I was in hell. They poisoned me with so much evil and death."

He rubbed his hair with his hand.

"My dreams have been dark, disturbing, images that will haunt me forever. I remember the things I said to you…the things I did to those people…I did horrible things, Elena. Horrible."

He stopped talking, and a shadow crossed his face. I reached out and grabbed his other hand.

My heart broke to see the pain in his eyes.

"That wasn't you, Jon. That was the black blight, the necromancers' black magic. It made you do these things, and it turned you into something else. It did the same to the poor infected souls we fought at the temple. They weren't in control of their actions either. The black magic was *controlling* you. You weren't yourself. Remember that. If you want to blame anyone, blame those necromancer bastards. I do."

"It would have killed me in the end, you know," he said softly. "I would have rotted from the inside *and* out."

"But it didn't. You didn't. We came back for you."

Jon nodded. "And just in time, according to Will."

"You've seen him?"

I felt a pang in my chest because I hadn't been the first to see Jon after he had recovered. I was angry that Will had been with Jon. I would see Fawkes next.

"Yes." Jon brushed back a loose strand of my hair. His callused fingers brushed against my cheek in a soft caress. The gentleness of it made my eyes burn.

"Will's been giving me detailed accounts of everything that's happened since I saw you last, since I became sick. Your trip to the witch realm, the trials you faced, the death of our friends. I've...I've been away for far too long."

A shadow passed over his eyes, and I could see his pain and regret.

"But you're here now," I said gently.

Jon caught me staring at his lips and smiled. "I am. And so are you."

"I'm sorry about Leo. I know how close the two of you were."

The smile slowly faded from his face.

"I'm sorry too. We go way back, Leo and me. Both of us were orphans in the Pit, always getting into trouble, stealing to eat, stealing for fun. Living on the streets was dangerous, and we grew up pretty quickly as we learned to survive. It was probably the worst way to spend your childhood, but I wouldn't have changed a thing. Not really. I'm just sad he's gone, and that I couldn't help to save him."

I reached out and trailed my fingers over his face.

"I'm sure wherever he is now, he's happy you're safe. Safe with me."

He leaned forward and kissed me lightly.

"You'll never be separated from me again, never."

Fire burned in his eyes, and another wave of desire washed over me. I wanted nothing more than to tear off his clothes and feel his hot skin against mine.

But I couldn't. The time wasn't right. I could easily have lost myself in Jon, but I dug my fingernails into my palms and stayed still.

"How did you know I was here?" I said, desperate to change the subject and clear my mind.

I withdrew far enough from him to study the familiar lines on his face, his long straight nose, his chiseled jaw, and his handsome cheekbones. I needed to reassure myself that he was actually here.

"Ada told me where to find you."

He opened his mouth, but then he closed it, as though he were struggling with what he was going to say next. And yet I knew from his tone and the way he glanced at the bed that he knew.

His gaze stayed on the spot where the rug used to be.

My throat ached. "They've told you about Rose."

It was my turn to avoid his gaze.

"I'm so sorry, Elena," he said. "I know how much you loved her. How much she meant to you."

He came closer, and his hot breath caressed my cheeks. "She was a great lady, your Rose. She never thought much of me, but I knew she was just looking out for you. She loved you like her own daughter."

I pressed my head into Jon's chest and sobbed as he held me. I closed my eyes and let the feel of his strong arms wash away my sorrow and make me feel that everything would be okay.

But it wouldn't be okay. I couldn't lose control now. There would be time for more tears later. We had to vanquish the necromancers and avenge Rose's death first.

I pushed back a little and looked into Jon's eyes.

"The witch king did it," I said.

"What? Are you sure?" He looked at me with a soldier's steady calculating gaze.

"Positive. He might not have done it himself, maybe he sent his general, but I have a feeling he did. But it must have been him. The way she was killed…"

I took a steadying breath. "It was too personal. It was meant to hurt me, to break me."

"I've only seen him once, and he barely looked at me," said Jon. "He did have that same royal arrogance as the priests and the nobles whom I've met over the years. They're all cowards and greedy for power."

Jon studied me closer. "Why do I have the feeling you have a lot to tell me."

"Because I do."

I smiled and told him everything: the failed first attempt at his retrieval, the journey to Witchdom, the witch trials, and what I'd learned about my mother. I told him about the matrimonial trap the witch king had set for me, and about his hatred for humans. I edited some of the parts about Aurion. It wasn't like anything had happened, so no need to go there. But when I told him about how the prince had helped me when I'd killed the witch queen, Jon's eyes widened.

"So he blames you for her death."

"She *was* trying to kill me. It was self-defense. It's not like I wanted it to happen. Even though I hated that cow, I just wanted to leave. She didn't give me a choice. It was either her or me. And I chose me."

"I know," said Jon. "But she was his *wife*."

"And a royal bitch."

I noticed the dark shadows and hollows in Jon's face. He looked tired, but his eyes were lit with a fierce resolve.

"And the queen's magecraft?" Jon looked concerned. "Do you still have it?"

My cheeks flushed. I still yearned for the stone, but I was ashamed that I still wanted it. I wasn't sure if Jon had seen my hunger for it reflected in my expression.

"No, Ada has it. She took it from me and she's not going to give it back. Not after what happened. Still, other witches use them. I really don't see the harm for me to have it. At least to use it just one last time."

"If Ada took it from you, I'm sure it was with good reason," said Jon.

I could sense that he was holding something back.

"The magic stones are tricky, Elena. Look what that damn Heart of Arcania has done."

"Trust me, I know."

Jon narrowed his eyes. "They're dangerous. Best to stay away from them. Especially you."

Heat rushed to my temples. "What the hell is that supposed to mean?"

Jon sighed, but there was only genuine concern in his eyes. "You know exactly what I mean. The witches warned you about the stones. I was there. I remember. They said that because you were a steel maiden it would be harder for you to resist them. I wouldn't trust their magic. From what the witches told me, the stones have a will of their own, and it's dark. You don't need them."

"I do need it," I said.

I let out a frustrated breath. "I could have used the magecraft to do good. I was able to wield it. I could use its power to make me strong enough to defeat the priests."

I told him about how I used the magecraft against the necromancer priest in the Dirty Habit. I watched his face closely.

Jon stepped away and rubbed his face.

"So you could have killed him? But you chose to save me instead?"

"It wasn't like that," I said. I was surprised that I felt angry, and I wasn't sure why.

When I spoke again, I made sure my voice was even tempered.

"I mean, he wasn't dead, and I'm not even sure I *could* have killed him. I don't know. It can't be that simple. There's something else I just haven't figured out yet."

I gripped his arm and pulled him to face me. I savored the strength in the corded muscle of his forearms.

"In that moment I made a decision. And it was the *right* decision at the time."

234

"Did you tell Ada and the other witches?"

I let him go and looked at him. I saw someone who, for the moment, had forgotten that he had ever been infected. All I saw was the man I loved, the man who had saved me.

"No," I said.

I clenched my hands into fists to keep from touching him again.

"How could I have told them when they had just surrendered me to the king and had thrown me into jail like a common criminal."

"Elena." Jon's eyes sparked with frustration.

"I wish we had more time together," he said softly. "I want to spend the rest of my life with you. I want to make up for all the time we've spent apart. Hell, I want to stay in bed with you for days…but we can't. There's no time."

The rest of his life.

My head spun. The warmth of his words soared through me, and I felt that my hopes and dreams might be fulfilled.

Of course, he was right. What was most important was to figure out what we were going to do next.

I searched his face. "What is it?"

The lines around his eyes deepened.

"I came to find you because, well, first because I *had* to see you." He grinned. "But mostly because you needed to know."

"Know what."

His expression changed.

"There was a meeting late last night."

"What kind of meeting?" But I already knew what kind.

"The kind where all the top leaders gather and decide the fate of the world," his eyes gleamed.

"I wanted them to wait until you were better, but it just happened so fast. I didn't think it right to proceed without you, especially after everything you'd done. You deserved to be at that meeting. You should have been there."

"It's fine," I said.

I tried to brush it off as nothing, but it pissed me off that I hadn't been invited.

They had seen me lose control when I'd found Rose. *What had they expected? That I would do nothing?*

"So, what happened?" I asked. "What did they decide?"

He clenched his jaw and hesitated slightly.

I knew it wouldn't like it.

"They're all gone," he said. "They left at sunrise. They're gone to kill the priests."

CHAPTER 26

Rose's funeral was beautiful, but it was the hardest thing I'd ever watched.

Torches had been placed in a circle around the pyre. It was a small gathering. Sylvia and Maya stood next to Ada and a handful of witches I didn't recognize. Even the concubines gathered around the pyre. And to my surprise, so did the two Coven Council witches, Ysmay and Forthwind.

It didn't take much time before the flames of the pyre had consumed her. I stopped crying when there was nothing left of Rose but a few embers that floated high into the sky and joined the stars. That's when I knew the Goddess had taken the Rose I had loved and would protect her soul forever.

I watched in silence as the ceremonial witch performed the blessing for the dead. Her white, shapeless linen gown flapped in a cool breeze, as she sang in Witchtongue. Her voice was as melodic and soothing as Celeste's, and I found myself captivated and drawn to her.

It was all over in a matter of minutes. The ceremonial witch gave a final blessing and stepped back.

I thought I heard the sounds of chanting, like hundreds of quiet voices carried on the wind. The hairs on the back of my neck rose when I thought I'd heard my name. But when I strained to hear it again, I could only hear the snap and crackling of the fire.

I studied Jon's profile. Even by the dim light of the dying fire, I could see the fierceness in his eyes. They weren't the eyes of a farmer or a prince, but the eyes of a warrior. He looked cool and calculating now, and yet just a few hours ago his eyes had been full of warmth and compassion. I still wasn't used to his short, cropped hair. It made him look years younger, but he was still my Jon. I still couldn't believe that only a few days ago I had found him dying on the ground. But the man who stood next to me now was different somehow. I couldn't tell what it was, but something about Jon was different.

Celeste and Will's shoulders brushed against each other. It was hard not to smile at the sight. They were still not completely open about their affection, but those of us who knew them could see it.

Lucas and Nugar had bowed their heads in respect. The wound on Nugar's shoulder wasn't dressed. Perhaps his injury hadn't been as serious as I'd fist thought, or maybe he'd allowed the witches to heal him.

A dozen men and two women I didn't recognize were also gathered around the pyre. Fawkes stood across from me, and I could feel his dark, green eyes on me. I wasn't ready to speak to him yet, and I didn't acknowledge his presence.

I didn't understand why Fawkes hadn't accompanied the prince. I thought the two of them were friends. I had no doubt that

Fawkes would have watched over him. Surely he didn't want to hit me over the head again?

So why was he here?

As the last of the flames flickered and died, I felt a part of me had died along with them. I was tired, but there was no time to sleep. I didn't care if the witch king died is his foolish attempt, but I didn't want Aurion to pay for his father's recklessness.

Ada looked tired and old. She leaned on her staff with both hands, and I could see a tremor in her legs. Even Sylvia and Maya seemed bent with age. They looked so different from when I'd seen them last, when they had been so full of excitement and light. Now there was only gloom and darkness in them.

The few fires that still dotted the castle grounds were tended by the elderly and by women and children. All the able bodied men had left earlier this morning. They had joined the thousands of witches who were heading towards Soul City to kill the priests.

It would never be that simple.

New information had arrived. According to the witches' spies, all the necromancer priests were gathered in Soul City. The king had argued that this was the only chance they would get to kill them all at the same time. Jon thought the king was probably right, but he had decided to stay with me anyway. And so he and his rebels had watched them go.

Jon and Ada told me the king and his guard of witches and humans had planned to surround the city first, to make sure there was no way for the priests to escape. Then a team of witches was going to go in, magecrafts blazing, and kill the priests.

The fact that all the priests had gathered in Soul City didn't rest easily with me. They had come together for a reason, and it was a dangerous one.

The witch king was a fool. He had no idea how strong the priests had become with the stone. It was going to be a massacre.

I wished I had been invited to their meeting. I could have changed Prince Aurion's mind. It came as a surprise to me when Jon told me that Aurion had willingly followed his father. Unless something had changed while I had been *indisposed*, the prince and his father weren't in agreement about anything.

So why had Prince Aurion followed the king?

I changed into my riding clothes and strapped my witch blade and two small daggers onto my belt. I felt ready. The only thing missing was the magecraft, but I knew I'd never get it back. I'd have to make do with my wits and my skills. I didn't have a choice.

I'm going to make this right again. For you, Rose.

First, I'd get the Heart of Arcania back, and then I'd deal with the king. When I found him, I was going to kill him.

I felt Jon's eyes on me. "I know what you're planning," he said.

I raised my brows. "Do you?"

Of course he did. He could read me like an open book.

"I'm coming with you," said Jon. "I'm not letting you out of my sight ever again."

"Are you sure you're up for it? You've only just recovered. I don't want you to exert yourself. Besides, the witches could use you here. They look like they need protection."

Ada's eyes were closed.

Jon said, "I'm fine, Elena. I feel better than I have in a long time."

"The witches and men have no idea what they're up against," I said. "A lot will die…maybe all of them. But they might create the distraction I need to sneak in and get the stone."

I hated to admit it, but I knew it to be true. "I'm good at sneaking."

Jon smiled. "I know you are. But if the humans and witches fail, we might be facing an army of thousands of infected soldiers. It'll be a lot worse than before."

"I know, but we can't let that stop us from trying."

He lowered his voice. "And the witch king? I know you're planning to kill him."

"Is it that obvious?"

"I know you, Elena. If it were me, I would have wanted the bastard who killed Rose to die, too. But what if you're wrong? What if it wasn't him?"

"I'm not." I knew in my soul that the witch king had done it. I wouldn't let doubt cloud my judgement. "And he's going to pay for what he did."

Even if it kills me, I thought. The bastard's already formidable blood magic was amplified even further by his magecraft. I might not survive. But it didn't matter. He needed to die.

"I have twenty of my best men who are ready to come with us," said Jon. "If we leave now, we might just catch up before things take a turn for the worse."

I stared at the ashes that marked the spot where Rose's body had been moments before. A dull ached formed in the pit of my stomach.

"Fine."

The gravel crunched behind me, and I turned around and scowled.

"You're not going anywhere until you spend a few hours with me," said Fawkes.

"I'll go anywhere I damn well please. I certainly don't need your permission."

If Fawkes had been shocked by my burst of anger, he didn't show it. He regarded me without expression.

"If you leave without some kind of training, the black magic in you will awaken, and you won't be able to resist it."

His eyes narrowed. "If you touch the stone…you'll be lost forever. You'll be consumed by its power, and you will become something else."

"I'm going."

Fawkes exhaled in exasperation. "Elena, just think for a moment. I know you're angry with me—"

"Angry?" I shouted. "You bloody hit me over the head! You knocked me out!"

Fawkes spoke gently. "I'm sorry. I had to stop you before you hurt anyone else. You couldn't see yourself. We could. There was something wild in your eyes, a madness, a darkness."

He paused.

"You looked like one of the infected."

"I'm not bloody infected!"

Fawkes began to open his mouth—

A great flash lit the surrounding woods, and a thunderclap cracked. The ground shook, trees swayed back in forth, and then another thunderclap boomed louder than the one before and reverberated into my bones.

When the noise stopped, the ground at my feet still shook as though the Goddess herself was crawling out from under it. The wind shifted, and a strong scent of sulfur rose all around. Every breath burned my throat and my lungs. My eyes watered.

People screamed as they scurried for cover.

"What's happening?" Celeste came rushing to me. Will, Lucas, and Nugar were not far behind.

"It's an earthquake," said Nugar. Lucas nodded in agreement.

I looked at Jon and shook my head.

"I don't think it is an earthquake." I didn't know how to explain why, but I just knew it wasn't an ordinary earthquake. This was something else.

Ada and the other witches looked terrified. I didn't know why.

"Our magic is spent," she said breathlessly. "We gave all we could. Anymore would be the end of us. We cannot protect this realm anymore. *I* cannot. The necromancers' reach is too great. The black magic is too strong. It's too late. The black blight will reach us, and it will destroy us all."

I was a fool to have thought I would have more time. I felt helpless and guilty.

"But we can still make it—"

And then I saw the coiling wall of mist rolling in from the north. The familiar white death moved relentlessly towards us.

It was going to devour Gray Havens.

CHAPTER 27

IT WAS IMPOSSIBLE TO see through the veil of mist, but I knew that within the first layer was a dark opening through which demons from the silence beyond could pour. No human or witch could survive in the demon realm. The air was toxic to anything mortal. It was death. Our world would die if we couldn't stop the necromancers in time.

As the ominous fog swept into Gray Havens like a strong current, I felt anew the massive weight of responsibility on my shoulders. So many lives would be lost no matter the outcome, and if I failed, the nightmare that was the necromancers' dream would come true.

How could we win against such powerful and complete evil?

My heart pounded in my ears.

"Damn you, devils," I snarled.

Was this the end? Had I really gone through everything only to be taken by that damn mist?

"Run!" I yelled. "Get away! Get away from the mist!"

The old and infirm who had not gone to fight in Soul City were frozen in fear at the sight of the mist, and I hurried to shake them out of their stupor. But they weren't fast enough.

The mist rose from the edge of the forest and rolled towards an elderly man with a cane. He scuttled away from it as fast as he could, but he was not fast enough. A layer of mist coiled around him, and he disappeared into its depths.

People screamed as they trampled over one another and scrambled for their lives.

But the fog didn't stop. It wanted blood.

A woman and her two young children disappeared into a spiral of fog. Their wails rose into the air and froze my blood. And then silence.

The mist kept rolling forward.

My worst fears were confirmed. The safest place in the world was just as vulnerable as the rest of the realm. No kingdom was safe, not anymore.

"Everyone in the castle! Hurry!" shouted Ada.

Witches ran to help the humans along. Everyone dashed through the grounds and into the castle in a mad frenzy.

Some didn't make it.

The mist stopped at the edge of the lake, as though an invisible wall forced it back, as though it could go no farther.

"It won't hold it forever," said Ada.

Somehow the witches' magic or just the grounds themselves had enough magic to keep the mist from approaching the castle.

"We'll be safe in the castle, but not for long."

"How long do you think it'll hold?"

"A day maybe," said the high witch. "Two at the most."

I watched as group of humans and concubines hesitated in front of the castle's doors. Their fear of the witches still played on their minds, and I thought they were going to return to their tents. But after a moment's hesitation they disappeared inside.

"Elena, you must find the source of the necromancers' power." Ada spoke to me as if I were the only one who could save them. "You must destroy it. You must sever their link. Shut them off completely. Find that source. Find the doorway where magic spills into our world and *close* it."

I tried to hide the dread I felt. That was barely enough time to make it to Soul City, and I had no idea what would happen when we got there. Anything could go wrong. It didn't leave me much time to deal with the king either. But I would make time for him.

"And the stone?"

Ada looked uncertainly at the two Coven Council witches. I could tell there had been many disagreements between them. I hated the way they looked at Ada with disdain, as though she was an inferior witch.

Ada turned back to me. "The stone cannot stay in the hands of the necromancers, or anyone else for that matter. The stone is its own master. No human or witch can wield it. Anyone else who thinks they can is a fool. You alone can take it from them. You *must* take it."

I opened my mouth to speak, but I hesitated. Ada was trying to tell me something. *But what?*

"The awakening?" pressed Fawkes. "If she touches the stone, without strengthening her mind, she will not be able to resist it."

"There's no time." Ada shuffled quickly towards me and pulled her pendant from her neck.

"Here," she said as she dropped it over my head. "This will protect you somewhat. It's the best I can do. I leave you in the Goddess' hands. Your blood magic will do the rest. I have faith in you, Elena. You can do this. You must hurry. The castle walls will not protect us from this evil for long."

Her eyes brimmed with tears, and I felt my heart break.

"It's not going to be easy," I said.

The mist at the edge of the lake still hadn't moved.

"The six priests have united their power, and they still possess the stone. There's a chance we might not survive this."

I let out a shaky breath. "I don't understand your faith in me. It's that same faith you had when you sent me to Witchdom."

I narrowed my eyes. "Why? Why me?"

"Because we have faith you will succeed."

I shook my head.

"How? One half-witch and a handful of men. It'll be a miracle if we get past the gates."

"Because you are not alone," said the high witch. "The witches will fight with you. They will fight for us, for the Goddess, and for this world."

"What witches?"

"These witches." Ada raised her head and gestured behind me.

I turned around and caught my breath. I stared, not quite sure what I was seeing.

Mounted on their horses was an army of a thousand witches.

CHAPTER 28

IN ALL THE COMMOTION and panic, I'd never even heard them approach. The immensity of it was staggering. Male and female witches of all ages and from all five clans sat straight in their saddles, waiting. Even without weapons of steel, it was an army ready for battle. Only a fool would think they were not powerful.

Despite their differences, their faces all shone with the same gritty determination. Their eyes shone with enthusiasm and hope. The hum of the witches and their magic surrounded me with purpose.

"What is this?" I asked. "Why are they here and not with the king?"

"Because they didn't come for the king," said Fawkes, shaking his head slightly. "Some still believe in their king, and they left with him and his guard. But not all witches agree with his methods. Most of them think it's time for a change."

My pulse raced and I frowned.

"What are you talking about?"

An army of faces looked at me expectantly.

"Fawkes?" I asked and turned around to face him.

Fawkes looked out over the army. "The witches came for you."

Heat rushed to my face, and I was glad for the semi-darkness because my heart was pummeling my chest as I tried to appear calm. I looked out at the mass of witches. They were waiting for me. It was unnerving.

"Why would they do this?"

"For Elena?" Jon's expression was grim and I could see that all of his attention was focused on me. I could tell in that moment that I was more important to him than anything else.

Fawkes answered for me. "Yes, for Elena, and because their prince ordered them."

"But how is this possible? I'm not a queen. I don't hold any sort of title. They would defy their king and follow me."

"Yes. Prince Aurion speaks very highly of you," said Fawkes.

My heart skipped a beat.

"We all saw you perform at the witch trials. We all know what you're capable of. Your strength, your blood magic, and your actions have made us into believers. And the prince shares our belief. You are the key. Not his father, the king, but you. This battalion of witches is here at the prince's command. They are here to protect you and to help you get the stone."

I began to panic. I knew they were wrong. I wasn't magical. Ada had confiscated my only source of real magic. I didn't understand why Aurion had placed so much faith in me. I wasn't what he thought I was.

Nugar whistled. "Good. With these numbers we'll have a real chance."

My rebels nodded in agreement. They all looked relieved, except for Lucas. He still looked at me suspiciously.

Nugar was right. One thousand was better than twenty. We might actually stand a chance of defeating the priests and getting the stone. Prince Aurion's actions never ceased to surprise me. I couldn't help but think he had an ulterior motive for providing this army. I just hoped he knew what he was doing.

Did the king know about his son's betrayal? Why had Aurion left with his father if he didn't believe he was capable of stopping the priests?

"What about the king?" I asked after a moment. "What does he believe?"

"The witch king believes in himself." Fawkes raised his brow.

My eyes darted back to the two Coven Council witches.

"And you? Did you come on the prince's orders?"

I knew they had their own agenda. I wanted to see if they were willing to tell us.

Ysmay smiled bitterly at me.

"We may not fully agree with our prince, but others do. And he has encouraged us all to take action, to follow the Goddess' path, and to protect our world from evil. We have come for that reason alone."

Bullshit.

"Whatever."

I knew I had to make things right again, but I didn't want to be responsible for all these witches. Moreover, I didn't want to see their faces when they realized they'd been wrong about me.

Ada turned to me. "Go now, Elena," she said. "You must hurry."

She read the expression on my face and said, "Don't worry about me. Celeste has been using her tonics to help with our stamina."

I smiled at Celeste. I could see how much we meant to her and how much she wanted to help.

"I need to focus my energy on those who are staying behind." Ada turned to me again. "Trust in yourself, Elena. You have it in you, the power. You don't need anything else."

Before I could say anything, Ada had turned around and shuffled towards the castle. Yellow light spilled from its many windows, and I could see the despair on the many faces peering down at us.

"I'll get the horses." Fawkes strolled away with Jon and the rebels.

Celeste and Will shared a few words. When she turned away, her cheeks were wet, and Will's eyes were red. I looked away before I embarrassed them.

Celeste squeezed my hand. "Be safe," she whispered and followed Ada without another word.

With a final glance at the mist, I made to move. But someone grabbed my arm, and I whirled around.

"When you get the stone, you bring it back to us," said Ysmay. Her coven partner loomed behind her.

"The prince commands it. He trusts us. We know how to take care of it."

I yanked my arm from her grip and stiffened with a sudden fury.

"He does, does he?"

"Yes. You can trust us," continued the coven witch.

Her smile looked false. Her hot, rancid breath in my face made me want to recoil.

"The stone will be in good hands. I promise. We are the only ones who can truly keep it safe."

She smiled that deceitful smile again, and then her voice turned soft, like a mother cuddling her favorite child.

"The Goddess has chosen you for this task. You alone can get the stone. She knows you will do the right thing and bring the stone back to *us*. We are just like you, but we have been entrusted by the Goddess to guard the stone. We alone are charged with its safekeeping."

"Guardians of the stone?" I mocked them.

Their smiles disappeared. They looked back at me with their usual masks of unpleasantness.

I struggled with the urge to slap both of them. They had never intended to help fight against the darkness. They had always intended to serve only themselves. I could see that they felt the same desperate hunger for the stone that I felt for the magecraft.

Power. They wanted it, and they wanted it badly. The Heart of Arcania stone was all they had ever wanted. They'd been manipulating us from the very beginning.

They might not have followed the witch king, but that didn't make them any more trustworthy. In fact, there was nothing good about them. They reminded me of the high priests. They had already been corrupted, and the stone would only magnify their danger.

I smiled at them. "When I do get the stone, and I assure you I *will...*"

Their greedy smiles widened, and their skeletal fingers twitched in anticipation.

"...you will never get your hands on it."

Without another word, I turned and ran after Jon.

CHAPTER 29

THE DEMON MIST HAD partly covered the main road south to Soul City, so we took a detour south through the forest. We knew it would take longer because we would have to ride slowly to protect the horses. When we finally hit firm level ground again on the other side of the mist, we'd already wasted four hours.

I was afraid the temple guards would discover us. Moving a thousand strong army wasn't a silent thing, and I was sure that all Anglia could hear us pushing through the forest.

The firm ground was better for the horses, and we dug in our heels and rode as if the demons themselves were chasing us. The ground shook with the loud sound of hooves tearing up the dirt road. The necromancers would surely hear us coming.

But what did that matter?

I was sure the high necromancer priest of Anglia would be waiting for me. He was the bastard who'd started all of this, and it was only a matter of time until I faced him again.

Only this time I felt naked without the magecraft.

A hot wind slapped my face, despite the winter month. Even in the moonlight, I could see that the black blight had spoiled the farms and their crops. Although I couldn't see any bodies, the familiar smell of rot was heavy in the air. It clung to our clothes and skin like the demon mist.

After what I'd encountered in the mist, I couldn't help but wonder how any army could stand up to the horrors that would be unleashed if the veil was finally broken. If the portals were opened, an unimaginable storm of demons would invade this world. Even an army of a million witches wouldn't be able to defeat it. We would all die. Everything with the light of life would be extinguished.

I gripped Torak's reins. The familiar bounce and smell of my horse was my only comfort. I watched our company as we rode. As usual, Fawkes rode on ahead of everyone on his great bull elk. I had no doubt that he knew Arcania like the back of his hand. He had led us through the forest without a misstep, and now I had the suspicion he could also see in the dark.

A group of twenty rebel men followed us on carthorses, which were smaller than the witches' horses but were sturdy and didn't scare easily. The travel-stained rebels bristled with weapons and rode with a solemn intensity. Most of them had lost parents, or wives, or their children. They hated the priests.

The witches had separated into different groups. Some travelled at the front with Fawkes, while hundreds more followed behind us. I recognized a few faces of witches who had traveled with us from Witchdom, but most of them were strangers.

Did they think their prince was mad?

I did my best not to dwell too much on what Aurion had done or why he believed in me. He was right about one thing, though. I was the only key that could unlock all this madness.

I was sad when we left Gray Havens because Ada had looked ill and defeated. Her magic wouldn't hold the mist at bay for very much longer, and I feared it was the last time I'd see her.

My usual companions rode with me. Nugar looked like a bearded wraith. He was armed to the teeth, and I suspected he frightened the witches who rode next to him. Lucas seemed to be in pain and was edgier than ever. He rode the same beautiful tawny stallion he'd ridden to Witchdom.

Will rode on my left side, and I was sure he did so because Celeste had asked him to protect me. His jaw was set, and he rode well, a strong figure among the other rebel men. But I could see he missed Celeste. It was the first time in months they'd been separated. I knew all too well what it was like to leave one's love behind.

Jon rode on my right. Even in the dim light, I could still see traces of the sickness in the luminous scar tissue on his face and in the pale gray veins that webbed his cheeks and neck. Other than that, no one would ever suspect he had once been near death. And he was still breathtakingly handsome.

His good looks and cutthroat image had seduced me at first, but what had finally taken hold of my heart were his loyalty and his selflessness. Jon was a special kind of man. Even High Witch Ada had noticed. The bond we shared was real. It made us stronger.

Jon commanded his horse, and besides being a top-notch swordsman, he was quick, strong and intelligent. He was the most experienced and logical choice to ride with me into Soul City. But at the same time I couldn't help but fear that I would lose him.

The memory of Rose's death was still very raw on my emotions, and if I lost Jon…

I blinked away my tears and studied his face. He looked as if he were the keeper of some secret power, that he was confident we could win.

But how could we?

We all knew what awaited us in the city, Jon especially, and still he followed unquestioningly.

I knew that none of us were a match for the high priests. My heart sank. Our whole task seemed hopeless.

I looked to the east. There were still at least four hours of night left. We still had a long way to go. The smell of sulfur, rot, and something I couldn't identify intensified the closer we got to Soul City.

We pushed our horses to their limits. Torak's back was covered in a sheen of sweat. He deserved better. I only hoped that one day this great big beast could have a normal life. I felt guilty that he couldn't run freely with other horses, that he was riding into death.

The sun rose, but we couldn't see it through the heavy gray clouds. We rode for hours and never stopped. My thighs burned, and my blistered fingers slipped from my reins, but my blood magic kept me from feeling too much pain. I couldn't help but wonder how the others fared.

I thought Fawkes might have gone mad with fear. I had seen the terror on his face when the first wave of mist had rolled into Gray Havens. Now he pushed us so hard that I was sure our horses were about to keel over. If we didn't give them rest soon, our horses would die, and we'd never make it on time. Ada and all the others would die. I was about to protest that we take a break when Fawkes ordered a stop. It was as if he had read my mind.

We slipped off our horses and brought them to a stream. Torak drank his fill, and I removed his saddle and hung his saddle blanket to dry on a nearby tree. I spent a half hour rubbing him down, and only when I was satisfied that he seemed rested did I drink from the stream myself.

I sloshed the water in my mouth. There was strange bitter aftertaste that I couldn't make out. But I drank again because I didn't know when we'd get the chance for any more water.

"There's an unpleasant flavor in the water." Jon kneeled next to me and tasted the water again. "Looks like the black blight's infected the waters as well."

A string of algae covered my fingers. It wasn't the usual green I'd seen before. It was black.

"Stop. We shouldn't drink it." Jon watched me, alarmed.

I looked around. "It's too late now. We've all had some and so have the horses."

I wiped my fingers on the grass. "Besides, it won't matter anyway if we all get sick."

Jon didn't say anything. We both knew that if we couldn't stop the necromancers, nothing would matter because we'd all be dead.

As I drank more from the stream, something caught my eye upstream. I gagged and spat the water out of my mouth.

Bodies bobbed up and down as they passed me and floated slowly downstream. Their flesh was wrinkled and rotten. It was impossible to tell if they'd been infected. They were so badly rotted that it was impossible to tell if they were male or female. Most were face down in the water, and no one dared touch them.

A bundle wrapped in a white cloth drifted past me. It was no longer than my forearm. I began to cry. It was as though an entire village had been killed and thrown into the river.

After that, we barely spoke to one another. Our entire company was haunted by a deep sense of foreboding. The air was thick with the smell of decay and blood. I could feel the witches watching me, but I did my best to ignore them.

What had I gotten myself into?

I thought of the mist and the nightmare that was inside it. It was such a great evil that you could actually feel it, like it was a tangible thing. The only way I could keep my fear at bay was to focus upon my hatred for the king. Rose's death haunted me, and I struggled to control my rising fury. I couldn't afford to make any mistakes.

After only an hour of rest, we got back on our horses and pressed on at a slower pace. The day went by in blurs of sick and dying trees that looked as if they had been burned. Occasionally we passed small farms where everything was filthy with ash and rot.

With the last glimmer of daylight, we finally left the forest. My ass was bruised and sore, and all I wanted to do was to collapse on the ground and sleep. But we had neared the city. Time was running out, and a new wave of adrenaline rushed through my veins.

Goddess, kept them safe. Please give us more time.

As if answering my call, a distant clap of thunder bellowed around us.

But this wasn't the Goddess. This was something else.

Another deep roll of what sounded like thunder sent the horses into a frenzy. I urged Torak forward and tried to distract him from the noise.

Jon and Will joined me as we made our way to the front line. Fawkes and his advance guard of witches had come to a halt, and no one turned around as we approached. Their gazes were all fixed at something below them.

I gasped when we crested the ridge beside them.

Soul City looked exactly as I remembered. It was surrounded by a thirty-foot stone wall, and the golden pyramid that represented the sun stood above the other buildings. I used to be amazed at the sight of it, but now I only felt a cold fury. The golden temple shone through the mist like a beacon. I cursed it.

It hadn't been thunderclaps I'd heard before, but rather the shouts and cries of thousands of men and witches at war. The clamor of metal hacking through flesh and bone echoed off the city walls. The witch king was at war with the infected army of the necromancer priests. And he was losing.

My stomach sank. It would take a miracle to get through the mist to the temple.

CHAPTER 30

I WAS NUMB. Everything seemed muted somehow: the sunlight, the sounds of battle, the stench, even the screams of the dying. The air was buzzing with energy, with magic. It was a strange mix. The sweet, wildflower and citrus smell of elemental and white magic mixed with the sulfur stench of rot and the rancid smell of burnt flesh.

Orange fire lit the skies as tendrils of silver and blasts of white and red energy shot into the air like fireworks.

The witches fought skillfully. They spun and waved their hands like skilled dancers. It was both beautiful and terrifying at the same time. I was in awe for a moment and forgot where I was.

But even the strongest witches were no match for the supernatural black magic of the temple guards and their infected soldiers. They encountered little resistance and cut through the witches as though they were harvesting fields of wheat. Dark puddles dotted the ground at their feet, and I knew it wasn't water.

I watched as an elemental female witch with long fiery hair sent a bolt of fire at an infected man. The fire consumed him in a blanket of fire, and he stumbled backwards. Even though he was still engulfed in orange flames, he brought his sword down on the witch and killed her instantly. I watched in horror as the same flaming man went on to skewer another witch.

The witches' magic seemed to have little or no effect at all on the infected soldiers. The black magic was protecting them somehow. I could feel it. The hum of magic was heavy in the air, just as it had been in Gray Havens. Like the buzzing of millions of bees, the magic seemed to emanate from the heart of the city. It felt as though the city itself was humming, as though it had a heart of its own and was alive.

The red, blue, orange, and purple colors of each of the realms caught the light and flashed through the chaos and smoke. An Anglian man slashed his sword, and an infected head rolled at his feet. He ducked and spun, moving skillfully through swarms of the infected fighters. He howled a battle cry and charged back into the fray, swinging his sword high before him. Three more of the infected died at his hands before he disappeared under a horde of the diseased.

A woman clad in the red and gold colors of Anglia skewered her blade through the eye of an infected female who slumped at her feet.

While the human metal weapons appeared to have more effect than the magic, it wouldn't be enough. We were outnumbered four to one.

I was amazed that the humans and their elected officials had followed the witch king at all.

Did they think he could overcome necromancers alone? Had he promised them something? Would they have supported him if they knew how deeply he hated them?

I spotted the witch king again. I couldn't see his magecraft, but I knew he was using it. It didn't matter. Although his coven guard blasted any infected that came near their king, it didn't even make a difference. As soon as an infected soldier fell, three more replaced him. The witch king was losing badly, and they hadn't even breached the city walls.

I started to tremble without even realizing it. I hated the king, but I didn't want the bastard to die. Not yet. Not until *I* killed him.

Jon reached out and put his hand on my shoulder.

"Once we get in, there's no turning back. You ready for this?"

"I don't think any of us are ready for this. But we have no other choice. I'd rather die trying than do nothing."

I searched the battle for the silver hair of the prince, but it was impossible to see or recognize anyone. I prayed that he was still alive.

I remained there watching for a moment longer. I knew the real threat lay beyond the city walls. Somehow I had to reach the temple.

Even though I knew it was my responsibility, I was unresolved. I only felt dismay. I knew I couldn't turn back now, and I struggled with my cold panic.

I looked to our company of witches, and for the first time since we had left Gray Havens, I saw real fear there. Perhaps they had thought their magic would be enough. Now they realized how wrong they'd been. Some of the witches whispered and shot doubtful glances my way.

Did they regret coming now? Did they realize their magic meant nothing against such evil?

If the infected didn't get them, the mist would.

I could already feel the mist wrapping its cold evil hands around my neck. If I didn't act soon, it would choke the life out of me, and the demons would feed on my soul. If the darkness breached the barrier into our world, nothing could stop it.

Fawkes and his elk drew closer. "Let's go over the plan again."

Next to him was Raken, a dark witch I recognized from our journey from Witchdom. Sweat trickled down the sides of his bald head. Like Fawkes, his face had that ageless quality to it, but his eyes had a dark hollow look about them now. He looked like the sort of witch you didn't want to cross. His hands were covered with the pale white scars that came from fighting with dark magic. He must have been battling for a lifetime to have scars like that.

"I won't waste our time going over preparations for battle," said Fawkes. "War is already upon us."

He raised his voice. "We knew what we were facing. This should be no surprise to any of you. I can see that some of you are doubting this quest, but hear me now. This is nothing compared to what will happen if the devils from the mist escape into our world. Never forget why we're here. We're here to *destroy* the necromancers and to *take* back the stone."

His eyes found mine. "The necromancers are humans, and they can be killed. But only if we find and destroy the source of their power."

His eyes darted back to the city below. "And we know it's in there somewhere."

"But what if you're wrong?" said a witch who looked like a pixie. "We never got actual proof that their source of magic is *in* the golden temple. Are you willing to sacrifice our lives on a whim?"

A few witches next to her nodded. I almost smiled at her challenge.

Fawkes glared at the witch, and I saw her flinch.

"I'm not wrong."

I recognized the furtive glances he gave to the humans. Fawkes had gone to war against the human nations years ago. This couldn't be easy for him, or for any of the witches who'd served in that war. Witches lived for a long time, but humans only remembered stories passed on from generation to generation. The wars with the witches had faded from human memory. I was sure that witches like Raken had been at war with humans, perhaps to get back the very land we stood on. They had real battle experience, but I could understand why they might have felt conflicted now.

I remembered what the witch king had said had happened to Fawkes' family. Working alongside humans was probably excruciating for him, but he was still here.

"First team's task is to get Elena and her rebels through the gates and into the temple," continued Fawkes.

"Elena's team has the responsibility to get the stone, and you're all here to make sure they do. Once inside the temple, we'll break out a second team who will go after necromancers. Raken will cover our backs."

It wasn't like Jon to take orders from someone else, especially a witch, but he seemed to give silent assent and nodded slightly with each point. Even my rebels followed Jon and my example and listened to Fawkes. I sensed a shift in the attitude between the humans and the witches. Will and Celeste's relationship was part of it, but I could see that the humans and the witches were beginning to accept each other. I hoped this newfound trust would last.

I could see that Jon admired and trusted Fawkes. I knew they'd been making plans while I had been indisposed. Apparently, there was a lot I missed.

No one talked about what would happen *after* we retrieved the stone.

Did Fawkes believe we'd die here? That we'd never make it back? Were we making some sort of sacrifice to the Goddess?

Perhaps Fawkes was prepared to die, but I wasn't planning on dying today.

"Elena is the only one who can retrieve the stone." Fawkes' voice shook me from my thoughts. "First, we need to get her inside that blasted golden temple. Whatever it takes, she *must* make it there. We will protect her with our lives."

Fawkes looked closely at the gathered witches and humans.

"Witches. Humans. We've got only one shot to get to the stone. We'll take the path through the north gate. The mist seems less there. Let's hope our eyes don't deceive us."

Fawkes dismounted. We followed his example and climbed down from our mounts. Fawkes leaned forward and whispered something in the ear of his elk. The great beast looked at him for a moment and then dashed back, away from the action. And to my surprise, the horses all followed him.

I rubbed Torak's neck. "You stay out of trouble. You stay safe." There was no way in hell I was going to risk my horse. "I'll see you later."

I smacked his behind, and he went galloping after the other horses. My chest tightened at the sight, but I was comforted at the same time. Torak and the horses would be safe, at least for a little while.

"May the Goddess protect us," said Fawkes.

I could hear the other witches pray to the Goddess, too.

And then we were moving. Fawkes led the way, and the witches aligned themselves in the front and boxed me and the rebels in, like a protective shell.

I concentrated on my breathing and tried to keep my focus. I felt my powers awakening in me like a rush of adrenaline. Ada's warnings flashed into my mind, but I managed not to think of them.

Jon and Will were on each side of me, while Nugar and Lucas had my back. Part of me was annoyed that I was being protected so thoroughly. How was I going to get a shot at the witch king while I was surrounded like this? Somehow, I'd have to break free and find the king.

Jon looked at me. His gaze was so full of love that I nearly started to cry. "Stay close to me. And if things go wrong, you find Fawkes. Promise me."

It took a moment before I answered because I didn't trust my voice.

"I won't have to. We'll be fine."

I strained to control the wild beating of my heart. "Just…just stay alive, okay?"

There was always the chance that he, too, might die. But if anyone could survive this, it was Jon.

"I'll be right behind you," he said. "I won't let anything happen to you."

I swallowed and nodded. I could barely breathe and I couldn't stop my teeth from clattering. I wiped my damp forehead with the back of my arm and blinked the moisture from my eyes.

The other rebels had all gathered around us. Most of them would probably die. I felt a rush of shame that I'd never even taken the time to learn all their names.

My knees shook suddenly, and I focused on my anger. Everything around me dissolved until there was only me and the golden temple. My fury, my blood magic, poured through my veins. No mist or black magic could deny me my vengeance.

At first I thought we'd have the element of surprise since the infected soldiers hadn't noticed us. But as though they had read my mind, a horde of them turned together and ran up the hill towards us.

"Shit. So much for the element of surprise," I grumbled.

"For better or for worse," said Jon. "Let's kill as many as these black-eyed bastards as we can."

"For Garrick," Nugar's rough voice always surprised me.

"For Max," echoed Lucas.

"For Leo," shouted Will.

Jon's face glistened in the dim light. His sword rose in his massive fist, and his muscles bulged along his arms. He howled a battle cry, and the rebels and witches did the same.

Blood pounded in my ears, and my heart raced with fear and fury.

"Let's kill these bastards."

I pulled out my witch blade, took a deep breath, and charged down the hill.

CHAPTER 31

THE FIRST WAVE OF the infected was immense, and they hit us fast. They moved like primitive animals. Some had weapons in their hands, but most used only their hands and fingers as claws. They advanced with a single purpose, to destroy every living soul in their path. Their skin barely clung to their bodies, and a yellow discharge and blisters covered most of their faces. Their eyes looked too big, and their noses and lips had rotted away to reveal bone and teeth.

I suppressed the urge to be sick. Their inhuman black eyes were empty and dead. Like Jon, the black blight had taken away their humanity and left them emaciated wraiths. They resembled the demons I'd seen in the mist.

The stench of infection was overwhelming. The stink burned my eyes and my throat with every labored breath. It felt as though I'd rubbed onions over my eyes and into my mouth. We all coughed and gagged, and for a few horrifying seconds, I feared we would be overwhelmed. But the line of witches held, and we began to make some progress towards the walls of the city.

Three infected men breached our lines. They appeared to be searching for someone, and when they saw me, they sprang like a pack of wild animals.

"They're coming from the left!" I yelled.

"Will!" bellowed Jon.

Will, Jon and I lunged forward and hacked at the heads and necks of our enemies. Somehow we knew we could kill them if we struck into their brains or decapitated them. They collapsed into heaps of bent limbs at our feet, and I tasted their sour acrid blood in my mouth. The wall of witches consolidated around us, and I was protected for the moment. But the way the infected seemed to be looking for *me* left a cold, uneasy feeling in my chest.

A handful of elemental witches rushed forward. They raised their hands and shot a booming blast of fire that illuminated the night as though it was daylight. The sound echoed off the city walls, and while the light only lasted a few seconds, it was enough for me to see beyond my protective wall of witches.

My heart sank. I looked to where I'd last seen the witch king. The infected who had been attacking him had left off their assault and were now making their way towards us. All their attention was focused on us now, on me. They'd forgotten the king because they *knew* I was here. They were coming for me.

At this rate we'd all be dead in an hour, and we'd never reach the gates to the city.

"Fawkes! We've stopped moving!" I screamed in a panic, and in a few great strides he was standing next to me.

"The other infected aren't attacking the king anymore, they're attacking us. They know I'm here, and they don't want me to reach the city. They've trapped us. If we can't move, we're not going to make it."

Fawkes appraised the situation, and his face grew grim and dark.

"Time for a new strategy," said Jon. He spoke quickly. "It's obvious the priests know Elena's here, and somehow the infected seem to recognize her. I don't know how that's possible."

"Magic," said Lucas.

Fawkes nodded. "Yes. Possibly."

"They know what she looks like," repeated Jon. He reached inside his cloak and pulled out a scarf. "So we disguise her."

I grabbed the scarf from him and wrapped it around my head and face, until only my eyes showed.

"What are you thinking?" asked Fawkes.

Witches and humans began to fall all around us. And so did my spirit. Jon's scarf prevented the others from seeing the despair in my heart.

"Let them believe she's here," said Jon. "Then we can sneak around them and head straight for the north gate. No one's guarding it, as far as I can tell. If we're quick, we can be inside the city before they even know she's gone."

"I won't be able to protect you," said Fawkes. "You'll be on your own. If they see you—"

"They won't," I said, my confidence building. "I'm good at being sneaky. I've had years of practice."

It was impossible to tell what Fawkes was thinking. "It's a very risky plan."

"I can do it," I pressed.

The carnage of battle around us was increasing by the second. We had to move.

"Trust me. This'll be the easy part."

"If something should happen to you…"

Fawkes' gaze darted from me to the mob.

"We'll keep her safe," said Jon. "I know it's a risk, but the odds of getting through the middle of this army of infected soldiers is not looking good. Even if we could fight our way through, we wouldn't reach the city before the mist. This is our only shot."

Fawkes' frown deepened. "Then you better make it quick before these abominations know we've tricked them."

I made to move—

"Elena, be careful," said Fawkes. "With the mist so close, the necromancers will be stronger now. I don't know what you'll face once you get inside the golden temple. It might be something you haven't seen before."

I could see despair in his face for the first time.

"I'll be careful." My stomach knotted. "I promise."

"And remember to control your *emotions*. Don't lose yourself to it."

I scowled at Fawkes. I knew exactly what he meant, that I hadn't had the necessary training, and that I was too weak to control the stone. But I wasn't, and I would prove it.

I turned away and followed Jon back towards the end of the line. The witches continued to engage the infected horde and gave us the window of opportunity we needed. We sneaked away easily.

I caught a glimpse of the witch king and his guards barreling through the north gate and making their way towards the golden temple. I spotted a flash of silver hair, but I couldn't tell for certain if it was the prince. I just hoped to the Goddess he was still alive.

We ran with stealth and speed. If we stopped, we died.

The dismembered limbs, severed heads, and entrails made our footing difficult, and I had to concentrate hard not to slip on the slick mess of blood and guts. While some of the bodies were infected soldiers, most of them were humans and witches. And there were thousands of them dead.

As we carefully picked our way through and over the dead, I heard the moans that rose from the carnage. Some were still alive. Tears welled in my eyes, but I couldn't stop. I couldn't help them. They were in the hands of the Goddess now.

The path that lead to the entrance of the north gate was clear.

Is this your doing, Goddess? Did you create this path for us?

Somehow, I knew in my soul that the Goddess was aiding us the best way she could. It was good enough.

By the time we'd reached the gate, our faces and clothes were covered in a sticky mess that I didn't want to think about. Still we didn't stop. We needed to make it to the golden temple.

Soul City had always looked a little eerie at night. But now, even in the gloom of this ungodly mist, I could see that the once manicured landscape of lawns and gardens had been reduced to rot and ash. It looked like Hell.

I thought of Fawkes and hoped that he would be able to fight his way through the infected horde and the mist. I pushed myself harder. My shirt stuck to my sweat-soaked skin, and the stench of rot intensified and turned to choking heat. But none of us stopped.

Finally the golden temple loomed over us at the end of the cobbled road. Its golden walls gleamed unnaturally, and soft yellow light spilled from the windows. We had made it.

I bent over to catch my breath for a second and looked behind me. Nugar and Lucas bounded into view, along with twelve of my twenty rebels. I couldn't think about what had happened to the others. I turned away before they could read the panic on my face. I had to look like I knew what I was doing. But I didn't.

The familiar walnut doors of the grand entrance were just in front of us.

"Why aren't there any guards?"

Jon wheezed and coughed, and for a horrible moment I thought I'd made a terrible mistake and he hadn't fully mended. But he recovered quickly, and his face was a healthy pink.

"Why have they guarded the outside of the city but not the temple?"

"Could we be wrong?" asked Lucas. "If the priests aren't here, we came all this way for nothing."

I could tell the others were thinking the same thing, too.

"We did *not* come for nothing," I snapped. My voice was louder than I'd intended.

I stared at the damn fog and felt the eyes of the demons staring at me, daring me to enter. The ground beneath our feet vibrated, and for a moment I thought I saw the temple walls expand and contract, as though the giant monument was breathing. The necromancers' power was potent here. Any fool could sense that we were surrounded by death.

I shrugged and straightened up.

"Enough of this horseshit. Let's do what we set out to do. They're in there all right. Don't let this fool you. We won't be pawns in their game."

Nugar swore loudly and gripped his axe with both hands. "I'm nobody's pawn. Especially the priests'."

I couldn't agree with Nugar more, but I suspected we had already been played. Now it was time to turn the game around.

"You know what'll happen once we go through those doors," said Jon, as though he had read my mind.

I looked to the entrance. My pulse raced and I let my anger feed me with much needed courage.

"It doesn't matter. We go on. We fight. It's all we can do. And if the Goddess allows it, we get the stone and live. I'm not planning on dying today, so get your heads out of your asses and let's do what we came here to do."

The longer I stood gaping at the doors, the more I felt my courage seeping away. If I didn't move now, I never would.

I unsheathed my witch blade and leaped up the stairs two at a time. Jon and Will bounded alongside me. We reached the two massive doors on the run, and I threw my shoulder against them hard.

They flew open, and my heart stopped.

The golden walls and black marble floors of the interior were not occupied by priests, but by demons.

CHAPTER 32

Hundreds of wolf-like creatures with long, dripping maws and hairless gray skin were waiting in the great hall. Their faces were distorted by hatred and their bodies were bent and deformed. They were armed with swords, and their mouths stretched unnaturally wide with their deep, savage roars. The rancid stench of feces and decay rolled off them, and their yellow animal eyes pulsed with magic as they appraised us.

I gripped my blade so hard it hurt, and I resisted the urge to take a step back. I barely had time to register what I was looking at. I felt the other rebels carefully taking their positions on either side of me.

The creatures loitered around us, but they didn't attack. It was as though they were waiting for something.

How had the witch king got through?

Scanning the room quickly, I saw a few crumpled bodies. And there was no mistaking the maroon puddles that covered the floors. But the bodies didn't belong to the king or his son.

I wished Fawkes and his company of witches were here. Maybe this wasn't such a good idea.

"Are these the demons you saw in the mist?" asked Will.

I shook my head. "No."

A cold panic welled through me as I realized what they were.

"These aren't demons. Look, they're wearing the temple guards' uniforms, and they are all carrying swords," I said.

"These are humans, or at least they were once. They were the temple guards."

Several of the rebels, including Nugar, made the sign of protection against evil. Some of the creatures even cocked their heads at the mention of *temple guards*, as though they were acknowledging that was what they had been.

"Make no mistake," I said. "These things are *different* from the other infected creatures we've seen. Their bodies look like they have morphed. Maybe this is a different kind of infection."

The air was thick with an energy I'd never sensed before. The entire temple vibrated with it. I could see that Jon could feel it.

The presence of these creatures confirmed my initial suspicion that the priests *were* still somewhere in the temple. The dome-like mist over the city appeared to emanate from here, too. Ada had charged me to find their source of magic. I knew it was somewhere in this massive temple.

But where was it coming from? Would I even recognize it if I saw it?

I looked out the doors behind me, and my breath caught.

The heavy mist had engulfed the street where we'd been just moments ago. The path we had used was gone. The unholy white fog coiled and swelled as it moved, and it was heading straight for the temple doors.

"Close the doors!"

Two of my rebels quickly pulled the doors closed behind us. I wasn't sure what was worse, the mist getting through or our being trapped in here with these creatures.

"Kill the bitch," said one of the temple guards.

I turned to face him.

His lips curled back as he growled between his long teeth. "Don't let her get away."

All at once the creatures came for me.

I didn't even have a chance to swing my blade before Jon pushed me behind him.

"Protect Elena!" he bellowed.

Nugar's huge form appeared at my side. Lucas was beside him, and Will moved to protect Jon.

The great hall erupted in a cacophony of earsplitting shrieks, roars, and clangs as metal hit metal and as metal hit flesh and bone.

Two creatures leapt from the opposite wall, coming straight for me. Nugar moved with frightening speed for someone so large. With a swing of his battle-axe, Nugar slit the first creature from its neck to its crotch. It fell into a mess of guts at his feet. Lucas spun, and with two quick jabs in the throat the other creature spat black liquid and collapsed.

Our tightknit group split up as we battled the flood of temple guard creatures. We were seriously outnumbered. I had to think of a solution before we were overwhelmed.

I had to find the stone.

"Jon, I need to get to the altar! That's where the priests are."

If they were here, I suspected they'd be praying at their altar. I was about to tell him where it was, but he nodded like he already knew.

"Okay. Stay behind me."

We dashed across the room, but we barely made it ten feet before a wall of possessed temple guards stood in our way.

"I'm going to taste your female flesh," spat a guard.

His yellow eyes sparked with the desperate hunger of hatred. His voice cackled into a wet, sick laugh, and he swung his sword at me faster than any ordinary man could.

I leapt out of the way, but I felt the tip of his sword through my shirt. Although the warm wet blood trickled down my stomach, I could feel that my healing powers had already begun to heal my wound.

Something caught Jon on the head with a sickening thud. His eyes rolled into the back of his head, and he stumbled and fell to the marble floor. Blood flowed from a large gash on his forehead. He was not moving.

"Jon!" I wailed, but he did not get up.

Anger, pain, and fear surged through me. I felt like my heart had been shredded. It had hurt when Jon had been infected. It had nearly broken me when I found him dying. But seeing him sprawled lifeless again nearly destroyed me.

I whirled at his attackers, seeking blood.

"You bastards! I'll kill you!"

The temple guard creatures glanced at me calmly, curious and amused. Their callused gray skin made me think of the tiny garden lizards I used to catch as a child.

"I've always hated you bastards," I hissed.

I brandished my witch blade and looked quickly at Jon. I hoped he was going to open his eyes and get up. But he didn't move, and I couldn't tell if he was breathing.

My vision blurred with tears, and I couldn't see the other rebels, but the sound of battle was everywhere.

"I'm going to skin you for what you did."

The guards laughed unkindly, and the largest of the three sneered. One of his eyes was milky-white, and a large scar ran from the lid down and across his face. He wore a belt of tiny skulls, and his voice was deep and commanding.

"You must have a death wish, witch bitch, to be as foolish as to come to our masters' temple."

I glowered at these beasts. "I'm not going to die. You are."

But even as I said the words, I realized how foolish it sounded. I didn't have the magecraft this time. I only had my blade and my blood magic. I prayed they would be enough.

"Aldus, let me kill the witch whore," said a guard with braids. His sword was still dripping with fresh blood.

"We can feast on her pretty flesh later."

"I can think of other things to do with her pretty flesh," said the milky eyed guard.

I kept my face straight. I wouldn't show them fear.

Part of my mind, the logical one, screamed to run. But brutal rage and my desire to avenge Jon and Rose possessed me and commanded me to stay and fight. I wouldn't abandon my friends. There was no turning back.

The guard called Aldus flashed his rotten teeth.

"There's no getting away. You're mine now, little witch."

He leapt at me, but I was ready.

With a quick flick of my wrist, I threw one of my hunting knives. Aldus' last words died in his throat as my knife pierced his right eye socket and entered his brain. Black blood spilled from his open mouth, and he toppled over like a big dead tree.

The two other guards roared in fury and charged like wild beasts. One of the guards hurled his sword like a spear, and I barely had time to duck as the massive weapon nicked my neck and buried itself in the wall behind me.

I pitched forward on the ground and rolled back onto my feet, surprised at how steady I was.

My fury had charged the black magic in my veins and filled me with a strength that was colder than that of my magecraft. It was different, but I knew I would lose myself if I couldn't control it.

Without giving the beast time to react, I kicked upward into his jaw and landed my other foot on his lower back. The guard staggered, but hardly looked injured. He spat some black blood from his mouth and smiled. His rotten teeth were smeared with blood.

His smile only aggravated me further.

"I'm going to slit your throat, witch!"

I bounced on the tips of my toes and brandished my witch blade. I narrowed my eyes and grinned darkly.

"Not if I slit yours first."

I let my intuition guide me. The guard lurched. I feinted left, spun, came up behind him, and sliced his neck.

I pushed the dead guard away from me, but then something slammed into me, and my witch blade flew from my hands. My breath escaped me, and I fell to the ground.

I cried out as searing pain attacked my shoulder. I managed to roll away from my attacker, but my warm blood was soaking my left side and front.

But even as the pain flamed in my shoulder, I could feel the warmth of healing power stitching up my sliced flesh and feeding me with new strength.

I spotted my witch blade on the ground between the two guards.

Golden light spilled from my torn shirt, and one of the guards faltered in confusion.

"Your magic won't save you now," snarled the other guard.

He launched himself at me ferociously with his sword high above his head.

Frantically, I raised my arm to parry the thrust, but the guard's violent strength sent a wave of intense pain through my arm and something snapped.

My attacker howled as he lunged again. I dodged backwards, but my right arm hung uselessly at my side. I could already feel it healing, but it wasn't going to be fast enough. I ducked as his sword brushed the top of my head. A few more inches and I would have been decapitated.

My heart hammered as I struggled to control my panic.

I had no more weapons. I was defeated.

I was sprawled defenseless on the floor, and I could only stare in terror as the guard bared his teeth and charged. His sword was aimed right at my heart.

CHAPTER 33

THE WORLD SLOWED, and I saw my life flash before my eyes.

The tip of the guard's sword was inches from my neck. I knew in that split second, that even if I moved it would be too late.

It was too late. I was going to die—

But then in a flash of movement a blade parried the guard's sword so that it only grazed my neck.

"Get back!"

Lucas had just saved my life.

He moved gracefully through the tangle of guards, slicing and dicing with blades in each hand. The guards around us fell in a matter of seconds.

I was stunned that Lucas had been the one to save me, but I was more than grateful. He had a strange, creepy smile on his face. At one time I would have sworn that Lucas wanted nothing more than to kill me. He was a more skillful fighter than I'd first thought. The other guards hadn't seen me yet, so I used the precious time Lucas had given me and rushed over to Jon.

I pressed my hands against his neck. There was a pulse.

"He's still alive," I said to myself quietly. Tears welled in my eyes. He had a large welt on his forehead, but his chest rose and fell in a constant motion.

"Jon, wake up!" I shook his shoulders. "Jon!"

But he wouldn't wake. I suppressed my panic because I knew he would wake up eventually. It was a good thing he looked dead because I had to leave him, and I needed the guards to think he was dead.

I searched the ongoing battle. I couldn't see Nugar or Will, but the other rebels still fought heroically. They were alive. I took that as a good sign.

With a new rush of adrenaline, I searched the hallways until I recognized the corridor that would take me to the altar. My arm had healed, so I grabbed my witch blade and ran for the north corridor.

"Lucas! To the altar!" I yelled.

Lucas bounded next to me like a cat, and we rushed past a few unsuspecting guards whose surprise and anger only showed after we had flown by.

We passed a blur of doors leading to other rooms as we flew across the marble floors. Heavy footsteps sounded behind us, but I concentrated only on getting to the altar and wrapping my hands around the high priest's neck.

The hall eventually opened up into the altar chamber. Two long ceremonial tables were covered with human skulls, and candles were positioned on either side of the altar. A large red ring with symbols inside was painted on the floor and circled the altar.

At first it looked exactly as I remembered when the high priest of Anglia had killed Prince Landon. But then the braziers that had once burned with green fire were cold and lifeless now. And the altar was empty.

The hairs on the back of my neck rose. There was no one there, no priest, no necromancer, no one.

I couldn't breathe. I skidded to a stop.

"I don't understand?" I panted. "They should be here. I felt their magic."

What if I had been wrong? What if the pulsing I had felt was something else?

I whirled around.

"Lucas—"

Lucas' eyes widened, and blood spurted from his mouth. The silver tip of a sword perforated his chest.

"No!"

I lunged at the guard just as he pulled out his sword to strike at me. But I was quicker, and my blade lanced through his open mouth and into his brain. With a smell of rotten eggs, the guard's body fell towards me. I pushed it away and rushed over to Lucas.

I knelt on the ground, the battles around me forgotten, and I pulled him into my lap.

His eyes flickered with pain and fear.

He whispered, "I'm. Sorry."

And then Lucas was no more.

I was hot and cold as I hung on to the young man who had once terrified me, whom I had thought I could never trust, and who had just saved my life.

And then I felt it—that reverberating pulse again. It was louder this time and seemed more intense. I pressed my hand on the floor and was shocked that the marble was warm and not cold.

And then I knew where the priests were.

Crashing sounds erupted. A mass of guards was heading my way.

I let Lucas fall to the floor as gently as I could.

"Goddess protect him."

I jumped up and ran across the chamber into the opposite corridor. My enemies were in hot pursuit behind me.

But my blood magic was strong, and I ran fast. But all the blasted hallways looked exactly the same, and I lost my way after the second corner. I searched for any familiar landmark and spotted a tapestry I had seen before. I knew where I was.

If I stopped to fight, I knew I'd be dead. My only option was to lose them. My advantage was that I knew where I was going, and they didn't.

I flew down the passageway, and after running in circles for five minutes I could finally hear less commotion behind me. Hopefully I'd lost them.

I'd wasted enough time. I had to move.

Torchlights flickered and sent long shadows shimmering against the stone walls as I ran. I neared the entrance to the prisons.

I'd been here just a few months ago when I had found Jon horribly infected. No one was around.

I focused on getting to the great wooden prison doors before the guards behind me.

Perhaps it was the Goddess, perhaps it was my blood magic, but I managed to get there in one piece.

I pushed the doors open and flew down the stairs into the blackness of the prison tunnel. In addition to the familiar smell of acrid air and rot, the humming noise had increased to a roar, and the smell of sulfur seared my nose and lungs.

There was only one thing that could be making that sound.

I wasn't going to the prison cells this time.

I landed on a platform, but instead of going straight, I turned to my left and saw another bolted door. If I was right, the layout on the main floor would be mirrored in the prisons below. There had to be more livable space in these underground levels.

I tried the handle and was surprised it wasn't locked.

Bracing myself, I pulled it open and stepped through. I was submerged into darkness immediately, but as I grew accustomed to the dark, I could see that a light glimmered through the gloom some fifty yards in front of me.

I heard loud footsteps, and I rushed to close the door and slide the metal bolt to lock it. I didn't know how long it would keep the guards out, but I didn't have a choice. I felt like I'd just sealed the lid of my coffin.

I turned around and gripped my witch blade tightly in an attempt to steady my trembling hands.

Listening carefully, I started forward. I heard the murmurs of voices, soft at first, but then they grew louder as I moved towards them. The air was thick with the reek of dark witch magic. It left a hard, metallic taste in my mouth.

But there was another putrescent smell, more foul than anything I'd ever smelled before. It smelled like hundreds of rotting corpses had been left in the sun for days and then piled in an enclosed space.

It was the reek of power and death.

My walk became a jog and then a run. I let my instincts guide me because I couldn't see more than two feet before me. I needed to get to that light.

The ball of light got bigger and bigger until I arrived at the threshold of another massive underground chamber.

I squinted as my eyes adjusted to the light. The chamber itself was about the same size as the entire first floor of the temple. There were no other rooms or corridors. It was just one giant space with rock and dirt walls and a dirt floor.

Tendrils of black and red and silver magic stretched and wove with one another and exploded throughout the chamber like a lightning storm. Red, yellow, and silver tendrils of magic bounced off the walls like rainbows. Blasts of magic ricocheted off the chamber walls and shards of fractured rock showered from the ceiling.

It was a war of magic between the witches and the necromancers.

The prince shot a blast of augur magic that sounded like a sonic boom, and white-hot energy hurled a diseased guard backward into the chamber wall.

The witch king and his coven guards stood with the prince and a mass of witches on the left side of the chamber. They were throwing everything they had at the six necromancer priests and their guards on the opposite side. Six strange shadow-like creatures in the robes of their priests cowered behind them.

No one had noticed me.

I could make out a wall of mist at the far end of the chamber. It rippled, coiled, and surged, slippery with death. Dark shadows moved inside the mist. I could see land and cities looming in the distance inside it. The seas inside the mist were black, and bodies seemed to float in the air.

The doorway to their world was nearly opened.

The humming sound wasn't coming from the mist or from the battle that shook the ground, but from a boundary of light that separated the two enemies.

I stepped closer and saw the source of the bright light.

In the middle of the chamber was a large opening, a crack. Thick smoke and brilliant white plumes of light poured through the hole like a fountain.

I knew instantly what it was. It was the crack in the world that Ada had told me about.

It was the source of the necromancer's power. And endless magic poured out of it.

CHAPTER 34

I'D NEVER SEEN ANYTHING like this. I was frightened of it, but I was also drawn to it. For a moment the magic called to me, and I forgot the dangers around me.

No one seemed to be paying attention to this outpouring of power. They were too busy trying to kill each other.

It all made sense now. The details began to fit together. The priests claimed this part of Anglia because they'd found an unlimited source of magic beneath the old king's castle in Soul City. They had retained the foundations of the old castle and built their golden temple above it. They had used the mask of a religion to keep it secret from the rest of the world. No one other than the priests had known about it, until now.

I had never felt magic of this magnitude. It was addictive and intoxicating. It was similar to the power I felt from the magecraft and the Heart of Arcania stone, only this was a thousand times stronger. I took another step forward, seeking more of that power, that magic. I wanted it. I needed to have it.

The earth screamed beneath my feet, as though it recognized and acknowledged me. I felt the magic's awareness. It was like a hurricane of knowledge and power waiting to be unleashed. I sensed it as it answered my desire for it with a great rumble.

Just as I made to move farther towards it, I heard rushing footsteps from behind me. The temple guards had broken down the door. I barely had time to leap out of the way before they came barreling into the chamber behind me.

Without a second thought, I rushed across the chamber to put as much distance as I could between myself and those creatures.

"Kill her! Kill the steel maiden!"

I didn't need to look up to see who was speaking. But I did anyway.

The high priest of Anglia's expression surprised me. It was the first time I had seen fear in those damned pale gray eyes.

Everyone turned towards me.

Aurion looked terrified, but I wasn't sure if he was frightened of me or his father.

The witch king sneered at me. The corners of his mouth were turned up in a self-satisfied smile as though he mocked me and gloated over Rose's death.

Bastard. I bared my teeth as I made my way towards him. I relished the thought that his life would fade from his eyes as my hands squeezed around his neck. I was going to kill him. I could feel the air shift behind me as the temple guards dashed in my direction, but I didn't take my eyes from the king. He was mine.

He turned his gaze away from me, as though I wasn't important, as though he hadn't seen the murderous intent in my eyes. He had turned towards the Anglian priest's staff, and his eyes gleamed with ravenous, desperate hunger.

"Kill her, you fools!" bellowed the Anglian priest to the temple guards.

The other priests barely glanced at me, and their arms flailed as they cast spell after spell at the witches across from them.

"Protect Elena!" shouted Prince Aurion.

A group of witches separated from the battle and rushed towards me shooting tendrils of magic through their fingers as they ran. Their magic whizzed over my head, and my cloak flapped around me from the blasts of magic that shot past. I smelled burned hair and heard moans and screams from behind me, but I didn't stop running towards the witches.

I made it to the first line of witches, and they managed to hold back the temple guards. They didn't realize I was here to kill their king. I knew they'd turn on me when I'd done the deed, and I seriously doubted I'd survive their wrath. All I could think about was avenging Rose.

The Anglian priest was still focused on me. I realized he was making a foolish mistake. The witch king took full advantage of the priest's preoccupation with me and roared something in Witchtongue. His magecraft blazed yellow, and with a quick flick of his fingers, a tendril of dark magic shot across the chamber and hit the Anglian priest square on the chest.

The priest flew off the ground with terrifying force and crashed back to the ground. He still clutched his staff tightly in his hand, but the metal cage on top had shattered on impact, and the stone slipped from its prison and rolled across the floor.

The priest let out a terrible cry, and as he crawled towards the stone, smoke coiled from his robes from where the king's magic had struck.

I could feel that the eyes of the shadowy creature who seemed always to accompany the high priest were on me. I looked away and stifled the creepy feeling in my chest.

The priest's outstretched hand moved towards the stone.

I made a wild dash for the witch king. But before I could reach him, a tendril of black wrapped around the stone, and with one easy flick, the stone sailed across the chamber and dropped into the witch king's hand.

Shit. Shit. Shit.

"Father, no!" Prince Aurion called out in a panic.

The coven general and the king's guards rushed forward and formed a protective circle around him. A tendril of black magic sailed over my head and flew towards the king. But it never reached him.

Roars blasted through the air as rays of black magic shot across the chamber at the king, but his guards repelled them easily. While some witches were blasted apart by the priests' nearly invisible tendrils of dark magic, other witches quickly replaced those who had fallen, and the king remained unharmed.

The stone was lost.

The witch king had the stone.

Anger, guilt, and agony hit me like a kick in the gut.

For some reason the Anglian priest stared inexplicably at the mist on the right side of the chamber.

I jumped back as a tendril of black magic exploded at my feet.

Prince Aurion rushed towards his father.

"You won't be able to wield the stone. It's too powerful."

I kept quiet, but a part of my heart broke at the pain in Aurion's voice.

Maybe I wouldn't have to waste my energy to kill the king, the stone would do it for me. *Good.* I just had to wait.

The witch king ignored his son and turned to me, clearly mistaking my hesitation for fear and envy. His grin widened as he marveled at the stone.

"See. Steel maidens are not the only ones who can wield a powerful magic stone like this. I told them a king could do it. These fools will regret the day they defied me. I deserve this power. I've waited three hundred years for it. And now it is mine."

"You never intended to help us. You only ever wanted the stone, didn't you?"

I looked over to the prince, and our eyes met. He knew. He had known all along, and he had followed his father here to prevent him from getting the stone. He had tried to stop him.

The chamber suddenly became too quiet. All eyes turned to the king. The witches and necromancers stopped fighting. Everyone watched to see if the king could truly wield the stone.

I could see the longing in the Anglian necromancer priest's eyes. He almost looked amused. Just like me, he didn't believe the king could handle the stone either. And just like me, he waited. Everyone did.

"It's mine," said the king again.

His eyes gleamed with greed as he admired his precious jewel. His general stood proudly beside him.

"The power is finally mine!" bellowed the king.

He had been consumed by dark madness, and I knew it was too late.

I watched transfixed. The witch king looked as if he might actually be able to handle the stone. I could barely breathe. He should have been blown to bits by now.

What if a dark witch could manipulate the stone? Could Ada and the others have been wrong? Did they even know?

If I could handle the stone with the small amount of dark blood magic in my veins, might the pure-bred dark witch king handle the stone as well?

I felt as though the world around me had stopped. An ice-cold feeling crept into my heart. Perhaps I'd been wrong. Perhaps we all had.

The witch king's cloak and clothes flapped in a sudden gust of wind. The creepy smile on his face grew even more disturbing. I could almost see the ideas forming inside his mind. I could feel his ancient malice and his hatred for humans.

He would kill us all, I realized. Every last human would be wiped from the face of the Earth.

"Father, listen to me!" Aurion stepped forward, but the general stood in his way.

"Father, please, let it go," urged the prince. "Forget the stone. You cannot wield it. None of us can. Not even a steel maiden."

He looked at me, and I knew deep down that he spoke the truth.

"You're a fool, my boy, if you think I'd let go of such power."

He gripped the stone in his large hand.

"Never. I will use this to eliminate the human scum once and for all."

"And how will you do that if you're dead?"

The king laughed. "Like all magic stones, it has recognized me as its true bearer. It is a conduit fit for a king."

"This is a mistake. This isn't right," said Aurion.

His voice was hoarse. He sounded broken.

"The mistake is you," growled the king. "You will never rule. You're too weak. Just like your mother was."

Something truly dark spread across the king's features. The stone was already manipulating him.

Pain flashed in Aurion's eyes. "Don't. Don't do this."

The king snapped. "Silence."

My blood pumped hot into my veins. I had failed. I had failed Rose. I trembled and felt myself diminished.

"Father—"

A sonic boom blasted into the chamber like the clap of thunder. Rock and dust fell from the walls and roof. I looked to the deep crack in the chamber floor, but nothing had changed. Only when I saw movement from the other end of the chamber did I realize where the sound had come from.

I could hardly breathe. The mist slowly began to evaporate, and to my horror a shape began to form inside it. It was a giant horned beast not unlike the demons I'd seen before, only much bigger. The toxic fumes from the demon realm burned my throat, and my eyes welled with tears.

The demons had breached the barrier to our world.

"Use the stone's power to stop the demons from entering our world," I yelled.

I became consumed by a fit of coughs, and soon all the witches began to heave and cough as well.

The priests and their guards looked on with sardonic expressions. They appeared to be able to breathe the toxic fumes.

The witch king glowered at me and tears welled in his eyes. Finally he noticed the creature that was about to step through the rift, and his madness seemed to dissipate for a moment.

He frowned suddenly and stared at the stone. It blasted yellow light.

"I don't understand." Panic flashed in his eyes, and his face paled. And then, just as I'd seen before when King Otto had held the stone, the witch king's flesh started to glow a bright yellow. His eyes opened wide with fear, and the yellow light broke through his skin.

"Aurion?" he gasped.

And then he exploded into thousands of bloody chunks of burned flesh.

Aurion's face was smeared in blood. He stood transfixed and stared at the spot where his father had stood moments before.

I looked to the ground for the stone, but there was only a puddle of bloody meat and bone.

The Heart of Arcania was gone.

Somehow the stone had been blasted away in the explosion. It could have gone anywhere. It looked exactly like the polished stone from which the chamber itself had been made.

I fell to my knees. "Aurion. Help me find the stone!"

I coughed as I searched through chunks of guts and blood and rock.

"Without it, we can't stop the demons from coming through."

Ada had omitted a crucial piece of information.

Even if I did find the stone, how would I use it?

The rocks all looked the same.

My chest felt empty. I had lost the stone.

CHAPTER 35

We were all going to die.

The toxic vapors in the air were getting stronger and every breath was like swallowing a bucket of broken glass. My head spun, and I struggled to keep from keeling over. Prince Aurion wasn't so lucky.

His pale face had turned pink as he fought for breath. He collapsed to the floor, shrieking in pain and coughing blood. All around us witches fell, all of them with blood spurting out of their mouths. Eventually no one was left standing.

Most of them were still alive, but it wouldn't be long until the toxic fumes killed them all.

But I wasn't dead yet. My blood magic was different, and I knew I had to keep searching for the stone. I still didn't know what the hell I'd do with it, but it was the only thing left for me to do.

I needed to get the stone.

"There's no need to keep fighting it," called a voice from across the chamber.

The Fransian priest was watching me. I recognized his deep-set eyes and has large girth. He looked like he'd fallen into a barrel of ale too many times.

"It's too late. You should just give up. You cannot stop the inevitable. The Unmaker will rise, and he will take this world as his own. You're all going to die."

"No," I wheezed and continued to search to search the ground. "I can't. I won't."

The priest laughed. "You won't find it. But even if you did, I'd let you keep it as a gift. It's no good to us anymore. It has served its purpose."

He smiled. "The master is coming, and all the light in this world will be extinguished."

He turned to the mist and raised his arms.

"Come forth, Unmaker, Lord of darkness. Banish dawn and the destroyer, sunshine. You are the master of shadows and the dark of night."

Together, the priests all turned toward the looming mist. There was something almost childlike about the expression of adoration on their faces.

Bile rose in my mouth.

"Use this blood, master," continued the Fransian priest. "Take this blood as you will take this world."

At first I thought they were going to sacrifice themselves, but then they drew daggers from their robes. As I watched, the remaining temple guards crossed the chamber, kneeled to the ground in front of their priests, and threw back their heads.

A chill ran through me. I saw the flash of their silver blades, and the priests sliced the throats of their guards. Their lifeless bodies toppled over, and pools of blood gushed from their throats.

Some kind of black magic within the mist seemed to be feeding on the blood.

The mist lifted slightly, and the priest began to chant in a strange language. It was haunting and guttural, nothing like the poetic lilt of Witchtongue. The language of their blood sacrifice was hard and vile.

The light in the great tear in the fabric of the earth began to glow. And then the priests' eyes changed from ice-gray to a deep crimson as they channeled the magic.

The shadows in the mist moved as though something inside it was climbing out of a hole. Slowly, a gigantic shadowy apparition disengaged itself from the roiling fog. Its yellow eyes gleamed with intelligence and malice. Its grotesque body was twisted and gnarled, and its yellow fangs dripped with black blood. I could see that its thick powerful arms and massive shoulders were roughly the shape of a man.

The great horned beast was wreathed in the shadows of smoke and fire. It raised a fiery sword in a gesture of triumph, as though it owned the world.

I realized I was staring at a god from the underworld.

The Unmaker was coming.

I could hear Ada's words inside my head.

When shadow and darkness cover the world, when the balance is lost, then the portals to the demon realms will unlock. And when they open, demons will have free reign over this world.

We were all doomed.

I searched the ground frantically using my witch blade to cut through the soil. I was going to pass out from holding my breath. I knew I couldn't last another five minutes. I crawled on my hands and knees, digging into the dirt with my fingers, desperately trying to distinguish the magic stone from the thousands of others. My fingers bled from handling the sharp rocks, and dirt stuck to the blood on my hands.

The Anglian priest rose in a fury.

"You might have escaped me, steel maiden," he said.

He moved closer to the great gap in the earth that separated us.

"But no mortal can survive the darkness of the shadow of death. The master will destroy the light of the mortal world. His kingdom will be a world of night. Unfortunately for you, you will not witness this event."

I turned from him and continued my frantic search for the stone.

Goddess help me. Help us.

"I will enjoy watching you die," he laughed. "And after the darkness takes your soul, you will rise again as my revenant. You will be my puppet, and you will do as I command. You will be my pet."

"Shut up," I coughed, and my blood splattered on the ground.

I scrambled on the ground, and although I could barely see through my tears I never stopped searching.

The Anglian priest chuckled at the look of panic on my face.

"Soon, little steel maiden, you will die. And then you will be mine. You're finished. Your world of light is finished. The dark lord will rise and take this world as his own. It was always meant to be. Even you, steel maiden, will be unable to resist. This world doesn't belong to the weak anymore. It belongs to the Unmaker and his faithful servants. We will be the overlords of his demon legions."

I remembered the words of the shadow knight I had met in the demon realm.

I choked a laugh. "I don't think the demons will regard you as their overlords, seeing as you are still men. You are fools if you think your god will share power with you."

A violent coughing fit overtook me, and I collapsed on the ground. I couldn't stop shaking.

"But they already have," said the priest. "For centuries. How do you think we've been able to live for so long? The master has been very generous in his gifts. But I cannot say the same for you."

He paused. "Where are *your* gods now? Why aren't they showing themselves? Why don't they save you? Because they can't. They don't care."

I fought the tears. They were pointless, anyway.

I could see Aurion. His face was contorted in pain, his eyes were bloodshot, and his mouth opened and closed like a fish out of water.

The priests were right. It *was* hopeless. We were all going to die.

And then I felt a tug of magic. It was faint, but it called to me. I rolled over. Though I couldn't see the stone, I could feel its magic, and I knew exactly where it lay. I could see a yellow light that peeked through a jumble of fallen rocks.

The Heart of Arcania. It was there. And I could reach it.

I felt a surge of renewed strength and hope. I reached out with my left hand. The stone wanted me to find it. When I grasped it in my hand, I was surprised to find it was warm and pulsing with life.

I was instantly filled with power. I had never felt so much power. Whether it was dark or black or white, it didn't matter. All that mattered was that I was strong again, and the stone was mine.

I panted and shook as the familiar magic poured into me. My skin tingled. The stone emitted a pulsing, beautiful, and terrifying stream of light. I knew the air was still toxic, but I didn't need it. It was as though my skin breathed in the energy and magic of the earth beneath me.

The magic and power was intoxicating. I could feel everything. I held the stone against my stomach, and my muscles fed from it and gathered even more strength.

And then I just knew what to do. It was like a little voice inside me had spoken.

Fawkes had been wrong. I could control the black magic I had awakened.

I smiled.

I scrambled to my feet and took a moment to let the new power flow through my limbs. A shudder went through my body. My vision twisted and faltered, and I lost my balance for a second, but I quickly steadied myself.

Finally, I took several slow steps towards the hole that had grown below the place where the stone had lain. I halted just at the edge and peered into its depths. All I could see was bottomless bright light. The air crackled as wind and magic swirled around me. It was cool on my skin.

Ada's voice came to me again, *The Unmaker is the ruler of darkness. His weakness is light.*

Light. All I needed was light.

The ground shook and echoed with thousands of cries. The unholy god was emerging from the mist and taking its first steps into our world.

The Anglian priest suddenly realized what I was about to do.

"No!" screamed the priest.

He hurled a filament of black magic directly at me.

But he was too late.

I had tossed the stone into the fountain of light and magic.

CHAPTER 36

As THE STONE DISAPPEARED into the depths of light, the priest's black magic hit me in the chest, and I sailed backwards.

I hit the ground hard. I should have been dead, but I felt pain, and that was a good sign. Even though my clothes were soaked with blood, I had managed to hold on to my witch blade. Even though I had avoided the full effect of the black magic, every pore, every breath, and every muscle hurt.

I could still feel the effects of the stone pulsing through my veins. I still had a little fury left in me. I rolled over and managed to steady myself on my feet.

The six priests stared at me, aghast with surprise and hatred.

And then I knew I really would die this time.

I braced myself for their blows. But they didn't come.

Instead, there was a massive boom. Brilliant white light shot from the hole in the ground and sent sparks in all directions. The entire chamber was bathed in the blinding light of a hundred suns.

I heard loud, mournful wails erupt from within the mist, and a strong breeze blew through the chamber and tugged at my clothes and hair. I covered my ears and blinked the brightness from my eyes. The ear piercing cries that filled the chamber were so desperate that they caused the hairs over my entire body to stand on end.

The mist churned slowly, folded in on itself, and then the cries stopped and the mist disappeared. The demons and the mist were gone.

Another boom exploded in a wave of heat and blew my hair back from my face. The walls of the temple shattered, and stone and dust fell like snow all around me. It was like an earthquake, but this time the earth did not split apart. It pulled itself together. The gap in the ground where the magic of the earth had poured out so freely slowly healed itself like a recovering wound. I watched mesmerized as the last of the magic disappeared, and the door to the earth's magic slammed shut for the last time.

I felt as if something that had been part of me had been lost forever. The power of the stone had abandoned me.

I stumbled back unsteadily.

But my blood magic soothed and fed my body. Although I was weak, I could still feel the rush of cool air coming back into the chamber. And then I heard faint moans coming from the witches whom I had thought were dead. I was almost overwhelmed with relief.

"What have you done?"

The priests were furious.

The Anglian priest closed the distance between us with a few easy strides.

"You meddlesome witch whore! I will crush every single bone in your body and boil your guts from the inside until you beg me to kill you," he hissed. "I want to be the last thing you see when you meet *your* Creator."

He flicked his fingers.

I braced myself as the priest sent blast after blast of deadly black magic into me again. The pain blinded me, and fire burned through every muscle, bone, and organ of my body. The air left my lungs, and I began to choke and convulse. I screamed and stumbled backwards.

The priest smiled. "I like the way you squeal. It excites me. It only makes me want to hurt you *more*. Come now, Elena. You're getting what you deserve, don't you think? I want you to beg me to stop. I want to kill you while you beg."

"Go to hell."

My limbs ached and my head pounded. I was exhausted. With nowhere to run, I was forced to stand my ground and face this bastard priest. I knew I couldn't protect myself for long.

"Let's show the world how well you can beg, shall we?"

The priest lashed out again, and filaments of black magic lanced into my wounded body again.

In my anger, I threw my blade like an arrow and heard it tear into the priest's flesh. But he barely flinched.

He looked down at my blade and smiled. He pulled it out, as though it had been nothing more than a tiny splinter. He didn't even bleed.

He tossed my blade down by my feet.

"You cannot kill me with any means you possess. We—" he glanced lazily at the other priests "—are immortal."

He glowered at me. "I underestimated you."

"I'm glad," I said. "Even if you kill me, at least you won't be able to bring back those demons."

The Anglian priest laughed. "You proved to be more resourceful than I anticipated. Still, it won't change anything. You might have been lucky with the stone, but there are other stones and other ways to open the doorways to the demon realm. You see, the magic is still here, still beneath our feet, and it is still easy to retrieve."

His smile widened when he saw I was confused.

And then he commanded, "Kill the witches. Let their blood spill into the earth."

The other five priests moved towards the fallen witches, towards Prince Aurion. The silver of their blades shone in the light.

"No. You can't do this!"

I stumbled forward. My legs tingled with my healing magic, but it wasn't acting quickly enough, and my legs were barely able to support me.

I strained to keep moving. "Stop!"

The Anglian priest smiled.

"Yes, you stupid witch. It only takes a few blood sacrifices to call forth the opening of the portal. It hasn't closed fully. Not yet. This fresh blood will open it again. You've failed."

I failed.

Something broke inside me. Anger. Desperation. Fear. I couldn't let these bastards open the portal again.

My blood magic surged through me. I spun on the spot as fresh blood pounded through my brain. The witches were still too weak to help me, so I needed to outsmart the bastard priests. I wasn't strong like the priests, and I didn't possess their kind of magic. I had no stone to help me anymore.

I needed something else...

I saw the shadowy creature that always lurked behind the Anglian priest. Its bulbous eyes always seemed to plead for something.

What did it want?

And then I understood.

Maybe it was the way the shadow creature always seemed to be in constant pain. It always seemed to be begging me to put it out of its misery, to release it from some pain that it suffered.

So I would.

And so in one smooth movement, I picked up my witch blade and threw it again. Only this time I was not aiming for the priest.

It flew straight where I'd intended, right at the priest's shadow. For a moment I thought my blade would go right through the creature, but the blade pierced the creature's heart as though it were made of flesh and bone and not of shadow and air.

"No! Impossible!"

The priest whirled around. The handle of my witch blade poked out from the creature's chest. The priest looked terrified.

"But—how? No one can see—!"

Black blood spilled from his mouth. His eyes bugged out of his head. His skin, cracked, blackened, and bled. He collapsed to the ground screaming. The reek of the black rot that was consuming him burned my throat, and I gasped for breath.

Finally his body withered and dissolved into blackened dust. All that remained was a crumpled pile of robes.

The shadow creature stood up. It smiled at me, and for the first time I saw that it had the priest's face. With a final farewell nod, the shadow creature dissipated like a puff of smoke.

My witch blade clattered with a thud to the ground.

"Kill the witch whore! Kill her!"

I snatched up my witch blade. I didn't have to turn around to know what was going to happen. I smiled. Now that I knew how to kill the necromancer priests, I wouldn't let the opportunity pass me by.

I ran faster than I'd ever run in my life.

The air was suddenly thick with filaments of black magic, and I jumped and ducked as I made my way towards my enemies.

The priests all attacked together.

Shit!

I could see that the five remaining shadow creatures had backed away from their necromancers. They stood together in a group and seemed to know what I was about to do. They *wanted* me to do it. They were waiting and ready.

The necromancers turned their attention away from me at the last minute and sent out filaments of their black magic to coil around their shadows and pull them back.

But their magic didn't work. Their shadows slipped away.

My blood magic stormed through me like a giant kick of adrenaline. I ran, twisted, kicked, and ducked as I moved amongst the necromancers. They couldn't stop me. No one could.

I avoided the priests and rammed my witch blade into the shadows where I believed their shadow creatures to be.

After I had hit my final mark, I turned, breathing hard, to see what the effect had been.

Nothing remained of the foul priests but the faint echoes of their shrill cries and five piles of robes covered in blackened dust.

I let out a shuddering breath, hardly believing what I'd done.

The necromancer priests were dead. They would never hurt anyone again.

I smiled amidst all the death. The darkness was gone, and we could all begin to heal again.

But just as I began to relax, I felt a presence behind me, and a sword lanced into my gut.

CHAPTER 37

I STUMBLED BACK, as blood gushed from my throat and spilled down my front. My breath came in rapid wheezes, and it felt as if toxic demon air had filled the chamber again.

I looked up into the face of one of the high priest's concubines.

"I know you can't die from a mere gut job," the concubine smiled.

"But..." she picked up another sword from a fallen guard. "I know you can't grow back a head either."

She waved the tip of the sword in front of my face.

"Helen?" Blood sprayed out of my mouth as I sputtered her name.

This was all wrong, wrong. It was too ludicrous to believe, but it was happening right in front of me. Helen was trying to kill me.

She was right, of course. I couldn't grow a new head.

My blood magic was nearly spent. I shivered and trembled, feeling hot and cold all at once. It was all I could do to keep from falling over. I winced as I pulled the hilt of the sword out of my abdomen. Golden light glowed from inside my body and spilled through the bloody gash, but Helen didn't seem surprised to see it.

"Why?" I gasped, "Why would you do this?"

I couldn't understand the hate I saw in her. I barely knew her and had hardly even spoken with her, and yet her hatred for me was palpable. She looked sick. Her once pretty face had become gaunt. Her eyes bugged out, and her cheekbones protruded and made her look skeletal.

"Why?" she repeated. "Because *you* ruined everything. You ruined our plans. It's all your fault."

I spat more blood from my mouth and tried hard not to retch.

"I don't know what you mean."

I felt my blood magic begin to heal my wound, but it was slow. Too slow. If she swung that sword at my neck, I wouldn't survive. I had to keep her talking.

"Why couldn't you just stop?" asked Helen.

She whined like a child and grazed my neck with her sword as she waved it around dramatically.

"Why did you have to poke your nose where it didn't belong? Why? Wasn't Rose's death enough? Why didn't you break? Any normal person would have given up. What is it about *you* that makes you keep going?"

I heard the words, but I didn't recognize their implications right away. Then I began to cry. I felt as though she'd gutted me again. My skin went cold, and bile rose in my throat.

"You killed Rose?" All this time I'd thought it had been the witch king. I'd been a fool.

Helen sighed. "Yes. Who cares? She was going to die anyway...I just helped her along, that stupid old bag."

"You murdered her, you sick bitch!" I yelled. "You tortured her. She was a defenseless old woman and you gutted her like an animal! How could you? Why would you do this?"

"Because it was necessary," said Helen.

"Necessary to kill an innocent woman who never hurt anyone?"

"Yes," said the concubine without emotion. "She had to die."

"Why?"

Helen slowly nodded her head.

"We knew you were trouble," she said coldly. "You were the only one who was a real threat to our plans. No mere female could have ruined them."

Dizzy, I drew in a breath. "What did Rose have to do with your sick plans?"

"We needed to break your spirit so that it would be easier to get you out of the way, you brat. She died because of you. We needed to make you unbalanced, to shake your core. We had tried to kill you before, but we failed. We thought up something that would have shattered an ordinary female. But it obviously didn't work."

An anger deep within me woke. "Who's we?" But I already knew.

Helen cocked her head. "Come on, Elena. Do I have to spell it out for you? I can see it in your face, but I'll tell you all the same."

She paused.

"The priests, of course."

She smiled, but then it faded and was replaced with an ugly snarl. "But now you've gone and killed them!"

She waved her sword at me again, and I barely avoided it.

There was no way a concubine like her should have been able to handle a large sword like that. Although her face was drawn and thin, her forearms were rippled with muscle, and her wrists were thick and strong. There were even small white scars on her hands and arms that I'd never noticed before, evidence of training. Helen had been trained in swordsmanship. There was no doubt about that. The confidence on her face argued that she was much better than me, and she knew it.

I trembled. I was too slow and weak. Helen's smile told me that she knew that, too.

"Rose was a means to an end," said Helen. "I knew you loved her like a mother. So of course, she had to go."

I staggered and spat more blood. I was furious that I had been betrayed by a woman who had once helped to bathe me.

"How can you have any love for those bastards?" I hissed through gritted teeth. "After everything they've done to us...to our families? To you? How could you?"

"My family left me for dead in the streets. I was born a girl you see, and girls were regarded as weak and useless in the Pit. I was just another useless mouth to feed...another burden for my parents. I was three years old when they dumped me by the side of the road to starve and die. The high priest of Anglia found me, fed me, and clothed me. I owe him everything."

I scowled. "That can't be it? You don't look like the kind of person who would kill innocent people out of some displaced sense of loyalty. You lived with them for years. You became their sex pet. It couldn't have been all roses and rainbows for you."

I watched her face carefully, but her expression was calm.

"What did he promise you? What did he promise you for Rose's death?"

The concubine smiled. "Power. More power than you can imagine."

"So you lusted for power instead of helping your own people find hope for a new and better life. Your heart is cold."

As Helen considered, her face brightened. "Power is everything. Without it, we are nothing."

"Lies," I hissed, and I almost laughed at her stupidity.

"You think he would have kept his promise to you? You think he would have shared with you the power that he most craved? His power? You stupid, stupid bitch."

The calm expression on the concubine's face contorted with anger. And before I could react, she darted forward and plunged her sword deep into my abdomen again.

She yanked out her sword abruptly, and I couldn't feel my legs. I fell back and crashed to the ground. My head slammed against something hard, and as I struggled for consciousness so much blood gushed into my mouth that I felt I was drowning in it. I couldn't breathe. I was dying.

Helen loomed over me with her feet apart, and then she raised her sword above her head.

"And now the legacy of the steel maidens dies with you, Elena."

I tried to move, but my body won't obey. Jon's face flashed in my mind's eye as Helen brought down her sword. My heart broke, and I closed my eyes.

The air moved next to me, and then I heard a thud as something warm brushed against my side. But I didn't feel the pain of the sword. Perhaps I was dead.

I opened my eyes. Helen was lying next to me, her eyes wide and lifeless. Blood spilled from around the hilt of a dagger that had pierced deep into her forehead.

"Elena!"

The voice of angels, I thought. Just this once I wanted to see him again. Just one more time.

I looked up into the face of the most beautiful man in the world. The Goddess had answered my prayers.

Jon kneeled next to me.

"By the creator! There's so much blood, Elena. I'm so sorry I wasn't here to protect you."

I saw his tears, and I couldn't control my own. I gasped as his hand wrapped around mine and made it warm.

I smiled despite the dizziness and pain. He was alive. I was alive. I looked again into his handsome face. His eyes shone with a grief and a sympathy that I could almost taste.

I heard other voices and footsteps. At first their faces were blurred, but then my vision sharpened enough to recognized one.

Prince Aurion looked down at me with the same love I had seen in Jon's face.

"She's bleeding out," said the prince. "We need to stop the bleeding."

None of that mattered. If I died now, if it was the Goddess' will, then so be it. I had done my duty as a soldier of light. I had made things right again.

I took comfort in knowing that for once in my life I'd done the right thing.

Rose would have been proud of me.

I smiled one last time and let the darkness take me.

CHAPTER 38

THREE MONTHS HAVE PASSED since the obliteration of the necromancer priests and the source of their power. The destruction of the golden temple was inevitable, and I watched with a smile on my face as a group of witches and humans tore it down to the very last stone.

Everything that the high priests had touched was destroyed. Their homes in Soul City, their banners, sculptures, and clothing, everything that reminded us of the Temple of the Sun empire was either burned or destroyed.

Although I wasn't there to witness the removal of the other temples in the other five realms, word reached us pretty quickly that all evidence of the necromancer priests had been destroyed throughout the land.

An elected council was formed as an interim government in Anglia, and we were able to rebuild our homes and rehabilitate the land until a real government could be formed.

Anglia had been hit the hardest by the black blight, especially the Pit and the surrounding farms. Although the land was blackened and diseased, the morning after the death of the high priests, I noticed a blade of grass among the gray ashes. More grass grew in the following weeks, and leaves budded on the trees. The rain washed away the ashes and the smell of rot as it fed the earth. The sun shone, and the land began to thrive again.

The remaining elected officials joined a council of witches under which King Aurion held court in Kindling Castle. Although Jon had announced that the rebel party was no more, he was still invited to be an advisor to the court. High Witch Ada invited me to join the government because of my role in the revolt. I was to represent change, and the new voices of Anglia. It was a new beginning.

And although the Girmanians and Romilians were still suspected of having aided the high priests in some way, a general pardon was signed, and the suspect realms swore fealty to the new government and to Witchdom. And every soldier, man or woman, who had been forced into the service of high priests was pardoned as well.

The black blight and all other traces of black magic disappeared hours after the rift had been sealed and the high priests had died. Those lucky enough to have survived the infection didn't remember much, and I suspect that those who did remember choose not to.

The council divided the land equally, and every family in Anglia got an equal share so that they could rebuild and start over. Although it would take years to rebuild the villages and to work the land so that it flourished as it once did, everyone was eager to start.

Jon and I both wanted to get away from the city and settle in the country where we would farm the land. It didn't take long for us to settle on a beautiful twenty-acre plot of rolling hills between

Gray Havens and the Pit. It was situated perfectly between the two worlds, just like me. I still had lots to learn about witches, and I wanted to continue my studies with Fawkes. With the help of Nugar and a handful of men, we built a modest home with oak and pine logs, like Kindling Castle.

I didn't know much about farming, but the neighboring Milton family had been prominent farmers for five generations, and they promised to help us if we helped them. It was too late in the year for us to plough our land and get it ready for seeding, so Jon and I helped the Miltons salvage their lands and get ready for harvest.

Some families decided to leave and go south. I didn't blame them.

Kayla and the other concubines headed west where they could build their lives again, and where no one would remember their past.

Every single family in Anglia and all of Arcania had been touched by the priests' black magic. The dead relatives we could find were given a proper burial, and eventually we found and burned others while we remembered those we'd lost.

The sounds of hammers banging nails, chisels carving stones, and saws cutting wood filled the air. Carthorses pulled wagons filled with stones from Soul City to be used for new constructions. And for the first time in months, I saw smiling faces and heard the laughter of children.

High Witch Ada found me. She had a strange smile on her face.

"Here," she said and placed bundle into my hand.

It was hard and cold and hung from a silver chain.

I immediately recognized it as the late queen's magecraft. My heart skipped, and I longed to feel its power again. But I only felt a profound sense of loss. There was no warmth, and no magic channeled into me like before. I turned the magecraft over in my hand and squeezed it. The stone was blackened and cold. It looked more like a piece of coal than a magic stone.

"What's this?" I asked, trying hard to hide my disappointment.

"What do you think? It's the stone you took from the witch queen."

"I can see that. But what happened to it?"

I wrinkled my nose at the faint smell of burnt hair it emitted.

"Dead," said Ada in an unusually cheerful tone. "Just like every other magic stone or magecraft in all of Arcania. Its magic is spent. Gone."

"But how is that possible?"

"I believe that when you sealed the opening in the earth, it cut off their source of magic. And now they're just stones. Just as they always should have been."

"You seem to be taking this news very well."

"Of course, as should you," answered Ada.

She became deadly serious. "Now the magic is where it always should have been, in its natural form, back in the earth."

I slipped it in my pocket. "I think I'll keep it. Just to remind myself of what happened."

"I thought you might want to." Ada's smile made her look years younger. "But it'll never waken again. Not ever."

I watched her walk away. Her back was straight, and she didn't need to use her staff.

"Elena."

Aurion stood so close behind me that I could smell the scent of lavender soap on his skin. He wore a gray tailored cloak embellished with silver stars set against a midnight sky and his glimmering silver hair was pulled back into a long braid that emphasized his elegant features. Tall and slender, he radiated beauty and power. I looked at his hands, but his magecraft was gone.

"I wanted to say goodbye," said the new witch king. He looked a bit flushed, but his eyes never wavered away from my face.

"You're leaving?"

I recognized his intense look, but I knew I could never surrender to it. I could never give him what he wanted. I blushed and looked at a spot on his shoulder.

He considered me for a moment, and then he said, "There's much to be done. When my father died, so did his legacy. There will be many changes back in Witchdom. I will not rule as my father did."

"No, you won't. You will be a much better king."

Aurion's white skin flushed.

"I'm not sure about that, but it all starts with our new alliance with the human nations. I know it'll take time, but I hope for peace between us. We must move forward from the ruins of the old and build anew."

"Will you keep the same Coven Council members?"

I remembered Ysmay's and Forthwind's selfish behavior and greed for the stone.

He smiled quietly.

"I'm sure the members will rotate, but that's up to the witches to decide. It will be a huge adjustment for a lot of the witches."

"For the humans, too. But it will be harder for us than for the children."

"I've asked the witches who chose to relocate in these parts to assist in the rebuilding efforts."

"Thank you. That's very much appreciated."

"It's a show of good faith, and I hope it's a good start."

Aurion cocked his head. "What will you do now?"

I let out a breath. "Good question. Live I guess. And be happy."

Aurion looked distant.

"Elena, I wanted to ask you something."

I gaped at him. "Ask me what?"

My mouth was dry, and my heart beat a little faster.

The witch king smiled at my reaction.

"How did you know that by killing those shadow creatures, you would kill the necromancers?"

It was not the question I had expected. I let out a breath and tried not to sound too relieved.

"I think those shadows who clung to the priests were their souls. I remembered Ada telling me that black magic required sacrifice. The priests had to sacrifice their humanity and their *souls* to borrow that black magic. I saw the humanity of the real priests in the eyes of those shadows. And then I knew. I knew they were their souls."

Aurion nodded. "Somewhere along the way, man and soul got separated because of the black magic."

"That's right. I knew I couldn't kill the high priest because he was already dead."

"So you killed his soul instead."

"More like released it."

"What do you mean?"

"I might be wrong, but I think somewhere along the way the priests became possessed by the black magic and couldn't turn back. They were trapped."

Aurion watched me. "I saw them, you know, the souls. But only after you'd stabbed them. I saw the shadow of the man flicker and then nothing. It was gone."

"I still don't understand why I was the only one who could see them. I asked Ada, and even she didn't know. The Coven Council witches weren't very helpful either. Ada called it a *great mystery*."

Aurion shrugged. "A mystery maybe, but it could also be the will of the Goddess."

"The will of the Goddess?"

"Yes. One of her many gifts to you, I expect. You're a special witch, Elena. I think the Goddess made it so that only *you* could see them. I always knew you were special. Since the first time I saw you in my father's court, I knew there was a reason why you had come to us. It seems I was right."

"I guess we'll never know," I said.

I was suddenly very self-conscious. "Do you think it will make a difference though? Do you think it's finally over?"

"Over for now," said Aurion. "There'll always be darkness in the world, but there's always a balance as well. As a soldier of light, you're living proof of that balance. One cannot exist without the other. Just as one accepts the good, one must also accept the bad. But I don't think you need to worry about it in your lifetime."

"I hope you're right," I said. "I need a few years to relax and recover. And I can't wait to start my new life."

The only one missing was Rose.

"Jon's a good man." Aurion held nothing back. "And a lucky one."

I could see the emotion in his face.

I swallowed hard and smiled. "Yes, he's very lucky to have me."

Aurion laughed. The intensity of his gaze returned.

"I'll miss you, Steel Maiden."

He started to say something else but decided against it.

My throat throbbed.

I said, "I'll miss you, too."

Aurion smiled despite the wetness in his eyes.

"I wish you all the happiness this world can give you. You deserve it."

He took my hand, and I could feel the warmth of his lips against my skin.

And with that the new witch king turned on his heels, stepped out the main door, and disappeared.

CHAPTER 39

THE FOLLOWING DAY I was honored to attend the wedding of Will and Celeste.

The afternoon sun was beautifully warm. The trees had blossomed into vibrant green leaves, and the grass was lush and soft. Although the land had not entirely recovered from the black blight, and some trees would never recover, the young trees had, and they would continue to thrive.

The wedding was the first between a human and a witch, and it symbolized the two nations' acceptance of each other. Will and Celeste had designed the ceremony themselves and created beautiful combination of both witch and human rituals. It was a very moving and honest ceremony.

Celeste had wanted a small affair in a garden wedding overlooking the lake, but it seemed as though all of Anglia has come to bear witness to this blissful and miraculous event. Hundreds of humans and witches gathered around the edges of the lake.

Will, Celeste, and Ada stood on a small dais. Celeste's long hair spilled down over her shoulders, and her traditional witch wedding gown of light green linen was embroidered with flowers and leaves.

White roses, daises, and purple pansies crowned her head, and her pale skin seemed to glow in the sun. She had never looked so radiant.

Will wore a matching green tunic, and even though he stood proud and strong, his eyes shimmered and he kept clenching his jaw as he struggled not to cry.

I didn't have anything fit to wear to a wedding, and so the witchlings surprised me with a beautiful red and gold gown. I was proud to wear the Steel Maiden clan colors. The neckline was low, and I was sure Jon would appreciate it. The fabric was a blend of wool and linen, not precious Witchdom silk, but to me it was priceless.

I felt the air move behind me, and when I turned I forgot to breathe.

Jon looked striking in his white tailored tunic. The snug fit revealed his broad chest and muscular arms, and the sun highlighted his chiseled and perfectly symmetrical face. He smiled at me sensually, and I had to turn away quickly before everyone saw the flush on my face.

As Celeste and Will took each other's hands and recited their vows before Ada, Jon and I took our places as witnesses, and the ceremony began.

My heart welled with happiness as I watched the happy couple.

And just as I felt tears on my cheeks, Jon reached out and lightly brushed my arm. My breath caught, and I felt desperate to feel his body against mine. I peeked at him under my lashes, but I couldn't tell whether he noticed the color on my face or the shifting of my body. But then he slipped his warm and calloused hand into mine, and I squeezed his hand in return. I resisted the urge to press my lips against his for now. There would be time for that later.

The wedding ceremony was over within a half hour, but the celebration continued well into the night. After the bonfire, I saw Celeste and Will sneak away into the castle, and with the happy couple gone, Jon and I retired to our rooms with a bottle of wine.

"Finally, I have you all to myself," he said.

He poured me a glass of red wine and raised his glass.

"Here's to our new beginning."

"To our new beginning." I raised my cup and drank deeply.

The effects of my previous three glasses had already made my head feel light, but the last glass awakened all my senses.

Jon leaned forward.

"Me and you together. It's all I've ever wanted. It's all I'll ever need. I can't promise it'll be perfect, but know that I'll always love you, no matter how stubborn you are."

"What are you talking about? I'm perfect." I could see the desire that flashed in his eyes.

The room felt deliciously hot. Jon took our cups and placed them on a dresser. And then in one swift move, he drew me onto the bed and kissed me. My hands sought his skin, and I tugged at his clothes impatiently and yanked off his shirt.

He pulled his lips from mine and grinned. "I love you, you know."

"I love you too, Mad Jack."

I closed my eyes and fought the tears that threatened to take over. I ran my fingers over his smooth, hard chest. He kissed my neck, and every part of my body hummed with waves of delightful heat.

"My Elena," he whispered.

Shivers raced along my skin. He was here with me, and I wasn't dreaming. We'd come through death and fire, and found each other again. The Goddess had indeed blessed me.

I reached up and squeezed him against me until my arms ached, and I began to shake.

"Why are you crying?" He breathed into my neck and then pulled away gently.

"Because," my voice cracked, "I never thought this could be real. Us. You and me, and a home, and land of our own. It's more than I could ever have imagined. I feel like I'm living a dream."

"Well," he said as he kissed my chin and my neck. "Get used to it because it's not a dream. It's real. And we're never ever going to be apart."

I wrapped my arms around him and pulled him close. I would never let him go again.

AUTHOR'S NOTE

Dear reader,

Thank you for reading *Blood Magic*. I hope you've enjoyed getting to know the heroes and villains and the world I've created for them. If you enjoyed this book, please visit the site where you purchased it and write a brief review. Your feedback is important to me and will help other readers decide whether to read the book too.

Again, thank you for coming on this ride with me, and I hope we'll take many more together. The adventures are just beginning. Happy reading!

Kim Richardson

The war of angels versus demons continues in this sequel to the Soul Guardians series. Coming soon!

THE SOUL THIEF

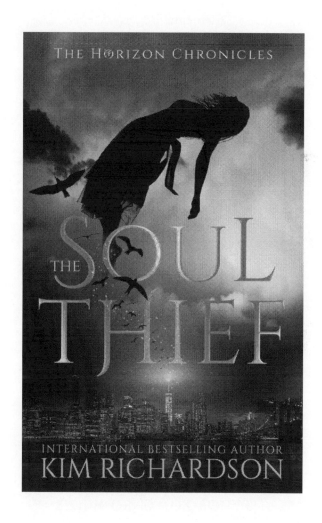

MORE BOOKS BY KIM RICHARDSON

SOUL GUARDIANS SERIES

Marked Book # 1

Elemental Book # 2

Horizon Book # 3

Netherworld Book # 4

Seirs Book # 5

Mortal Book # 6

Reapers # 7

Seals Book # 8

MYSTICS SERIES

The Seventh Sense Book # 1

The Alpha Nation Book # 2

The Nexus Book # 3

DIVIDED REALMS

Steel Maiden Book # 1

Witch Queen Book # 2

Blood Magic Book # 3

THE HORIZON CHRONICLES

The Soul Thief Book # 1

ABOUT THE AUTHOR

Kim Richardson is the award-winning author of the bestselling SOUL GUARDIANS series. She lives in the eastern part of Canada with her husband, two dogs and a very old cat. She is the author of the SOUL GUARDIANS series, the MYSTICS series, and the DIVIDED REALMS series. Kim's books are available in print editions, and translations are available in over seven languages.

To learn more about the author, please visit:

Website

www.kimrichardsonbooks.com

Facebook

https://www.facebook.com/KRAuthorPage

Twitter

https://twitter.com/Kim_Richardson

Printed in Great Britain
by Amazon